FROG

Joffre White

Book Guild Publishing

First published in Great Britain in 2010 by
The Book Guild Ltd
9 Priory Business Park
Wistow Road, Kibworth,
Leics, LE8 0RX

Typesetting in Century Schoolbook by
Nat-Type, Cheshire

Printed and Bound in Great Britain by
CPI Group (UK) Ltd, Croydon, CR0 4YY

A catalogue record for this book is available from
The British Library.

ISBN 978 1 84624 711 8

For Chris, my pride and joy

Prologue

Another world. Another dimension ...

As the sound of birdsong and the musical chinking of
his horse's bridle created a soothing symphony to his
ears, a brave knight rode his horse along a woodland
track. Sunlight dappled through the trees and reflected
off his armour, sending out flashes of light into the
surrounding foliage.

His thoughts turned to the start of his journey. He
had been sent on a quest to cleanse the kingdom of
three terrible witches who roamed the lands, spoiling
harvests, poisoning wells and streams and spreading
sickness in any animals and good folk who happened to
cross their paths.

Saleeza, Farella and Belzeera were sisters in wicked
witchery. The deadliest of them was Belzeera, for she
was a powerful shamanic witch who had long defeated
and killed all who had the misfortune to come into
contact with her. The knight had taken counsel with
the great Wizard Gizmo, who had armed him with
various charms and placed protective spells on him. He
recalled Gizmo's parting words.

1

'Good luck,' he had said as he watched the knight mount his horse to begin his quest. 'You'll jolly well need it!'

He had been journeying for two days and now followed the directions of some villagers whose livestock had mysteriously dropped dead in the fields while grazing. His horse's ears suddenly pricked up and he pulled back on the reins to stop their progress. He could hear the low murmur of a woman's voice coming from somewhere through the shrubbery and he carefully dismounted and drew his sword.

Saleeza was in a clearing, with her familiar, a jet-black crow perched upon her shoulder. She was stooped over a poor village child whom she had caught out alone gathering berries. With cruel excitement she busied herself tormenting the girl with demonic visions and apparitions; so involved with her own depraved enjoyment that she did not hear the knight coming. With one swift swing of his sword he separated her head from her body (the only sure way to end the life force of a witch who practised the Dark Arts). He also managed to catch the tail feathers of the crow before it flew awkwardly away to refuge in a tree. As he administered a calming potion to the child, the remains of the witch shrivelled and dissolved into nothingness. The crow cawed loudly as it flapped itself away, its ragged backside disappearing over the tree-tops. The knight gathered the girl up into his arms and, safe now, high in the saddle of his horse with him, he returned her to her grateful parents.

A few days later and further into his quest, his encounter with the second sister was more of a challenge. Farella had been warned of his coming by the crow whose rear end he had de-feathered. He had been mounted on his horse, slowly crossing a narrow, but deep river ford. Halfway across he had heard the caw of a crow which sounded like a mocking laugh.

'Cawhawhaw.'

The crow could not contain its delight in knowing the trap that had been laid for him. This, however, was the knight's saving, for had he not looked in the crow's direction he would not have seen the great wall of water silently churning down the river towards him. Those precious few seconds allowed him to spur his horse on and scrabble up the bank. However, the height of the wave was still enough to catch his horse broadside and dismount him, leaving them both to flounder in the aftermath of the water.

From her hiding place in a large tree which overhung the river, Farella had descended on him with the wailing of a banshee. She flew down on her enchanted hazel branch and leapt at him fiercely before he could stand. She lashed at his face with her long, dirty, venomous nails. He grabbed her wrists, but her strength was powerful and he struggled to force her arms back.

She was spitting and screaming into his face.

'You killed my sister! I'll suck your eyes out! I'll rip out your tongue and deafen your brain!' Her mouth drooled a green and yellow slime, the stench made him feel faint and darkness was beginning to cloud his eyes as his arms weakened.

Then, in an instant, she was gone. A wailing screech

followed his release and he opened his eyes just in time to see her land heavily in the grass a few metres from him.

Looking quickly to his side, he saw the still twitching rear legs of his horse, green slime splattered on its hooves from the kick that it had just administered.

'Good fellow, good fellow,' he said as he rose and drew his broad, shining sword. 'Go wash that muck off in the river before it does you harm, while I dispatch another witch.'

As he approached her, the witch was trying to come to her senses, but the horse's kick had dazed and blinded her. Before she knew of the knight's presence his sword had swung down in an arc and another head was separated from its owner's wicked body.

Sir Peacealot had been travelling the countryside for more than a month after his encounter with Farella and he was beginning to think that his quest would be a lifetime task. The trail for Belzeera had gone cold – no news of her wickedness had reached him, it was as if she had completely disappeared. He thought of returning to the realm of his king to seek further counsel with the Wizard Gizmo and finally resolved to do so the following day. That night he made camp in a clearing at the foot of a waterfall, a full moon dominating the sky above him and its image rippling in the pool fed by the water. The fire that he had made earlier to cook his supper on still crackled and hissed with burning wood which sent sparks dancing up into the night sky. He was staring dreamily into the flames when the presence of evil came.

Without warning the fire froze and the flames turned ice blue, the air around him became deathly cold. He could see his breath escape him in the night air even though it was a mild summer's evening. He knew the signs, the Wizard Gizmo had educated him well and so he stood, sword at the ready, with his back to his horse. In an instant the sound of the waterfall was quelled and he looked towards it to see it frozen and suspended in ice. The pool itself was a solid white circle of frost. Nothing moved in the sudden silence.

Then came a grinding and groaning as the surface of the pool splintered and cracked apart, shards of razor-sharp ice flew at him and he shielded his face. From the fissure in the pool rose a large figure, a distorted frozen man, his body creaking and cracking. He clambered onto the bank and towards the knight. The voice, when it came, was mournful.

'The witch Belzeera awaits your company at the ridge of the waterfall. She will grind your bones one by one while you scream your way to death, a sweet revenge for her sisters. That is after I have had the pleasure of administering some cold torture upon you, you feeble knight.'

The figure drew itself upright to almost twice the knight's height and directed its vicious icicle fingers towards him. With unexpected speed it moved forwards, intent on piercing his body. Sir Peacealot moved directly at the oncoming figure and at the last moment doubled up and slipped himself between its legs. In one movement and before it could turn, he gripped his sword in both hands and with all his strength drove it upwards and into the frozen body.

The result was shattering – literally. As the creature exploded into thousands of fragments it emitted an ear-splitting scream. Sir Peacealot dropped his sword, closed his eyes and clamped his hands over his ears in case he was struck deaf. He waited to be pierced by a thousand daggers of ice. Instead he was drenched in freezing water as the remains of the creature, now harmless, washed over him. He opened his eyes. The pool had returned to normal and as he looked towards the now flowing waterfall, there, hovering in the air above it, was the witch.

'Such a shame that you spoilt my fun. Now it's time for you to meet your doom. I'll be waiting for you up here by the willow tree, but hurry, my desire to enjoy your slow demise could soon dissolve and you may meet a swift end where you stand. Either way, you'll not be taking any more heads after I've finished with you. I will avenge my sisters and then I will ravage the land until nothing but misery remains. Your head will sit prettily on the end of my broomstick for all to see!' She cackled as she disappeared from view.

The path was steep up to the top of the waterfall but Sir Peacealot's horse was foot-sure and steady on the rough ground. The knight was now fully attired in his battle armour, his visor raised and his shield ready in case the witch threw an unwelcome object at him.

As he neared the top of the path, he could see the source of the waterfall, a lake spreading out to his left, its flat surface mirroring the pale, full moon. Ahead of him, standing as a dark silhouette, was the sad-looking, leafless form of a large willow tree, its foliage blackened and lying in heaps on the ground at its base.

'Is nothing left untainted?' questioned Sir Peacealot sadly to himself.

The trunk of the tree exploded as though struck by lightning and from the billowing black smoke flew the witch, screaming and wailing with wretched glee. She arched her arm in the air as a fireball formed in her vile, clawed hand and with one swift movement, she released it at him.

He was ready and brought his shield up to glance the fireball sideways and into the lake where it sizzled and popped before sinking, extinguished and harmless.

'Just something to warm you up, how about some brimstone, you tin fool?' she cackled as she flew over his head.

He had just enough time to bring his shield up for protection as the pellets of white-hot sulphur rained down on him, bouncing off the metal to burn furiously in the grass about him.

'You'll have to try harder than that, you ugly old hag!' he shouted after her. 'If you want to prove how good you are, why don't you come down and face me? Or haven't you got the nerve that your sisters had?' he taunted.

He could sense her growing rage.

'If you're as powerful as they say you are, you shouldn't have any problem facing a mere knight like me.'

'Oh, I'll face you and you'll stare into my eyes. You'll see death as it approaches and not be able to stop it. You'll feel my sisters' pain ten thousand fold, I'll boil you alive in that steel suit and serve up that horse of yours in pieces to my goblins!'

She touched the ground no more than five paces in front of him. The grass withered and blackened around her and a fetid rotting stink filled the air.

Gathering all his resolve, Sir Peacealot addressed her.

'As you have come to ground, then I shall dismount from my horse and meet you standing, I shall fight as a knight should, with only shield and sword.'

He dismounted, keeping his eyes firmly on the witch. 'I ask only one thing,' he continued as he settled himself before her. 'That you let my steed go; he has been faithful and deserves no merciless end.'

The witch grinned her wicked smile. 'You expect mercy? You expect too much!'

She reached up and flicked the black feather which curved from the brim of her hat. In an instant, three dark, needle shapes flew forwards and past the knight. He turned and his eyes followed their path. All three pierced his horse's chest and without a sound it closed its eyes and collapsed to the ground, dead.

'There's your mercy,' she jibed. 'And you'll be begging for such a swift end for yourself pretty soon.'

Rage gathered inside Sir Peacealot's heart and it took all of his focus to control it. He knew that if he allowed his emotions to rule his actions then he would surely be doomed. Up until this moment he had been carrying out his duties for his king and the good folk of the realm – now it was personal. Avenging his noble and trusty steed would make destroying the demonic creature all the more satisfying.

He knelt on one knee as if in prayer.

She mocked him. 'Call upon whatever god you like,

you fool, there is no one who can help you now, my black arts have the power of my brother, the Dark Lord himself, and soon I will path the way for his return by darkening the skies and scouring the earth.'

He knew that if he could distract her, make her too confident, then he would have the advantage and so he encouraged her to rail and screech.

'What makes you so sure that you will meet his expectations, you old crone?' he goaded.

'You dare to question my abilities?' she spat.

As she lectured him and cursed him with all manner of profanities he quickly took advantage. He reached inside his breastplate and found the cloth bag given to him by the Wizard Gizmo. Turning his shield towards him he tore the cloth open and smeared the contents across its shiny surface. He stood, pulled his visor down and unsheathed his sword, bringing it up to cut through the cloth in his gauntleted hand so that the blade was drawn through the material from hilt to tip.

She railed on at him. 'I see that you are eager to meet your end, but I am afraid I will have to disappoint you. I have a much slower death in mind for you; let's see if we can relieve you of a few limbs first!' Her hand curled in mid-air and a green glowing orb appeared in her fingers. 'This has the power to slice though steel, let's see how you stand with a leg missing, you clanking pile of waste.'

He was right. She was too confident and he was ready for her.

The orb flew from her hand and towards him; he dropped on one knee again but brought the shield across and struck the sickly green object to one side.

No steel was sliced; the orb fizzed and then imploded on itself, vanishing with a final 'crack!'

She shrieked with a mixture of surprise and rage. 'What trickery is this? What fool thinks they can defeat me with lesser magic?'

She threw another orb and another, and each time he deflected them with his shield to the same end. Her rage increased with each second; she spat curses and chants at him, but to no effect – he was for a while protected by the Wizard Gizmo's preparations and secret sorcery.

Thunder rattled overhead as she raised her hands skywards, summoning forces of death and destruction. Two lightning bolts struck the earth in front of her. Chanting an incantation, she dug her clawed hands into the blackened ground which boiled and gave off a sickly colour through her fingers. The orb that she gradually shaped was much larger than the previous ones, its green much darker and more vile and, as Sir Peacealot watched, it seemed to pulsate and throb. He summoned all his remaining strength and courage just to stop his legs from giving way under him.

'You want to play with magic, you little man?' she jibed at him through black and wicked teeth. 'Your fate is for your body to be split into pieces and those pieces will be spread across time and space, forever searching for your soul and mind. Prepare for your endless torment!'

Both of her hands raised the pulsating mass above her head and with a mixture of fury and glee she hurled it at him.

The orb was an arms-length away when he sliced

through it with his sword and everything from that moment was as if in slow motion. One half of the orb spun from the sword and struck his shield which reflected it back towards the witch who now seemed frozen to the spot, unable to move, her mouth open in a silent scream as her own creation of destruction streaked back and struck her body. Sir Peacealot's shield exploded into pieces while the other half of the orb attached itself to his sword, slowly melting into it and causing the blade to shimmer and fade from a sickly green colour to a bright electric blue; golden runes appeared along the length of the blade.

His last memory was of being engulfed by the bright blue light from his sword and the sight of the witch becoming transparent as she produced a small wand in her hand and, pointing it at him, shrieked a curse just before she stretched into nothingness and disappeared.

'Know this foolish knight, by my last powers I cast you into the sleep of time and other worlds, but one day, past or future, I'll find you, for all the white magic since the time of knowledge will not keep me imprisoned and I'll reap my revenge!'

The blue light blinked out and Sir Peacealot was drawn into dark oblivion.

11

1

The Orchard

Present day ...

Chris Casey was a very confident twelve-year-old and
although being on the small side, what he lacked in
stature he made up for in character. His mop of tousled
mousy hair along with his long eyelashes and toothy
grin ensured that he stood out amongst his peers.

It was late on a warm Monday evening in July; the
school holidays were barely a week old, but he was
already bored. Today, three more of his school friends
had left for their annual summer holidays with their
families, three more friends who wouldn't be around to
play with him for a couple of weeks. He sighed as he
leant on the window ledge and stared out through the
glass at the moonlit orchard below and the fields
beyond.

The orchard was the size of a very big garden made
up of half a dozen apple trees and a couple of old pear
trees, what was left of a large area of fruit trees that
had been split up and divided between his home and
the two neighbouring properties when the land was
built on in the late 1800s. The house that he lived in

with his mum was a detached, three-storey Victorian building with high ceilings, large windows and creaky floorboards. Not long after they had moved into the house, Chris had been allowed to choose his own theme to decorate his bedroom with and in the end he selected a wallpaper with planets and astral landscapes, as this was the subject that intrigued him the most. He had become really interested in astronomy and how the planets and solar system worked. He had started to research information about the subject on the internet and a telescope was already on his birthday wish list.

It was no surprise this evening, then, that Chris found his eyes straying to the clear starry sky above. Fortunately, there were no street lights at the back of the house and therefore no sodium glare to dim the clarity of the main constellations. With just a small bedside light on in his room, it was surprisingly easy to pick out some of the smaller formations tonight, even with a full moon hovering overhead. His eyes picked out the bluish-hued stars that formed the shape of the 'Big Dipper' which he knew was part of the Ursa Major constellation.

His concentration was broken by his mum calling up the stairs.

'Chris, it's well past time for bed now, lights out.'

'Okay Mum. Just a couple more minutes,' he replied as he gazed at the distant shimmering diamonds of light.

'Now,' he wondered. 'Where was Orion's Belt?'

From the corner of his eye he caught a bright flash from about halfway down the orchard and turned his focus to where he thought it had come from, but

13

whatever it was had gone and so he resumed his stare to the heavens. A few moments later it was there again, a bright flash down by one of the apple trees. His eyes scoured the area, squinting into the silver-grey landscape. Nothing, just shapes and shadows outlining the trees and untidy clumps of grass left on the ground from where he had mowed the area earlier that day.

'Probably a piece of silver foil or a sliver of broken glass turned over by the lawnmower,' he thought to himself and continued his search for Orion's Belt.

Again he caught a flash in the corner of his eye but this time he did not allow his gaze to be distracted, he continued to look skyward. The light at the edge of his vision grew brighter as if trying to attract his attention but something told him not to look in its direction; instead his eyes were slowly drawn to the face of the full moon.

'Wow!' Chris mouthed to himself as he stared wide-eyed at the moon's cratered orb which was now surrounded by a growing, pulsing halo of light.

'Double wow!' he exclaimed as a silver stream of light stretched out from the moon's surface and across the sky to connect to a small, shimmering shape lying in the grass of the orchard. As he gazed down, transfixed, a ray of clear white light snaked up towards him. It hovered against the window pane just centimetres from his face. He blinked; there was a blinding flash and he fell backwards onto the floor, black dots spinning across his eyes and a dizziness spreading through his head. He sat there for a while, watching the dots swirl and fade from his vision then, slowly, he got to his knees and cautiously crawled to

14

the window. He peered out into the sky. The moon was looking bright and normal, hanging where it should be.

He turned his attention to the orchard, squinted his eyes. Could it be? Yes, there was definitely something glinting in the grass, something real and permanent to his normal vision now. His imagination fed his mind, all sorts of questions crowded his head and all sorts of ready-made answers appeared.

'*Aliens! It's the first landing of aliens! It's going to be like* War *of the* Worlds. *But why here? Why in our orchard?*' Whatever it was, it was up to him to investigate and warn everyone. He would be a hero – he would save the world! But then, what if it did turn out to be nothing, just the moonlight playing tricks on his eyes? He'd be made to look a right twit!

A plan. He needed a plan.

He grabbed a couple of items from the corner of his room. First of all he needed to see exactly what he was dealing with and that meant going down there, going down to the orchard in the spooky dark and getting close to whatever it was. He looked at what he was holding in his hands – his wind-up rechargeable torch and a toy light sabre!

'*Is that the best I can do?*' he thought to himself. '*Hmm. Perhaps I need to think this out; perhaps I need to think of a strategy. I'll sleep on it and if we're all still here in the morning, it'll be a good sign.*'

Five minutes later he'd been to the toilet, brushed his teeth, washed his face, changed into his pyjamas, drawn his curtains (without looking into the orchard again) and settled himself comfortably under his duvet with his light out.

'*Yes, if it is aliens,*' he said to himself, '*I'm sure they'd much rather meet someone after they've had a good breakfast.*'

With that thought he drifted into a restless sleep where he dreamed he was 'Enforcer of the Universe' and saved worlds from destruction and alien invasions.

Chris opened his eyes to the friendly purring of a cat, the gentle stroke of its whiskers tickling his nose and brushing across his cheek.

'Tabby!' he cried as he sat up and gave it a hug. Stroking the animal he wandered over to the window and drew the curtains apart as the events of the previous night unfolded in his head. He stared out into the orchard, wondering if it had all been one big dream, and then the hairs on the back of his neck stood up as he caught the glint of something in the grass.

He got himself dressed in double-quick time, pausing only for a token splash of water on his face and a quick brush of his teeth. Dashing downstairs he crossed the kitchen and reached for the handle to the back door.

'Where's the fire?' enquired his mum.

'What fire?' he asked.

'The rush, what's the rush?' she continued. 'Where do you think that you're going?'

'Got to save the planet,' he replied.

'Not until you've had some breakfast,' she instructed, smiling.

'Oh. But Mum … ' he protested.

'Sit down and eat your cereal and drink your orange juice or you won't be going anywhere.'

He knew that he wouldn't win and surrendered to the fact that the aliens would have to wait. However, he amazed his mum at the speed that he devoured his breakfast.

'You'll get indigestion,' she said as he got up and opened the back door. 'Where are you off to?'

'Down to the orchard,' he replied as he quickly made his escape.

'Don't wander off,' his mother shouted after him.

Chris was halfway down the path when he started to shorten his footsteps and slow down his pace.

'Whoa, there boy,' he said to himself. 'Where do you think you're going in such a hurry?'

He hadn't even thought of what he was going to do when he found the object, never mind what he would say if it really was aliens.

'Greetings, we come in peace,' he thought. 'No you idiot, that's what they're supposed to say. What about "Take me to your leader"?'

Then he had another thought. What if they actually said, 'Die, earthling die!'

Ten minutes later he was still sitting in the grass by the side of the path with no idea of how he actually would save the world. Finally he decided that there was only one way forward – he would sneak up on them and spy out the situation.

From where he was, he couldn't see anything reflecting in the grass, although as far as he could recollect, it was near the fourth apple tree down from the end of the path and in the middle of the orchard. He decided to follow the side of the orchard down to where he would be opposite the tree and then crawl slowly towards it until he could see the object. He crept as low as he could and made his way forward until he thought that he was in the right place. Then, dropping onto his stomach, he crawled commando-style towards the tree.

Everything was going well until he was a couple of metres from the tree, where he stopped, conscious that something was not quite right. He turned over and looked down at his legs. He had his baggy skateboard shorts on, which went down to his knees, but below that the skin on his legs seemed to be *moving*. Moving and red!

'Ants!' he shouted. 'Flipping ants!'

He was on his feet instantly, brushing his legs with his hands, stamping his feet, twisting around in circles, picking up clumps of grass and rubbing them on his legs in an effort to wipe off the army of ants that was in danger of actually invading his pants.

At this moment his mother looked out of the window to see her son dancing around like a hyperactive chimpanzee.

'We've got to find that boy some new friends,' she said to herself, shaking her head and turning back to her work.

Meanwhile, Chris had managed to weave in and out of the apple trees in his efforts to repel the ants. So far, none had made it above his thighs, but he was fighting a losing battle. Fearing the consequences of a mass invasion of his private regions, he made a quick and desperate decision and with three rapid steps and a jump he splashed knee-deep into an old ornamental pond, that until this moment in time had enjoyed a rather quiet and uneventful existence. However, it now experienced a small boy splashing water, pond weed and the odd surprised goldfish up the ends of his baggy shorts.

After a few minutes of sloshing around, Chris waded from the pond and following a brief inspection he was relieved that all ants had been repelled with only a few minor bites to himself. Looking into the pond he was also satisfied to see a brown scum of ants floating on the water with the occasional goldfish breaking the surface to feed on the unexpected but welcome delicacy. He sat down on a rock by the pond and removed his soggy trainers and socks along with his hooded top, as the sun had now burnt off the morning mist and the temperature was beginning to rise.

He looked down at himself. What a state. So much for the element of surprise. He'd made enough commotion and noise to wake up the inhabitants of Pluto and beyond. If there were any aliens in the orchard there was no doubt that they knew he was around. In fact, if they weren't friendly he would have been vaporised by now along with a couple of hundred ants!

'Okay, let's see what we've got,' he said as he wandered slowly to where he thought the mystery object would be. Unfortunately, because of his dance with the ants, he had disturbed most of the newly-mown area and he was now resigned to turning over the clods of grass in order to find anything. Getting down on all fours he started to brush the loose grass into piles. After ten minutes of searching he stood up and surveyed the scene. All he had succeeded in doing was to create a number of tidy piles of grass around the centre of the orchard. He looked at his hands. They were green. He looked down at his feet. Green. He looked at his knees. Green and covered in brown blotches. He bent down and on closer inspection discovered that the blotches were in fact rabbit droppings!

'Oh, paleese!' he exclaimed.

He grabbed another handful of grass and quickly wiped his knees free of the offending lumps.

'This is ridiculous. Stupid grass!' he shouted as he kicked out at the closest pile. His foot connected with a hard concealed object and a sharp pain exploded up through his big toe and into his ankle. Chris grabbed his foot with both hands, rubbing it to numb the pain.

'Ow! Ow! Ow! Ow!' he shouted as he hopped around in circles.

His mum looked out of the window for the second time that morning only to see her son hugging his foot and hopping around, whooping like an American Indian on the warpath. He then proceeded to sit down and tried to put his foot in his mouth!

'We've got to get that boy out more often,' she said to herself.

Thankfully, his mum did not see him hop back to the pond and immerse his foot in the cool water. This, at least, gave Chris some relief and the pain gradually faded. As he sat there wondering if it would have been better to have been vaporised, he noticed that a large clump of ants was floating towards him. He also noticed that they were in fact wriggling frantically, their many legs moving desperately and, in his opinion, intent on renewing their acquaintance with his legs. Suddenly any pain receded, he was healed and to prove it he was out of the pond and back under the shade of the apple tree in one athletic bound.

As he stood there and took stock of the situation, Chris realised that there was a good chance that the object which had connected with his foot was in fact what he had been searching for and he made his way to the demolished clump of grass. After satisfying himself that there were neither ants nor rabbit poo in the area, he knelt down and slowly cleared away the remains of the grass. He held his breath as he was finally faced with a curved metal object rising just a few centimetres out of the ground. He cautiously ran his fingers over it. It was shiny and smooth to the touch and looked not too dissimilar to a section of a large steel football.

'It doesn't look like a spaceship,' he thought. *'It must be recent whatever it is; otherwise if it had been in the ground for a long time, it would be rusty.'*

All fear now disappeared to be replaced with the excitement of adventure.

He knew that he would need to uncover more of the object to see if he could free it from the ground and inspect it further, so he carefully started to pull away the grass surrounding it. He then tried to scrape away the earth with his fingers, but as it had been quite a while since there had been any rain, the ground was too hard and compact and would not give way.

'Right,' he said. 'This is going to be a major excavation. I need tools.'

Chris ran to the garden shed which had doubled up as his father's workshop, opened the door and went to an old workbench where he excitedly pulled open a drawer and retrieved a rolled-up bundle. He unrolled the cloth and stared at the contents. It was a spare set of his father's archaeology tools. Suddenly he realised again how much he missed his dad and his mind drifted back to the day, over a year ago, when his mother had received the fateful telephone call.

His dad was an archaeologist who specialised in ancient languages and symbols and had been away working on an exciting project with the Global Archaeological Society at a site in the western Sahara.

A Bedouin robber had been caught trying to sell some strange artefacts on the black market and on inspection they had turned out to be small pieces of animal skin inscribed with hieroglyphics the style of which had never before been encountered. Such was the interest and importance of the find that his father had been contacted late one evening and arrangements were made to fly him out to the site the very next day.

Under police questioning the robber had disclosed that he had 'acquired' the items from a friend who worked at the massive Bou Craa phosphate mine. Further investigations directed the authorities to a rock formation some five kilometres west of the mine, and it was here that a small cave had led them to what turned out to be a simple burial tomb. The sarcophagus had been broken into by grave robbers and all that remained were the disturbed bones of its occupier. A Moroccan historian from the city of El Ayun had been sent out to inspect the site, and confirmed that the hieroglyphics that were carved into the shattered stone lid of the sarcophagus were much the same as those that were etched into the animal skins. Photographs of the lid samples and the animal skins were emailed to the Global Archaeological Society headquarters and this was when things started to escalate very quickly.

A team (including his dad) were contacted from all over the world and in a few days they were all assembled at a field camp constructed at the site of the tomb. Three days later, a secret passage was discovered behind a sliding stone wall and an exploratory party led by his dad had set off down the torchlit passageway. Within minutes, there was a loud rumbling and the roof to the tomb and the cave collapsed. The only survivors were those outside who watched in disbelief and horror as the entrance was sealed in a landslide of dust, sand and impenetrable rock. The tomb had lived up to its purpose and his father had not been seen or heard of since that day.

Chris could feel the warm tears welling up and he wiped his eyes with the palms of his hands. He took a deep breath.

'Okay Dad,' he said, picking up the bundle of tools. 'It looks like you're not the only archaeologist in the family.'

Twenty minutes later he was staring and slightly trembling at what he had uncovered so far. It was a helmet, the type that usually accompanied a suit of armour, and as far as he could make out there was indeed the beginnings of a breastplate. The helmet was turned at an angle, which was why only the curved side of it had been originally visible above the grass and earth. One exposed eye-slit stared darkly back at him and there was also a pointed, ventilated grill that appeared to have a hinge mechanism so that it could be raised. However, because of the sideways position of the helmet, it was not possible to open it at this moment, even if Chris could summon up the courage to look inside.

It wasn't long before he'd uncovered the shoulder-plates and the arms which ended in chain-mail gloves. The main body of the suit was now visible down to the waist. He became conscious that it was in very good condition and had somehow been preserved with hardly a scratch on it, and the last thing that he wanted to do was mark or dent it himself. In fact, he noted that there were so few obvious markings on it that the previous occupier had either been excellent at defending himself, or had not been involved in fighting at all.

'Chris! Lunch! Come in and wash your hands.'

His mother's voice startled him from his thoughts and he rose to survey with great satisfaction the work he had done that morning .

'Chris, did you hear me?'

This time her voice was much clearer and looking up Chris noticed his mother was making her way down the gravel path. He didn't want anyone to know about his discovery yet and he knew that if his mum found out she'd certainly have something to say about it.

'Coming Mum,' he said, getting up and running towards her.

'What are you up to, young man?' she said as she surveyed his hands and knees. 'Just look at the state of you, what have you been doing?'

'Just digging,' he replied.

'Just digging? You look as though you've wrestled with the compost heap, and where are your trainers and socks?'

'Oh, I took them off 'cause I fell into the pond.' (He thought this would get him some sympathy.)

'Fell into the pond? I hope you didn't frighten the fish!' she exclaimed.

'*So much for sympathy,*' thought Chris.

'Come on,' she said. 'Let's get you cleaned up, and don't you make a mess of my bathroom.'

'I'll just get my trainers and socks, be with you in a second,' he said and before his mum could object he was on his way back to the orchard.

'Right, but don't you be long,' she shouted after him, then thankfully she turned back to the house.

He hurriedly spread grass over the exposed armour and when he was happy with its concealment he made his way back to the house for his lunch. After he had been escorted to the bathroom and made to change out of his damp and mud-stained clothes he was issued with his combat pants and a T-shirt. Clean socks and trainers were issued with strict instructions to stay away from the pond!

'So, what's the plan for this afternoon?' asked his mum as he gulped down the last of his pizza. 'I thought we might take a trip to the park and then into town,' she continued.

'No thanks, I'd rather stay in the garden,' he replied.

'Why do you want to do that?' she asked.

Chris knew that if he didn't come up with something convincing he would be dragged off to the park and then on to the shops which would be totally boring.

25

'I'm going to tidy up the grass,' he announced. 'I thought it would save you having to do it.'

'Well, you've got to finish the job off properly if you want some extra pocket money, you don't seem to be doing a very good job of it so far,' she commented as she looked out of the window at the orchard. 'It looks in a worse state since you've been out there this morning. I mean, what are those mounds and that long lump by the apple tree? I don't call that tidy.' She turned to remonstrate further but he had already gone.

'Don't you go getting into any mischief, my boy,' she called after him.

2

Sir Peacealot

Chris had steadily worked through the afternoon and past tea time, when he had taken a short break and convinced his mum that as it was such a nice day he would like to eat his tea as a picnic under the trees. And so he found himself sitting against one of the old pear trees munching his way through an apple and studying the results of his activity.

It was fantastic! He had worked as carefully and as slowly as his excitement would allow him, scraping and brushing dirt and grass away from all of the joints and seams until a gleaming suit of steel was stretched out before him with no visible hint of age or rust.

He had not, as yet, attempted to move any part of the suit although he was now sure that he'd sufficiently freed up the arms and legs to do so. In fact, the whole figure appeared to be resting on a bed of earth. As he inspected it from head to toe, his eyes fell on the gleaming hilt of the sword which lay firmly in its scabbard that was buckled to the suit. It then dawned on him how strange it was that not only did the armour and chain mail look in incredibly good condition, but the leather straps which held it together were untouched by age.

'*Surely,*' he thought, '*at least that would have rotted away?*' The grip of the sword had a hand-guard fashioned into the shapes of two lions heads, The detail was intricate and small ruby-red jewels glistened in place for the lions' eyes. Staring at the shining stones he became mesmerised.

'I wonder,' he whispered to himself as he tentatively crawled towards the suit. He knelt down, studying the patterns on the hilt of the sword and the brightness of the red ruby stones. His hands reached out and grasped the handle – it was warm and somehow comforting. A tingling sensation began to grow in his fingers which spread up and into his hands and arms.

'Free me. Free me,' a deep voice whispered.

A sensation similar to that of static electricity bristled the fine hairs on Chris's arms and with a yelp of surprise he released his grip on the sword and fell backwards. He shook his head to clear the drowsy feeling that had crept up on him.

'Who's there?' he called, turning his head this way and that. 'You don't frighten me,' he added.

There was no reply as he stood there staring around the orchard from tree to tree. There was no sound or movement except for the gentle early evening breeze shifting the leaves on the trees.

'I've definitely been out in the sun too long today,' Chris mused and began looking for the water bottle that he'd been drinking from earlier on, eventually locating it in the grass and taking a gulp of the now very warm and stale water that it contained.

'Yuck! That's too gross!' he exclaimed, spluttering

and coughing the warm liquid across the back of his arm. Another breeze rippled through the trees and this time the early evening air was cool enough to bring out goosebumps on his arms. He retrieved his top from the rocks by the pond and was glad of its warming comfort.

'Let's see if my imagination is playing tricks on me,' he breathed to himself, and with a mixture of stubbornness and curiosity he once again knelt before the shining hilt of the sword.

He grasped the handle and felt the tingling sensation work its way into his hands. This time he noticed that all noise around him faded away, no birdsong, no rustling of leaves and, just as before, the voice whispered to him.

'Free me. Free me.'

Somehow he was unafraid; he gripped the handle tighter, the static electricity was crackling around him now and the small ruby stones in the lions' eyes glowed like hot coals on a barbeque. The same white light that he had seen from his bedroom window the previous evening now surrounded him, visible and bright even though the sky above him was still blue prior to the evening sunset.

His hair stood on end, the static making it ripple and shimmer. He looked down at his hands still firmly gripping the sword which had somehow released itself from its sheath, the blade gleaming like a polished mirror and as he watched, a strange luminescent writing began to appear. The letters scrolled their way from the tip towards the hilt as he stared, transfixed. Suddenly, chaos broke loose.

Either he was spinning or everything else was spinning around him, he was too confused to tell. The light became intense and he had to close his eyes. He squeezed them so tightly that it hurt. This made bright sparks explode in his head, dizziness claiming his senses, and then with one stomach-churning lurch, darkness smothered him and wrapped him in its sleep.

A noise echoed in his head. It was a familiar noise, a somehow comforting noise in the darkness which gradually gave way to grey and then bright light. He opened his eyes and the sharp pain of sunlight pierced his eyeballs, making him blink furiously. Then the source of the noise rubbed his face with its warm furry body.

'Tabby! Boy am I glad to see you,' he said, and shielding his eyes with one hand he curled the other around the cat and hugged it close to him.

He raised himself slowly on one elbow, his mind gathering together the memory of what had just happened; thoughts and images were merging together until he could make sense of what he had experienced. Chris's eyes fell upon the sword which now lay unsheathed by his side.

The blade was clear to see in all its magnificent glory, it was as if the surface rippled with different hues of light and colours which danced across the strange and beautiful writing etched along the length of mirrored steel. A fine, delicate mist hung around its edges, refusing to be moved by the now constant evening breeze.

All this Chris drank in, in wonder, distractedly stroking Tabby and allowing his mind to revisit what had happened when he had grasped the sword's handle.

'Well Tabby,' he said absently. 'We're either in big trouble or something amazing has just happened.'

'Or it could be both, young squire,' came the voice from behind him.

Chris looked up at where the suit of armour should still have been resting on the earth, only to find it no longer lying there.

Tabby chose this moment to sink his claws into Chris's leg. The cat spat and hissed while arching its back and straightening every strand of hair on its sleek body. With a piercing screech the cat leapt at least a metre into the air and shot with incredible speed across the orchard like a demented furry hovercraft heading towards the neighbouring foliage, with what Chris felt was most of the skin from his thigh trailing after it.

'Reeeeowwww!' shrieked the cat, rocketing between the trees, scattering clouds of grass in its wake.

'Yeeeeeowwww!' howled Chris, clutching his leg as the burning, stinging pain that only a cat's claws can inflict on human flesh spread across his recently ant-bitten skin. It was the third time that day that Chris felt the need to exhibit his ability to perform a weird and wonderful dance movement induced and fuelled by pain. He leapt to his feet, using the palms of both hands to rub and massage what precious skin that he felt was left intact beneath the material of his combats while almost defying gravity by leaping up and down on the spot.

The sound of tearful laughter gradually caught his

attention as the pain receded into an acceptable stinging and throbbing. He steadied himself and opened his own tear-filled eyes which took in a sight that had the effect of numbing all feeling of pain into a distant memory.

There, no more than two metres in front of him and sitting against the trunk of one of the pear trees with its legs splayed out before it was the suit of armour. However, the helmet was now placed upright on the ground next to the figure whose head protruded from the suit.

The knight's face was bright red and he spoke with an effort between bursts of laughter, his steel-encased hands and arms clutching at his stomach.

'My dear young squire, I have not witnessed such entertainment since the court jester was trussed up like a suckling pig with an apple in his mouth and presented for all to see at King Hector's All Hallows feast last season, 'tis merriment of the highest order,' he said.

Chris stood there trying to put some response together, some words of cautious curiosity. However, he was more than a little annoyed with what he saw as someone who obviously did not appreciate the work and effort that he had applied to free them from their earthly grave no matter how unexplained their revival was at that moment.

'I'm glad that you think it's so funny,' Chris started. 'Of course, if I had known that you were going to be so rude, I'm not so sure that I would have dug you out of the grass in the first place. You're not what I imagined a knight to be like at all.'

The knight stopped mid-laugh, his face remained red but now took on a stern and serious expression.

'Who's your master, what title and colours does he go by?' he barked.

Chris took a step backwards.

'Come on, boy, if we're to compare manners, then where's the ceremony and courtesy of your introduction? Speak up I say.'

'You go first,' said Chris in his bravest voice. 'You're the one with all of the gear, you're the one who's supposed to be a knight.'

'You have a strange way about you boy, but as you've given me such entertainment, I'll return the favour on this occasion and humour you.'

With that he picked up his helmet, stood up and tucked it ceremoniously under one arm while he made a fist of his other gloved hand, placed it on his hip, spread his legs and steadied his stance.

'Sir Percival Peacealot, knight of His Majesty King Hector the First, lord and ruler of the kingdom and protector of his loyal subjects.'

It was so impressive that Chris could almost hear a fanfare of trumpets and cheering crowds echoing in the distance.

Chris studied the knight's features. His face was now very pale which seemed to make his green eyes stand out bright and piercing. His nose was sort of pointed but not in an ugly or oversized way. His hair was thick, greyish and untidy and he had a ragged moustache which curled up at the ends and occupied most of his upper lip. There was the wisp of a goatee beard on his chin. He reminded Chris of pictures that he had seen of the character Don Quixote.

'Are you or are you not a squire?' enquired the knight.

'I suppose that I might be,' replied Chris, playing for time.

'Then I would be grateful for water,' said the knight.

Chris looked around for the discarded water bottle but then remembered how foul it had tasted.

'I'll need to fetch some, be back in a minute,' he announced and before the knight could object, he was heading up the path to the house. Minutes later when he returned with two plastic bottles of spring water he found the knight once more sitting against a tree.

'Here you go,' said Chris sitting opposite the knight and handing him one of the bottles.

Staring at the bottle, the knight hesitated.

'What witchcraft is this?' he whispered.

'What are you on about?' asked Chris.

'The water is hard and yet it moves,' said the knight in wonder.

'It's a plastic bottle of water, look,' Chris said as he took the bottle, unscrewed the cap and offered it back to the knight. 'Go on, it won't hurt you,' he encouraged.

The knight tentatively took the bottle and holding it up to the sky looked at it closely. He then turned the bottle to examine it further, however this was when he tilted the open end downwards and gravity pulled a stream of liquid onto his upturned face. There followed much coughing and spluttering and Chris had to be quick to catch the bottle before it spilt the rest of its contents over the convulsed knight.

34

'Steady!' he cried. 'You'll be rusting up if you're not careful.'

The knight pulled off his steel, chain-mail gloves to reveal reddened but strong-looking hands.

'How can you control such vessels?' he asked as he wiped his face.

'Look, it's easy,' Chris replied and demonstrated drinking from his own fresh bottle. He handed the other half-empty bottle back to the knight, who this time slowly copied Chris's actions and as he swallowed each mouthful his thirst gave him confidence and he swiftly drained the contents.

The knight stared at Chris for a few seconds and then finally said, 'I do not know what your standing is boy, but something tells me I must take counsel with you. I am gradually becoming aware of old memories which are clearing the confusion in my mind and I now know all is not as it should be for me.'

'Okay,' said Chris. 'First question, what year is it?'

'Why, the year of our king, fourteen hundred and thirty-two,' announced the knight.

'Who is on the throne?' asked Chris, holding down his excitement.

'King Hector the First, son of Eduard the Fallen,' came the reply.

Chris searched his memory and knowledge of English kings. He could not recollect these names as much as he tried, however, he would give the knight the benefit of the doubt for now as there was a strong chance that he may not have been paying attention when his teacher had mentioned these particular names.

'I'm afraid that I've got some rather surprising news for you,' he announced.

'Believe me, dear boy, I have encountered many things in my life from the enforced visions of witches and wizards to the floating trees of the Emerald Forest and the living ghosts of the Wastelands. Nothing can surprise me as my mind is open to all possibilities.'

'Well, let's see how surprised you are with this,' continued Chris. 'Somehow you've slept through the last five hundred and seventy eight years. This is the year two thousand and ten.'

The knight's face was creased with concentration.

'She couldn't have,' he murmured. 'The power would have destroyed her in doing so surely?' He paused. 'Unless she lies sleeping also.' His mouth became dry.

'I would favour some more of your water, no matter what the vessel, would you oblige me, boy?' he asked.

'You can have mine,' said Chris, passing the knight his bottle. 'I do have a name you know.'

'Which you have yet to reveal,' corrected the knight as he gulped down the water.

'Chris, my name is Chris.'

The knight inspected him, staring intently.

'Hey!' said Chris. 'Don't you know it's rude to stare?'

'I apologise, young Chris, but I am wary of your motive and I need to be sure that you are not one of her disciples.'

'One of whose disciples?' asked Chris.

'The wretched hag that I suspect has cursed me to this world – Belzeera!'

He looked around him cautiously and Chris noticed

that a chill breeze disturbed the leaves on the trees and made him shiver uncomfortably.

'Her power crosses time and worlds. She still exists somewhere but her influence is very weak,' whispered the knight. 'Let us hope and pray that she does not find an accomplice to free her in this world.'

'So, who exactly is this Belzeera?' ventured Chris.

The knight leaned his head back against the tree, closed his eyes and dug his hands into the grass.

Chris sat and waited in silence, studying the knight's features again. It was as if he was gathering his will, using the peace and the quiet to call on a hidden strength. Chris could see the colour filling his face and he noticed a change in the man's features, slowly a transformation was taking place, and as he watched it was as if he was becoming healthier, more alive in his features. Even his hair had darkened from a greyish shade to a thick shiny black, the moustache and beard were less ragged and more trim.

The minutes passed and the tired, pale figure that Chris had unearthed gave way to a conditioned and rejuvenated, younger-looking man. Even the armour seemed brighter, keener.

Sir Peacealot proceeded to tell Chris of his quest and how he had defeated Saleeza and Farella and his encounter with the ice monster, ending with his confrontation and battle with Belzeera. Chris sat there open mouthed; he could see the cold sweat on the knight's brow, he could feel the tension, he could almost smell the wretchedness of the witch.

The knight turned to Chris. 'And so young man, here I am, lost, alone and friendless except for your company.

Guide me if you can for I feel that you have much to play in my future.'

He looked up at the evening sky, streaked red and blue with the onset of a summer sunset.

Chris raided the kitchen once more and this time gave Sir Peacealot a large bottle of water, half of which he consumed in frantic gulps.

'Here's something you might like, it's good for energy,' said Chris, passing him a chocolate bar. He watched in fascination as the knight unwrapped it and took a bite. The look on his face was of absolute pleasure.

'I had heard of such delicacies, but thought they only existed in the minds of fools,' smiled Sir Peacealot.

'It's called chocolate and I don't think that it was discovered until the fifteen-hundreds,' said Chris. 'I've seen something on the internet about it not being introduced to Europe until then, so you definitely wouldn't have known about it in England at your time.'

Sir Peacealot looked at him with a frown.

'You speak many strange words to me, some that I do not understand.'

'What words aren't you sure about?' replied Chris.

'Well ...' The knight paused, running the words though his mind. *'Internet. Urope,* and *ingland,* these are unfamiliar to me.'

'I can understand that you don't know what the internet is,' said Chris. 'And I don't think they used the word Europe in your time but surely you know the name of your own country?'

'My country?' said Sir Peacealot quizzically. 'My

country and the kingdom of my birth is Castellion and I know it by no other name.'

Chris looked at him.

'Either you've got a really bad case of amnesia or you've been living in a totally different world.' It was then that the possibility hit him. 'That's it, what did that witch say to you? Something like, "I cast you to sleep for all time and in other worlds".'

'I cast you into the sleep of time and other worlds,' corrected Sir Peacealot quietly.

'That explains it,' said Chris excitedly. 'You're from another time *and* another world, like a parallel world. I've read about them in some of my science books, about black holes and things that warp time.'

But Sir Peacealot was not listening. Chris followed his gaze skyward to the now pre-dusk sunset of blues, reds and greys with the first shining diamonds of stars appearing. A pale twilight illuminated the orchard.

The expression on Sir Peacealot's face told Chris of his longing to return to his world, his land and his life.

The chatter of a bird heading for its nesting place for the night brought them out of their thoughts and Chris looked at his watch. 21.18 it read.

'Well, what are we going to do with you?' said Chris. 'I suppose I could try to smuggle you into my room for the night but it's going to be a bit dodgy with you clanking about in that armour. Look, I'll tell you what, you can spend the night in the shed, nobody goes in there these days. I'll get you a blanket and some more food and you can hide there until we figure out what to do next.'

'Hide?' responded Sir Peacealot, raising his voice. 'I am a knight, I do not hide!'

'Okay, okay, keep your armour on,' said Chris. 'What I meant was that it will be somewhere comfortable and no one will disturb you.'

'Hmm, blanket and food you say? Would it include any of that wonderful chocolate?' asked the knight hopefully.

'I'll see what I can do,' replied Chris, standing up. 'Meanwhile you'd better not leave this lying around.' He reached down into the grass and gripped the handle of the sword. It seemed unnaturally light in his hands as he brought it up in front of him, pointing the tip to the starry sky.

'Here you are,' he offered, but as he took a step, the true weight of the sword returned and it tilted forwards in his hands. The momentum pulled him towards Sir Peacealot who watched in alarm. Chris tried with all his strength to stop the blade from descending, but it was no use as the grip twisted in his hands and he stumbled with the sword falling towards the knight. He closed his eyes. Even to the last second he hung on to the sword, even as he felt it drive home.

'It's a good job that I've still got my reflexes,' Sir Peacealot said and Chris opened his eyes to see the sword firmly planted in the earth between the knight's splayed legs. 'Here, let me have that before you do some real damage.'

He clasped his hands around Chris's to draw the sword from the earth and in the final light of dusk they both saw the electric-blue glow from the sword's blade. As its intensity increased, a single note filled the air, sounding very much, as Chris would explain later, as if someone were running their finger around the rim of a glass.

The runes on the blade shone a golden colour and burned through the steel until it looked transparent. The blue glow enveloped them both now and try as he might Chris could not release his hands.

'What's happening?' he shouted as a whirlwind erupted around them.

'Magic!' shouted back Sir Peacealot. 'Powerful White Magic!'

Chris held his breath as the shadows of the orchard blurred into a grey mist which was then replaced by a curtain of stars that slowly wrapped themselves around him and his new companion.

He looked up at Sir Peacealot who had his eyes closed. Chris tried to speak but when he opened his mouth there was no sound except the constant ringing tone that seemed to emanate from the sword itself. He couldn't tell if the stars were revolving around them or if they were the ones who were moving. The spinning intensified, making him dizzy. The last thing he remembered was saying over and over to himself, *'Don't let go, don't let go,'* then, the soft dark cloak of unconsciousness wrapped itself around him.

3

Castellion

The smell of fresh green grass drifted into his senses as Chris awoke, and he opened his eyes to a cloudless, powder-blue sky. His head was clear and he felt refreshed as his thoughts calmly put together his last memories.

'Wow!' he murmured. 'What a dream, I've got to stop eating so much just before I go to sleep.' He lay there enjoying the warmth of the sun and the feeling of being totally comfortable.

'This grass must be the softest grass I've ever slept on, I must tell Mum to get some more,' he thought as he turned on his side. As his vision took in the view and reality kicked into his consciousness, he froze, open mouthed.

He was lying on a grassy hill looking down across a green rolling dale. A river glistened in the sunlight as it made its way out of a wood and towards an enormous stone castle in the distance. Even from here he could clearly see the turrets and buttresses with flags fluttering in the breeze. The drawbridge was down and he could just make out a horse and cart making its way into the castle.

'You have got to be kidding me!' he said aloud, pulling himself up to a sitting position. 'This can't be real.'

'I'm afraid it is, young squire,' said a familiar voice behind him.

Chris swivelled himself around and there, before him, sitting cross-legged and in his cloth garments, his armour placed to one side, was Sir Peacealot, his face beaming with a friendly smile.

'I thought that you were going to sleep for all eternity. The sun has been risen threefold and breakfast has been caught, cleaned and cooked.' He indicated to a small fire with what looked like the remains of a rabbit sizzling above the flames.

Chris looked at his watch; the face stared back at him and he read out the numbers, 21.20. *'But it's daylight,'* he thought.

'What's happened, where are we?' he asked.

'Come here my friend and I'll tell you what I know while you breakfast on some of this delicious rabbit and fresh field mushrooms.' Sir Peacealot could see the concern on Chris's face. 'Don't you go worrying about your safety now. No harm will come to you while I'm around.'

Chris didn't actually feel afraid. Everything still felt like a dream to him and so he sat himself next to Sir Peacealot and took the hot piece of meat that was offered to him, blowing on it and passing it from hand to hand to cool it down.

'Well, my young friend, the first thing I must tell you is that you have a purpose here and whether you know it or not there is some magic about you. Listen to me well as this concerns our past and our future.'

Sir Peacealot proceeded to tell Chris that the Wizard Gizmo had come to him in a dream while they travelled through what he now knew was called the Slipstream, a passage of time and space, accessible only by using some of the universe's most ancient Magik. The knowledge of this power had been a closely kept secret since the dawn of creation, handed down only by those known as Guardians.

There had always been a Guardian for each of the Dimensions. Castellion was one such Dimension and Gizmo was one such Guardian. He possessed the power of the rare and ancient Magik to protect Castellion and the gateway to the other Dimensions.

For the first time known, an individual outside the Guardians had gained access to the secret knowledge of time and dimensional travel and was preparing to use it on behalf of the darkest and most evil of beings, Lord Maelstrom!

Lord Maelstrom intended to use the power not only to conquer the lands and world of Castellion but to spread the endless night across all of the Dimensions. The individual concerned was Belzeera, Lord Maelstrom's elder sister, and she was just beginning to build up the knowledge that she needed to control the full force of the ancient powers. That was why Gizmo had armed Sir Peacealot with the protection of the high Magik among many other spells.

As he had told Chris before, Belzeera was a shamanic witch, the distinguishing element of shamanic witchcraft being the knowledge and use of certain plants to effect mental transitions between worlds. However, this did not transport her physically. Somehow she had come into the possession of a lost Rune Stone, and Gizmo suspected that Lord Maelstrom had something to do with this. This Stone, when combined with her power, gave her the full ability to travel through time and the Dimensions. But one last ingredient was missing to make the power complete, and that was the blood and soul of a pure and steadfast person. The problem was, it would need such an individual to also defeat her, that person was Sir Peacealot.

Gizmo's most powerful Magik was conjured into Sir Peacealot's shield and sword. Secret unseen runes were implanted into both, enough to deflect most dark or evil magic. Gizmo knew that he would have to use the witch's own powers against her if she were to be defeated and so the bag that he had given Sir Peacealot contained a potion of the plants which gave her her shamanic powers and he had instructed Sir Peacealot as to when to apply them to the sword and shield and so bring the high Magik into effect. From what Sir Peacealot could gather, the wizard hadn't expected the knight to be transported into another Dimension and affected by the witch's final curse.

In the dream, the Wizard Gizmo had also told Sir Peacealot of a prophecy that a boy not of this world would be instrumental in Castellion's future. Strange days and strange Magik were coming to the kingdom. New friends and old foes would be thrown together in battle.

Sir Peacealot had woken from the dream and found himself lying in the grass, and on seeing the castle he knew that he was home again. His stomach had complained of hunger and he had decided to wait until

Chris awoke naturally and used the time to go hunting in the nearby woods, where he had caught the rabbit and picked the mushrooms.

Chris had listened intently to the tale, deciding to save his questions for later, and had concentrated on satisfying the hunger pains in his own stomach. By the time Sir Peacealot had finished, Chris had devoured most of the rabbit; he had never tasted anything as delicious and although he didn't usually like meat (in fact, he had often thought of becoming a vegetarian) he had to admit that he would quite happily eat roast rabbit again.

Sir Peacealot removed what was left of the carcass from the fire and proceeded to pick at the bones.

'If you wander to the bottom of the hill, there's a small stream where you can wash the food and the journey from your hands and face,' he told Chris.

He found Chris a short while later, sitting by the stream with sadness on his face.

'What's the matter my young friend?' he asked.

'What's going to happen to me?' asked Chris. 'My Mum will wonder where I've gone. How am I going to get home?'

'Fret not and fear not, I'm sure that you will return to your rightful place and time. We'll see Gizmo and he'll put everything to rights, just you wait and see. Come on, we have adventures ahead of us, the first of which is to find that crafty old wizard.'

Sir Peacealot climbed into his armour and the both of them started their journey towards the castle. Along the way the knight explained the etiquette of court and how a castle's society worked.

'We don't want to alarm people or give them the knowledge of what's happened,' he explained. 'They must not know that you are from another Dimension, another world, so we must make up a story between us. What I would suggest is that I say that you come from a little known part of the realm seldom visited by outsiders and that you are my new squire in training that I have acquired on my travels. How does that sound?'

'Okay,' said Chris. 'But you're going to have to tell me a bit about what a squire does, and what about my clothes?' He looked down at his trainers, combat trousers and Disney T-shirt and gestured to the hooded top that he carried over his arm.

'They're going to think that's a bit strange.'

'Oh, I'm sure you'll think of some explanation if I don't,' said Sir Peacealot, who then proceeded to tell Chris about the duties of a knight's squire.

By the time they were on the track leading to the drawbridge, Chris's head was spinning with so much information on sword carrying, horse grooming, armour cleaning, cooking, washing and other squire's duties that he wished that he had never asked.

I'll make it up as I go along,' he thought. *'No one will notice.'*

As they approached the castle he looked up at the flags fluttering from the turrets. They all had the same colours and motif on them: a pale blue background with a golden-rayed sun in the centre.

When they eventually walked onto the large wooden drawbridge and up to the portcullis gate, they were immediately challenged by two of the castle guards who were the biggest, most ferocious-looking men Chris had ever seen. The same blazing emblem that adorned the flags was resplendent on their tabards.

'Halt, who goes there?' said one very gruffly.

'Friend or foe of Castellion?' said the other as they both pointed their sharp-looking pikes at Chris and Sir Peacealot.

'What's this?' questioned Sir Peacealot from behind his visor. 'Why such formal aggression towards strangers?'

'Orders of the king,' barked the larger of the guards. 'These are troubled times. Now state your loyalty, your business and your names.'

'My loyalty is to the one and only ruler of the kingdom, King Hector and my business is with the royal court and His Majesty. I am Sir Peacealot, defender of the realm, quest knight and loyal subject and this is my trusted squire and page,' he announced, lifting his visor.

The guards looked astonished, their pikes dropping to the ground.

'It was rumoured that you were dead my lord, slain by the vicious hag witch Belzeera,' said the first guard. He turned to the other guard. 'Brother, go and send the news to the king and arrange an escort for Sir Peacealot and his squire. Go on, don't just stand there gawping, make haste.' As the second guard disappeared into the castle, the first motioned Sir Peacealot and Chris to enter.

'You are welcome to rest in the keep until your escort arrives, my lord.' He motioned them to the guards' room at the base of one of the towers.

'No bother,' said Sir Peacealot. 'We'll wait in the courtyard.'

The guard looked concerned. 'I would advise otherwise, my lord.'

'And why should that be?' asked Sir Peacealot.

'There are those that thought you dead sire, and rumours are believed that you had been transformed into a servant of Lord Maelstrom himself and taken into his service to plot against the realm,' he said, and carefully eyeing Chris added, 'The boy dresses strangely and could be taken for a witch's familiar.'

Sir Peacealot noticed that a small crowd had gathered just inside the castle gate and people were eyeing the scene, some with curiosity and some with concern.

'The boy's attire is of foreign lands,' said Sir Peacealot, raising his voice. 'We have travelled long and light since we were relieved of our belongings by vagabonds and thieves while we slept one night and the boy is not yet equipped nor fully trained in his duties as my squire. He has many strange customs and uses unfamiliar words, but one thing I can assure you of, is that he is no witch's familiar and I am no servant of the Dark Lord.' He stepped in front of Chris protectively and drew his sword, brandishing it at the crowd.

'I will openly challenge anyone who rumours otherwise,' he announced.

Just then, the crowd parted and a figure familiar to Sir Peacealot appeared. The midnight blue cloak with its gold and silver runes shimmering in the material gave presence to the unmistakable features of Gizmo, wizard of the realm. He was not a tall person but those close to him seemed to diminish in size as he passed by them. His silver hair was pulled back into a long pony tail which curled around his neck and was plaited with symbols, ciphers and charms. A silver beard was similarly plaited and a trim moustache framed his beaming smile.

'So, you did survive! I knew it, I knew it,' he said, his face joyful with pleasure. 'That old hag was no match for my Magik. I kept telling them. He'll be back, sooner or later and, well, here you are. I might have expected it to be sooner. What's taken you so long?'

Sir Peacealot opened his mouth to explain when the wizard cut him off.

'No matter, no matter. Show me the boy,' he said eagerly.

Chris peered out slightly in awe from behind Sir Peacealot.

'A real live Wizard,' he thought. *'I wonder what he wants with me?'*

'Come out boy, come out and let me see you properly, I've been waiting a long time to meet you,' said Gizmo.

'I can't believe that you've been expecting me,' said Chris curiously as he stepped out from behind Sir Peacealot.

'We've all been expecting you,' said the wizard, gesturing with his arms.

'Everyone?' said Sir Peacealot.

'Well, those of us with the foresight,' corrected the wizard. 'But more of that later. Now let me take a good look at you boy.'

He caught hold of Chris by the shoulders and stared intently into his eyes and his ears.

'Open your mouth,' he ordered.

Chris was so shocked at the command that he obeyed immediately. Gizmo peered in. 'Hmmm,' he murmured. Then he turned Chris around in a circle, felt for the muscles on his arms and stood back.

'You're not very tall, are you?' observed the wizard, a finger crooked across his chin.

Now, Chris had always been aware of his short stature. In fact the bullies and spiteful individuals at school regularly reminded him of it. That made Chris quite defensive about it. So it was no surprise that he blurted out, 'You can talk, have you looked in a mirror lately?'

The wizard's face changed as his skin's pallor darkened, his eyes glowed ice white. The sun disappeared behind a cloud that materialised from nowhere and a rough breeze swirled around them. A roll of thunder shook the ground and Chris noticed that even Sir Peacealot had stepped a little away from him.

The wizard seemed to grow in front of Chris. Two metres, three metres, four metres, towering over him.

'Am I not great in stature now?' boomed Gizmo.

Chris stood still with his mouth open, looking up, as the echo of the wizard's voice rumbled into the distance. Then for a moment there was silence and no one dared to move.

'Chirrup! Chirrup!' came the sound from Chris's pocket. 'Chirrup! Chirrup!' It sounded again with some urgency.

Not taking his eyes off the wizard, Chris put his hand into his pocket and retrieved the object.

51

'My Tamagotchi,' explained Chris, holding out the blue plastic toy while it continued to chirrup its little tune. Chris glanced at the display. 'It's hungry and I need to feed it,' he said, as the tune became more erratic and insistent. 'I've got to feed it or it will get sick and die, this is tenth generation and I don't want that to happen.'

'What wonder is this?' enquired Gizmo as curiosity broke the spell and he shrank to his normal size, the pleasant sunny day returning as if nothing had happened.

'A Tamagotchi,' repeated Chris. 'It's an electronic toy.' He turned the screen towards Gizmo as he proceeded to study the little screen and press the appropriate buttons, the Tamagotchi beeping and chirruping with approval.

The wizard's long slender hand reached out and curled itself over Chris's hands and the toy. He turned his head to observe the king's herald who was approaching, closely followed by a company of the royal guard.

'Best hide this Magik and keep it quiet for now; there are those whose minds are not yet ready for such marvels and would use them for the wrong reasons. All in good time, you and I will discuss such things. But, for now, be discreet with this and any other wares you may have brought with you from your world.'

'You mean, you know?' gasped Chris.

'I know many things concerning you my boy, and there are others who may share an insight to your coming and who would seize you for their wicked motives. The least you say to anyone for the moment the better. I don't want either of you giving away any information.' He glanced at Sir Peacealot. 'Or even mentioning your name until I've had the chance to have a long talk with you myself.'

Chris set his Tamagotchi on pause and put it into his pocket.

'Sir Knight,' commanded the Wizard. 'Sheath your sword before it gets you into more trouble, stay close by my side until we are safely inside the royal court and don't say anything until I tell you to. The same goes for you, boy,' he said to Chris. 'But obviously without the sword bit,' he added as an after thought.

The wizard turned and then everything seemed to move at breakneck speed. Suddenly, they were off, Chris and Sir Peacealot striding alongside the wizard who was shouting at soldiers and people alike, announcing the return of Sir Peacealot and command- ing them to keep their distance lest he turn them all into sheep or toads or even a mixture of the two. (The latter threat having the greatest effect on even the most inquisitive individuals who dared to get too close.)

Chris had no trouble keeping up with the two men; it was as if he was being carried along, his legs effort- lessly striding forward. The royal guards, however, seemed to struggle with the pace, stumbling over the cobbled yard and tripping into each other in their efforts to keep up. The herald, keen to get in front so that he could be ready to announce them into the court, became sandwiched between two of the burly guards, his long trumpet becoming entangled with his tabard.

By the time they had all reached the tall wooden doors of the throne room, every guard was red-faced and distinctly out of breath. The herald was nowhere to be seen. Gizmo pulled at a strand of his silver hair and plucked it from his head. He let the strand fall towards the flagstone floor, and as it fell it thickened and lengthened until it formed a bright silver cane covered in strange patterns and carvings. Gizmo reached out and caught hold of the stick as it hovered before him.

'Piece of cake,' he announced. 'Now let's have some fun, shall we?'

4

Don't Look Down

The giant wooden doors arced open effortlessly to the movement of Gizmo's hand and the babble of the crowded court receded as heads turned in expectation of Sir Peacealot's return. To Chris, everything seemed just how he imagined a king's court to be from pictures and descriptions in history books. Before him was a great circular room with tall stone arches and pillars supporting the wooden struts and beams of the roof. Multi-coloured banners and tapestries hung from the walls.

What light could enter, streaked down from the high stone windows, dust motes danced in the shafts of sunlight and grey smoke drifted in the air from the burning braziers and the hanging iron chandeliers which were alight with hundreds of yellow wax candles. Birds fluttered in the eaves and shadows teased themselves around the walls. The floor was strewn with straw and Chris could see glimpses of the flagstones exposed in random patches.

They strode forwards through the gathered ensemble of colourful individuals. Knights, squires, courtiers, guards and ladies in waiting all filled the court, and

Chris even spotted what he thought was a gaudily clothed jester, sitting amongst four or five very large black dogs grouped at the base of one of the stone pillars.

Gizmo brought them to a halt a short distance from some rising steps where two more large dogs lounged, their pointed ears alert for any untoward movement and their sharp, ivory fangs just visible through their partly open pink mouths.

In front of them, an enormous blue tapestry hung against the far wall from ceiling to floor. At its centre was embroidered a giant, blazing, golden sun. Sitting in front of this, on a carved wooden throne that was raised up on a dais, was unmistakably the king, resplendent in a blue tunic and leggings braided with gold and silver, a simple gold band with lettering engraved around it adorning his head.

His careworn face carried the lines of responsibility rather than of age and was framed by greying shoulder-length hair. Either side of his throne stood two knights. The one to the right was wearing armour that seemed to be dark crimson in colour. The candle-light reflected oranges and reds on the steel suit so that flames danced and flickered across the metal. The wearer had a round and pleasant face and his hair was a striking shade of light brown. Chris thought that his skin looked tanned, as if he had spent much time in the sun.

Chris's eyes moved to the other knight, who up until then had been turned to one side, speaking to one of the guards. The figure now faced Chris and he nearly gasped with surprise, for there, dressed in a suit of white, steel armour was a woman, her thick black hair in contrast cascading over her shoulders like a long mane. She was now examining Chris intently with her strange, smoke-grey eyes.

'Your Majesty,' announced Gizmo. 'I present to you, your noble knight, long thought lost to us but now returned victorious, Sir Percival Peacealot and his new squire enlisted from foreign lands.'

He bowed and stepped to one side. Sir Peacealot knelt on one knee and lowered his head before the king. Chris was brought to his senses with a sharp jab in the side from Gizmo who gestured for him to follow suit. He did as he was told and his knee connected with the stone floor with a thump.

'Trust me to find a gap in the straw,' he thought.

Nothing immediate seemed to happen and Chris wondered whether he should look up when two leather-clad feet appeared on the stone steps before him.

'Arise my knight,' said the voice above him. 'It was thought that your presence would never be seen again, our hopes for your safe return have only been encouraged by the Wizard Gizmo and we have waited many months for this day.'

From the corner of his eye Chris saw Sir Peacealot stand and wondered if he should do the same. As if reading his thoughts, Gizmo whispered to him.

'Wait your turn, you'll know when.'

Chris knelt there while the king made a speech to the court celebrating Sir Peacealot's return and a sharp pain jabbed in his knee and started to spread pins and needles down his leg.

'Oh great,' he thought, 'just what I need.' He tried to

shift his weight but this only sent more sharp pains down his leg. In desperation he slowly reached down and grabbed a wad of straw. He lifted his knee, gritting his teeth at the pain and, as quick as he dared, he slid the small clump under his knee. Immediately he felt relief, the softness cushioning the floor. Just as he was congratulating himself for being so clever, the smell hit his nostrils. It was unmistakable.

'*Dog poo!*' he grimaced to himself as he felt the dampness soaking into his combats and he realised too late what the straw was strewn around for. Things were just about to get worse.

'Arise young squire and present yourself to the king,' came Sir Peacealot's voice.

Chris hesitated but was then persuaded to stand by another poke from Gizmo's silver cane. Chris stood up and the clump of straw and dog muck defiantly remained attached to his leg. He felt that everyone in the court was looking at it with disgust. He reached down self-consciously to brush the offending lump off but to his horror it detached itself from his leg and stuck to his hand. He shook his hand but to no avail, it wouldn't shift. It clung to him like a troublesome, sticky toffee paper. He stood there going redder and redder with a damp patch on one knee and a smelly lump of straw and dogs mess on his hand. He just wanted to disappear.

Thankfully, the next best thing happened and Gizmo came to his rescue. With a touch of his silver cane the lump evaporated in a puff of smoke and the patch on his combats faded, though unfortunately the smell remained!

'What strange attire,' observed the king, taking a

step backwards as the offending smell reached his nostrils. 'I'm sure we have much to hear from you but first we must know your name.'

Chris opened his mouth to introduce himself but all that came out was, 'Blurble, blurble, piffle wick!'

There were several gasps from the court.

The king leaned forward. 'What's this?'

'Blibble, pobby blip sla, sla, slallop,' stuttered Chris, totally confused as he could hear himself saying his name in his head but he also heard the gibberish escaping from his mouth.

Murmurs now started to surface from several corners of the great hall.

'Sir knight, explain,' demanded the king.

Sir Peacealot opened his mouth, looked at Gizmo and closed it again.

'If I may explain, my king,' interjected the wizard, moving forward. 'The boy is from a region vastly unexplored and rarely visited by outsiders. Their language is a complicated one to such a point that I will need some time alone with him to successfully cast a speech spell to convert his tongue to ours.'

The king looked down at Chris. Chris smiled back weakly. The king looked at Sir Peacealot.

'How have you managed to talk with the boy?' he asked.

'Sign language,' blurted out Sir Peacealot. 'And hand signals,' he added, waving his arms wildly for good measure.

Gizmo looked skywards in disbelief.

'Well, demonstrate for us now so that we at least can exchange names,' commanded the king.

59

Gizmo moved forward. 'If I may have a private word, my king?'

The king nodded his approval and Gizmo leaned forward and whispered into his ear.

'Oh, I see,' said the king briskly, stepping further back from Chris and Sir Peacealot. He turned and addressed the gathered crowd.

'Sir Peacealot and his squire have journeyed long to reach us and no doubt have many tales to share, however I feel it would be wise to give them time to recover from their travels before we put them to the court's questioning. I myself am tired from the day's events and therefore I declare this gathering at an end until tomorrow when we shall have all manner of festivity to celebrate our brave knight's return. Clear the court.'

Amidst much mumbling and some gentle protesting, the royal guards ushered the crowd through the big doors and out of the room. The king and the two knights left the dais and disappeared through a gap in the tapestry which hung behind the throne.

Gizmo beckoned Sir Peacealot and Chris to him.

'What did you say to the king?' asked Sir Peacealot.

'I told him that you may be infected with a sickness spell and that it was best for me to cleanse you both before you had any further contact with him.'

They both stared back at him accusingly.

'Well, it worked, didn't it? Now let's move on, shall we?' he snapped. 'Follow me and don't stray,' he said as he touched one of the large stone pillars with his silver cane. Silently, granite blocks slid aside and a rough, door-shaped opening appeared. Gizmo stepped into the darkness.

His voice echoed from the shadows. 'Come on, don't just stand there gawping.'

Chris followed the wizard with Sir Peacealot close behind.

'Hold tight and don't look down,' ordered the wizard as the stone pillar closed in front of them and they were bathed in a grey, eerie light. There was a rushing of air from below them and Chris looked down in horror to see that there was no floor. They were suspended on a thin grey vapour and he could see the stone pillar walls dropping below them into lost darkness.

'Crikey!' he yelped, grabbing hold of the wizard's cloak.

'I told you not to look down,' growled Gizmo, and Chris closed his eyes.

Then with a start, they were lifted on a soft cushion of air, their clothes billowing around them as they travelled upwards. Chris thought he saw a flickering of coloured lights through his eyelids and so he opened his eyes. The stone wall was inches from his face as it raced past at an incredible speed, flickering and flashing colours as if it were a fairground ride. Looking up he saw nothing but blackness. He glanced to his left at Sir Peacealot who was also staring up, the colours dancing across his face. The knight smiled down at Chris.

'Here comes the bit that I like,' he grinned.

'You mean there's more?' asked Chris.

The wizard reached out and touched the wall with his silver cane and the wall became a curtain of mist.

'Get ready to step forward,' he instructed Chris.

'You have got to be joking,' yelled Chris. 'Haven't you noticed that there's nowhere to go to?'

'Of course,' said Sir Peacealot. 'That's the fun in it.'

'Now, one, two, three, step!' commanded the wizard.

Once again, Chris closed his eyes and hung on to Gizmo's cloak, for good measure he also grabbed Sir Peacealot's arm, then he stepped forward with them. It was like walking through a veil of thin material and as it passed across his face, Chris realised he was again standing on something solid. Slowly, he opened his eyes. It was amazing; they were standing on a stone balcony overlooking an enormous circular room with a high, domed ceiling.

'Where are we?' he asked in wonder.

'The wizard's private apartments. Very few have had the privilege of visiting them,' said Sir Peacealot.

Chris stepped forward to grasp a thick iron railing. Spread below him was a vast space comprising a confusing mixture of apparatus and objects.

The right-hand side of the room was dedicated to an array of test tubes, bowls and laboratory equipment. Coloured liquids bubbled and gurgled their way through a maze of glass pipes. The left-hand side was laid out as what looked like an indoor herb garden, with plants of all different shapes and sizes in pots and trays, all bathed in a strange orange glow. In the centre of the room was the strangest construction that Chris had ever seen. It resembled a cross between a giant telescope and a hang-glider. A wooden seat was suspended under the end of the telescope which itself was mounted on a large revolving wooden wheel. The hang-glider style wings formed a canopy above the seat. To the right of the seat was a series of levers and knobs and to the left a curious glass jar filled with multi-coloured marbles.

On the far side of the room a semicircle of steps led up to a large stone fireplace, where a fire burned with vivid blue and orange flames generously licking at a blackened pot hanging over it. What loosely resembled a kitchen was tucked away in an arched recess, with all manner of spice jars filling wall racks and bunches of dried herbs hanging from shelves. Just to the left of the fireplace was a carpeted area encircled with large colourful cushions and sheepskin rugs.

The domed ceiling was supported by strong wooden arches and beams. As Chris tried to take in the view, he caught a movement amongst the beams, and a small dark shadow scuttled out of sight. He strained his eyes to follow it but it was too quick for him.

'Come along boy, we haven't got all day,' shouted the wizard from below.

Chris scampered down the curving stone steps to join him and heard Sir Peacealot, who was excitedly describing the wonders of chocolate to the wizard.

'The taste!' exclaimed the knight. 'It could be worth a king's ransom and would enchant the fair ladies of the court. I'm sure that the boy could share its secret and many other wonders from his world with us.'

'I've no doubt that he could,' replied the wizard. 'We just have to make sure that he keeps such information to himself.'

'Keep what to myself?' asked Chris.

Gizmo turned and looked worriedly at Chris. 'This world is not yet ready for many things, no matter how trivial they may seem. You have the power to bring us knowledge that can destroy us all, my boy, but the same power can save us from the desolation planned by Lord Maelstrom and his followers.'

'I don't like the sound of that at all,' said Chris nervously.

'Then prepare yourself for the greatest burden you may ever know. We must sit and I will educate and acquaint you with my knowledge concerning your future in both this world and your own,' instructed the wizard.

They sat amongst the sheepskins and cushions while Gizmo revealed what he knew, of things past and how the future could unfold in different ways. He recounted the history of the rôle of the Guardians and how the witch Belzeera was planning to conquer time and space for Lord Maelstrom, which would mean the conquest and complete devastation of the Four Dimensional Worlds. Time would cease and the living dead would reign over all those who were not annihilated in the process.

Although Gizmo's Magik and Sir Peacealot's courage had brought Belzeera's actions to a halt, it would seem that she had merely been delayed from opening the gate to the Dimensions for Lord Maelstrom and his armies.

'She lies sleeping in the earth also,' said Gizmo. 'And it is only a matter of time before someone awakens her in much the same way as you awakened Sir Peacealot. Dark activities have been reported from the Ice Mountains and Frozen Wastes and it would seem that Lord Maelstrom is encouraging the Hidden People to rise against us. This will be the first of many battles to be won if we are to defend Castellion and the Dimensions.' He paused and closed his eyes for a moment.

'The coming of a boy, not of this world was revealed aeons ago to the elder Guardians. This boy, it was prophesied, would have the powers to allow good or evil to triumph and bring a final destiny to the Dimensions. His abilities and knowledge would need to be harnessed if good was to prevail, for he would bring the science of the future in his mind and if this were applied in other Dimensions then catastrophe would follow for all. So you see, young squire,' he said, addressing Chris, 'even a trinket such as this could give the forces of evil victory if it was in the wrong hands.' The wizard held aloft Chris's Tamagotchi by its short chain.

'How did you ...?' said Chris, amazed that the wizard had taken it from him without his knowing. 'Anyway, it's just a game,' Chris protested. 'It's like a small computer, you have to instruct it what to do.'

'Oh, I see,' said the wizard. 'You mean like this?' He touched it with his silver cane and threw it out in front of him. Before it hit the ground, the small screen burst open and a miniature figure jumped out, then another and another, until there were half a dozen black, distorted Tamagotchi men grouped together on the carpeted area in front of them.

'Enough!' commanded the wizard. 'Grow!'

Sure enough the figures began to grow in size until the wizard made a movement of his hand and they remained at about a metre in height.

'Now, fight!' he ordered.

Immediately the figures attacked each other with incredible ferocity, tearing at each other, intent on destruction. Sir Peacealot jumped to his feet and drew his sword.

'Stay, Sir Knight. They will not harm you unless commanded,' said Gizmo.

The wizard allowed the carnage to continue for less than a minute before he clapped his hands and the now grotesquely damaged figures shrank and spiralled back into the Tamagotchi screen.

'So my young friend, you say it's just a game and you only have to instruct it what to do. In this world, the game is deadly when the wrong person gives the instructions.' He tapped the Tamagotchi with a long index finger. 'Herein lies an army of thousands just waiting to be released and commanded.'

Chris sat and stared at the toy as Gizmo handed it back to him. He didn't really know if he wanted it any more. Sir Peacealot sheathed his sword but remained standing, anxious should the figures appear again.

'I will be your guide and counsel my friend, but you must understand that some things that may seem harmless to you, in fact, have immense power here,' said Gizmo.

Chris looked up at Gizmo. 'I'm not a coward, Mr Wizard, but I think that you've got the wrong boy. I think that I should go home, if it's all the same to you, as my Mum will be worried where I am by now.'

'Home, you say? Well I have no power to return you, it is said that when your task is complete the Dimensions will return you. As for your mother, console yourself, she won't even miss you.'

Chris stood, anger welling up in him. 'That's not true; my Mum loves me, if I was missing she'd be searching for me. She will miss me, she will miss me!' he tearfully shouted at the wizard.

'Calm yourself, boy,' soothed Gizmo. 'Of *course* she loves you, but she will not miss you in the sense of time. Only a second or two divides our worlds, nothing more, and nothing less. Whenever you are returned it will be as if you had never left.' He placed a hand on Chris's shoulder and a calm ran through Chris's mind, chasing away doubts, fears and confusion. He knew all of a sudden that somehow, everything would be all right.

Gizmo produced a small wooden box, carved with distinct runes, and opened its lid.

'Put the rest of your other-world belongings in here for safe keeping, we wouldn't want any of them getting into the wrong hands, would we?'

Chris put the Tamagotchi in first and then searched his pockets: two marbles, half a rubber, an old conker and finally a wine bottle cork were placed into the box.

'Can I keep my watch?' he asked.

'For your own comfort of mind, yes. It will be of no use if worn by another, but, keep it hidden, all the same,' the wizard replied.

'And what about this?' Chris asked, holding up half a packet of chewing gum.

The wizard took it, put it up to his nose, sniffed and put it on top of the other items.

'That definitely goes in,' he said with disdain.

Gizmo passed his hand over the box, the lid silently closed and the carvings and joints just melted into the grain, leaving no hinge or visible means of access. It looked to all accounts like a solid piece of wood.

'You'll get them back all in good time,' he said, and placed the box on top of the great stone fireplace. He turned and faced Chris, his gaze looking deep into the boy's eyes.

'You have strength about you my little friend which even you have not reckoned with. Take this time to be at peace and calm your mind. Your education is about to start with urgent matters that you will need to know. Sir Knight, I would suggest that you divest yourself of your armour. Now will be the time for knowledge not battle. I'll arrange some sustenance for us all.'

Gizmo turned to where the pot steamed over the open fire and busied himself while Sir Peacealot removed his armour.

Chris sank back into the soft cushions, his head swimming with thoughts and his eyes staring up at the domed ceiling.

There it was again. The small shadow darting amongst the beams.

'Have you got rats?' Chris enquired, eyeing the rafters.

'Rats?' asked the wizard, turning to Chris, a ladle in his hand. Chris pointed upwards.

'Oh!' replied Gizmo. 'He'll be down when he's ready. He's more than likely *catching* rats if anything.' And he turned back to the fire.

Chris felt the soft warmth of the cushions melt into him but he was not aware of his eyelids closing and taking him into a half sleep. He became conscious of the wizard's and Sir Peacealot's voices in conversation and the strange sensation that he knew he was awake but still caught in the dream of his cat, Tabby, lying on his chest as he stroked him. He slowly opened his eyes, aware that the weight on his body and the fur running between his fingers were no longer part of a dream.

The eyes that stared back were jet black; as was the whole face and head that filled his vision. The whiskers were sleek and long, a glimpse of white fangs was the only break in the monotone colour. Chris craned his head back to take in the full size of the animal. It was a *giant* cat. The word 'panther' materialised in Chris's head and his hand trembled and froze, mid-stroke. A low rumbling growl emitted from the animal.

'I'd keep stroking if I were you,' said Gizmo. 'I think he likes you.'

'Oh,' murmured Chris. 'That's comforting.' He nervously resumed stroking the sleek, black fur. 'Nice kitty, good kitty,' Chris encouraged.

Another growl and the fangs were exposed a little more.

'By the way,' advised Gizmo. 'He doesn't like being called kitty.'

'Thanks for that,' replied Chris, stroking frantically. 'Anything else that I should know?'

'Yes, he's probably hungry as he's not yet had his tea, but I imagine he's been snacking on the odd rat so you should be safe.'

Chris said a silent prayer and stared heavenward. He wondered how an animal so big could negotiate the small spaces in the ceiling above him.

Eventually Gizmo called the animal and it slid effortlessly from Chris and padded away across the room towards the wizard.

'Here you are, Storm,' he said.

Chris caught a glimpse of a lump of raw and bloody flesh placed on the floor by the fire. The large cat settled down with its food and proceeded to crunch away at the bones and tear at the flesh. Chris had suddenly lost his appetite.

5

Introductions

A large crusty chunk of bread and a steaming wooden bowl were placed in front of him and Chris eyed the contents suspiciously.

'No magic,' said the wizard. 'Just good, wholesome food.'

He was right. As it turned out, the food was some of the best that Chris had ever tasted and his appetite returned with the first spoonful, although he resisted the temptation to ask exactly what was in it and he could not stop himself from asking for a second helping.

Sir Peacealot couldn't, or wouldn't, stop talking. He was asking questions furiously, so fast in fact that not only did neither Gizmo nor Chris have a chance to answer, but they couldn't figure out which questions were directed at whom. Gizmo kept telling the knight to shut up and eat his food and finally, after several attempts to encourage him to eat, the wizard had to resort to the, 'I'll turn you into something nasty if you don't do as you are told,' threat, to get the knight to comply. Finally the three of them sat in relative silence, enjoying the meal and the opportunity to gather their thoughts.

Chris considered what had happened since discovering the buried knight. He still felt that everything was a dream and that he was really curled up in his own bed at home.

'Well, let's see what my imagination can come up with, it beats spending half the summer holidays looking for someone to play with,' he thought to himself reassuringly.

Sir Peacealot on the other hand was in a state of complete confusion. He had the equivalent of a mega-long-haul version of jet lag. His body told him that he needed to sleep but his mind kept telling him that he needed to stay alert and think of questions that he should be asking the wizard. It was as if there was a big hole in the back of his head that swallowed everything he thought of. In the end, all he could focus on were the two pieces of carrot floating in his food bowl and how much they resembled goldfish!

Chris finished his second bowl and looked up to find the wizard staring at him intently.

'How are you feeling now, my young friend?' he enquired, taking the empty bowl.

'Fine, thank you,' replied Chris. 'Although I think it's Sir Peacealot you should be worried about.'

The wizard followed Chris's gaze to see the knight sitting motionless, his blank face staring into the bowl that he cradled in his lap.

'The lights are on but no one's at home,' observed Chris.

'Oh, dear,' said Gizmo. 'I was afraid this would happen, it's the time shift you see. He's been in your world for so long that now he's back here his mind can't cope. There's been this lengthy period of inactivity which has created a void, a time gap in his memory. I was hoping that he would have eaten enough of the broth by now to counteract the effects.'

'You said that there was only food in the bowls and no magic,' said Chris, a little disappointed that the wizard might lie to him.

'Only in his,' said the wizard. 'You see, I have no idea how long he was suspended asleep in your time. In this world he has only been gone for two phases of the moon, but I suspect that this may equate to many years in your world.'

'I don't understand,' said Chris. 'You said that our worlds were separated by only a second or two, and how come I haven't been affected the same way?'

'It's simple,' said the wizard, matter of factly. 'You haven't been affected because you were not a victim of a time lapse spell and therefore have no void created in your memory.' He paused. 'Oh dear. Just a moment.'

Gizmo reached across and with a small cloth wiped away the dribble that had started to accumulate on the knight's chin.

'Oh, that's gross!' said Chris. 'I hope he doesn't need to go to the toilet while he's like this!'

'Quite,' said Gizmo with obvious concern. 'I've had enough trouble house-training Storm.'

Chris looked in the direction of where the panther had been enjoying its meal and was a little alarmed to find that it was nowhere to be seen.

'I'm not going to give you a lengthy lesson in time configuration, matter particle acceleration, black holes, quantum physics and dimensional light fusion, so you will just have to accept that the rules governing your ability to travel between our worlds and the Dimensions within a mere second is just simply how it is,' lectured the wizard. 'Now, let's get our friend here sorted out before he does have an accident that we will all regret.'

Gizmo reached across, took the knight's bowl and stood up. Cradling the bowl in one hand, he tilted Sir Peacealot's head back and leant forward, whispering into the knight's ear. Sir Peacealot closed his vacant eyes and opened his mouth, into which the wizard slowly poured the remaining contents of the bowl. It smoothly disappeared down his throat without creating any reaction from the knight. Finally Gizmo closed Sir Peacealot's mouth and leaned him back onto the cushions.

'That should do it,' he said, with obvious satisfaction. 'He'll sleep for a while but he should be all right when he wakes up.'

There came a low rumbling sound followed by a loud burp.

'Oh, well,' said Gizmo, shaking his head. 'Better out than in, I suppose.' He wandered off with the empty bowls towards the kitchen area.

'Do you mind if I have a look around?' asked Chris.

'Look, but don't touch,' came the wizard's sharp reply.

Chris wandered down the stone steps towards the area of equipment that resembled a science lab. He reached the bench and studied the maze of glass bottles and connecting tubes which contained the colourful liquids fizzing and squirting their way around. He noticed that several large bowls of bubbling liquid were heated from beneath by small, dancing blue flames. The strangest thing however was that there was no obvious source that powered the small flames.

He slowly walked around the large display of apparatus, mesmerised by the various fluids, blending, diluting and reforming into a myriad of colours.

He felt a soft pressure against his leg and looked down to see a handsome black cat curling its tail and rubbing its body affectionately against him.

'Hello puss,' he said, as he reached down and stroked the cat which purred loudly and pushed its head against his leg.

'You're very friendly,' said Chris, picking up the cat, cradling it in his arms and stroking it behind the ears. The cat purred with obvious delight. 'My cat Tabby loves to be stroked there. I wonder what he's up to?' he added absently. 'Probably curled up on my bed fast asleep.'

The cat nuzzled Chris under the chin.

'Let's see what other surprises there are around here, shall we?'

Chris wandered over to the strange, giant telescope and studied the levers and the large glass jar filled with coloured balls. He found it too tempting to resist, and reached out and touched the glass.

All of a sudden the jar vibrated and the contents started to rattle and move around. Alarmed, Chris stood back as a hole appeared in the centre of the glass lid and a blue-coloured ball shot high into the air. Both Chris's and the cat's eyes followed it intently as it arced and came back down towards them. Just as the ball was above his head, a hand shot out from behind him and caught it.

'I told you *not* to touch,' said the wizard sternly. 'I would advise that you be more careful in future. If you had gone poking around amongst my little garden over there, my vampire plants would have had a couple of your fingers off!'

Chris brought his hand up and continued to stroke the cat as if to reassure himself that his fingers were still attached and in the right order.

'I just wanted to know what all those coloured balls were for,' he said.

'They help me to focus on the stars and con-stellations while I spend many hours searching the cosmos for answers and signs,' said the wizard.

'Do you use them to represent the planets?' enquired Chris.

'No, they're much more fun than that,' Gizmo replied, popping the blue ball into his mouth. 'They're gobstoppers and they help me to concentrate! Now, you didn't touch any of the levers, did you?'

'No, no,' said Chris. 'I was just being curious, that's all.'

'Curiosity killed the cat, that's what they say isn't it?' Although I don't think Storm would agree, would you, my friend?' He gently ruffled the cat's fur.

'St ... Storm?' stammered Chris, looking around nervously.

'Nothing is as it seems, my young friend, and Storm here is your first lesson. There is a saying, "If you change the way you look at things, then the things you look at, change".'

Chris looked down at the cat which looked back at him with deep, dark eyes and Chris felt the tips of the cat's sharp claws flex themselves through his sweatshirt.

'I should carry on stroking him for a while until he decides that he's had enough. He's not due to morph again until he gets hungry so you've got plenty of time to get acquainted,' advised the wizard as he made his way towards the laboratory. 'Now you must excuse me while I tidy up before our guests arrive.'

Chris held on to the cat which somehow felt much heavier now, or was that just his imagination?

'Nice kit—' he began and then stopped himself, suddenly remembering the earlier warning. 'Nice cat, nice Storm.' The response was a purr which was much too loud for the size of the cat in Chris's arms.

Eventually, Storm jumped down and sauntered off. Chris collapsed on to one of the large cushions, vowing to give Storm a wide berth in future. A few minutes later he saw the cat dart across the beams above him, in pursuit of a smaller shadow.

'*Well at least that explains one thing,*' he thought to himself as he felt his eyelids grow heavy and the warm comfort of sleep tempted his tired mind to rest.

The low sound of conversation eventually woke him and he opened his eyes to see a group of people gathered around the fire, each with a tankard or goblet in their hands.

The wizard turned, as if sensing that Chris was awake.

'Ah, I hope you are now refreshed, my young friend, for now is the time of introductions, questions and revelations. Come and join us and I will get you a reviving drink to sharpen your senses,' he coaxed.

The other members of the group turned to Chris. There was the lady knight, Sir Peacealot (minus any dribble on his chin, Chris noticed thankfully,) the knight with the tanned skin and, in the centre of the group, the king. The two knights were out of their armour and dressed in brown leather leggings and jerkins. Both were still armed with swords and even without their armour they looked formidable.

Chris sat there feeling awkward and not sure what to say, but his predicament was solved by the lady. She placed her goblet on the stone hearth and moved towards him, putting her hand out to help him up.

'Come, young squire, do not be afraid or shy, you are among friends. Friends that according to the wizard's instructions should afford the same duty to you as they do to their king and protect you with their lives.'

Chris was impressed by her words, but it was the sound of her voice and her radiant face that enchanted him. As she took his hand, she smiled and for an instant he was lost dreamily in her smile, then all of a sudden the smile disappeared, her face hardened and the grip on his hand tightened as she pulled him sharply towards her and down to the floor where she stepped over him and drew her sword. There was a shout behind her and the sound of other swords being released from their scabbards.

As he turned around on the floor behind her, he looked up to see a dark shape with venomous red eyes and blood-red needle teeth swooping down from the rafters towards him, its black furry body propelled through the air by a pair of leathery bat-like wings. She held her hand out in front of her, as if instructing the creature to stop, then with little more that a metre separating it from her, she brought her blade over her shoulder and sliced it neatly in two. The halves dropped to the floor, each wing still flapping, still trying to reach its quarry.

Two streaks of blue lightning shot across the room and struck the quivering remains, and the bloody carcass disappeared in a puff of acrid smoke.

Chris felt hands lift him and he was placed beside the king as Sir Peacealot and the tanned Knight closed ranks and stood in front of them, acting as a barrier, their swords at the ready.

The wizard stepped forward, cupped his hands, and an orb of blue light appeared in his palms. He spoke some strange words into the orb and it rose and floated up to the rafters.

'Shield your eyes!' shouted the wizard, and they quickly followed his command. The flash of bright light that bathed the room for only a second shone through their raised hands and pierced their eyelids with its intensity, causing them to blink.

'If there were any more of the creatures hiding anywhere they will have met the same fate as the last one,' said the wizard. 'I don't know how it managed to get in and past Storm, but none will be able to follow. I have now sealed the room with Magik strong enough to ensure our safety.

'What was it?' asked Chris nervously.

'Bat-rat,' replied the lady. 'A spy of Lord Maelstrom

and a carrier of plagues. One bite or scratch and within an hour you become one of the living dead.'

'Definitely not my idea of fun,' said Chris.

The king turned to Chris. 'Gizmo said you had spirit, now let's have a good look at you boy.'

Chris moved a pace back and the three knights joined the king in a semicircle around him, which made him feel very self-conscious.

'Sheath those swords,' ordered the king. 'There'll be plenty of time for him to get used to the sight of them.'

All three obeyed, but Chris could see that their hands did not stray from the hilts and their eyes were alert for any other movements from above.

Gizmo brought Chris a small goblet.

'Here, drink this, it will revive and refresh you, no magic I promise you, just good to honest fruit and herbs.'

Chris took the goblet and gave the contents a sniff. Satisfied, he took a sip.

The king laughed and the others followed suit. 'I see he has the measure of you, Master Wizard. He has already learned to use his intuition before trusting his new acquaintances.'

'Trust will separate his friends from his enemies and his intuition will save his life and hold the future of our world in the balance,' said the wizard. 'These things will come to pass and so let us now bring the boy into our confidence and inform Sir Peacealot of matters he has missed. Unbuckle those swords and let us sit in conference.'

They all took their places amongst the cushions and rugs, all three knights doing as they were told but choosing to keep their weapons close to them. The lady knight patted the cushions between herself and the king and motioned for Chris to sit there. He looked at Gizmo who nodded in agreement. Once they were all seated, Gizmo spoke.

'Now is the time for proper introductions to the boy.'

'Excuse me,' said Chris. 'But I do have a name you know, other than "boy" or "squire". My name is Christopher, Chris for short.'

'In your world, maybe, but it cannot be widely used in this one. Not yet at least,' said Gizmo. 'Your real identity must be guarded closely.'

'Well, what are you going to call me?' asked Chris.

'The name will not be selected by us,' said the wizard. 'But when it is given to you it will be accepted by all. Until that moment you will be referred to as Sir Peacealot's squire. Now, to introductions. I would suggest we start with you, my lady.

In the moment that Lady Dawnstar turned and spoke her name to Chris, he knew that he had met someone who was going to be very important to him. He wasn't sure whether it was because, in the back of his mind, she reminded him of his mum (although she looked younger than his mum), or because she had certainly saved his life earlier. He also noticed her eyes again. This time they were a lighter grey, almost a moonlight grey.

She told him that she was in fact a cousin of the king but had grown up not wanting the trappings of royalty and had rebelled at an early age. When other members of the royal household were at court, behaving and socialising as royalty should, she was missing. She preferred the company of the ordinary children, and especially to join in with the boys and their rough and tumble games. She had quickly built up two reputations, one at court for being troublesome and unruly and the other with the town's children for being able to beat all of the boys at arm-wrestling and most forms of mock battle games. As she grew older, her skills in combat had become legendary and she was the first young girl not only to enter the tournaments but also to win most of the trophies!

She had earned her knighthood (she would not have had it any other way) when she had rescued some villagers that were being attacked by a vicious Stone Org. Single-handed, she fought with it for many hours, finally defeating and slaying the monster. This had confirmed her status in the land as a heroine and protector of the people. Now she was a member of the Chosen, an elite group who were dedicated to defending Castellion and the Dimensions from evil.

'You have been sent to us to help us in our endeavours, and I in turn pledge my breath and blood to protecting you,' she said as she reached inside her tunic and brought out an object which she offered to Chris.

'Take this, it is a token of my pledge, carry it with you always, you will only be able to use it once in this world and that will be when there is no other help in sight.'

Chris took the object, which was a small crystal glass whistle with an ornate silver cap around the mouthpiece. He turned it over in his hand, the delicate frosted pattern reflecting the light of the candles.

'I'm afraid that I'll break it,' he said.

'You mean like this?' said Lady Dawnstar, taking it back from him and throwing it onto the stone floor. He looked in dismay as she stamped on it and ground it with her heel.

'Why bother to give it to me if you were going to break it anyway?' asked Chris.

'Remember, things are not always as they seem,' she replied, and lifted her foot. Lying perfect and unbroken, was the whistle. She handed it back to Chris.

'Do not fear, you cannot break it. It was made from diamonds, liquefied and shaped by the glass smiths of Lire and is very rare. The Bird Men of the Eastern Highlands used them once to train their flocks. Many years ago a great plague visited the land and nearly wiped out all the birds of the air and so they took the surviving few and retreated to the mountain passes and high peaks where they shut themselves off from the rest of our world. No one truly knows if they survive, but it is said that one day they will return when they are needed to save the skies from darkness. Perhaps you will be the one to use it and summon the Bird Men when the time is right.'

Chris looked at the whistle in his hand. It still looked fragile to him so he tucked it carefully away into the leg pocket of his combats.

The dark-skinned knight stood.

'My name is Sir Cassius Dragonslayer. I am the king's crusader and protector. I, too, give my oath to shield and defend you with my breath and blood. Take off your jerkin and come here,' he ordered, not unkindly.

Curious, Chris stood and removed his sweatshirt.

'The undergarment also,' prompted the Sir Dragon-slayer.

Chris self-consciously removed his T-shirt. He was so glad that he had kept up his tae kwon do exercises, as in the last year he had grown from a somewhat scrawny frame to a more muscular and wiry shape.

'Try this on for size,' said Sir Dragonslayer, passing Chris a bundle of leather-like material. Chris unfolded it. It was a waistcoat of sorts, but instead of buttons, the front had strings of leather to tie together. He put it over himself. It felt soft to the touch on the inside but the surface was strange, with small overlapping diamond shapes of a dull brown colour which reminded him of fish scales.

'Here, let me help you,' said Sir Dragonslayer, securing the ties. 'How does that feel?'

'Fine,' replied Chris. 'It's very light and comfortable.'

'You wear it under your other garments,' instructed Sir Dragonslayer.

'Why?' enquired Chris.

'In case something like this happens,' he replied, and walked across the room.

Suddenly Sir Dragonslayer turned, drew a small dagger from his belt and threw it.

Chris did not have a chance; he was frozen to the spot as the dagger flew towards him. He watched it as if in slow motion as the handle spun and the point of the blade arrowed its way to his heart. He closed his eyes. There was a dull thud as it connected with his chest and bounced off, rattling away across the floor. He opened his eyes and looked down at the garment;

there was not a mark on it. Then with relief and amazement he looked at Sir Dragonslayer. 'Dragon skin,' he said, retrieving his blade. 'It will protect you from most things but it does have its limitations, as its previous owner found out.' He grinned. 'You took it from a dragon?' asked Chris.

'The toughest, meanest, most cunning and vicious old dragon that walked this world,' said Sir Dragonslayer. He indicated for Chris to sit as he made himself comfortable on the cushions.

'I am a dragon-hunter by profession, choosing to track down and tame them rather than kill them. They are valuable resources in battle and once you have their allegiance they will never betray or fail you. It's not easy though, they are normally solitary creatures and do not get on well with their own kind. They will defend their treasures ferociously and unfortunately they do have a taste for cattle and sheep. You also need to speak their language, they communicate telepathically, so all that most people hear are hisses and grunts. But, once a dragon fixes a link with you, then you can talk to all dragons. This takes great trust and understanding as you have to convince them that you do not want to take their treasure and you have to get them to agree to stop attacking farms and roasting the livestock! When you get an agreement with the townsfolk in the farms and villages (which is sometimes just as hard as taming the dragon), they will breed stock as food for the dragon in exchange for gold or jewels and protection from other dragons or robbers.

'Unfortunately, you can come across the odd rogue

dragon who just wants to terrorise the countryside and not only has a taste for farm animals but is also quite partial to humans. They're usually in the service of the darker forces whose mission is to cause death and destruction across the land. That's when my negotiating skills are put away and my sword comes out. Our old friend, a part of whom you are wearing, was one such dragon. This is my gift to you.'

'Thank you,' said Chris.

Sir Peacealot spoke. 'I have a lot to thank you for, you released me and brought me back to my world and my friends. I must admit I have no idea how long I would have lain there undiscovered.'

'It really was an accident,' admitted Chris.

'Accident or no, you have conducted yourself well and destiny has brought you to us. I would be proud to have you as my squire and companion and I, too, pledge my life's breath and blood to your protection. Here, take this as a token of my bond.'

He handed a decorated leather scabbard and belt to Chris; the handle of the short sword it contained was of a grey metal with runes etched along it. Chris steadily unsheathed the blade which flashed and reflected polished steel.

'I'm not sure that I should really have this, I've always been told to keep away from knives and weapons,' he said.

'In your world I'm sure that is good advice,' said Sir Peacealot. 'But here it is a different matter. It was given to me by the wizard and it has his mark on it. Wear it with pride and draw it only when needed, it will help in your transformation to appear as a royal knight's squire, for that is all you must seem until the time is right.'

'But, I don't really understand what you expect of me,' said Chris.

Up until this point Gizmo had been standing back by the fireplace, listening and watching. Now he stepped forward.

'You are the future, you are the past. You are our survival or our destruction. You are the prophecy and the legend.'

'But I'm just an ordinary boy,' protested Chris.

The wizard leaned forwards. 'How many more times must you be told? Things are ...'

'I know, I know,' interrupted Chris. 'Things are not always what they seem.'

'Exactly,' smiled the wizard. 'Now listen to our noble King Hector.'

Chris turned to face the man, who despite his position as king, had been sitting patiently and quietly throughout the proceedings.

'Let me be honest with you, young man, none of us knows for certain what the future will bring, not even our most trusted wizard and Guardian,' he indicated to Gizmo. 'We only know that there are two paths in destiny, one good and the other bad. We stand for the path of good as do all the Guardians of the Four Dimensions. There is now, and always has been, a force, which follows the dark and evil ways. It rises like a wave through history and time to challenge us in its quest to bring chaos and misery to all worlds. A new wave is on the horizon, there is uncertainty across the land, a restlessness.'

He paused and took a drink.

'Disturbances are reported from many places, accounts of crops and wells being tainted, unearthly creatures moving in groups are causing mischief and destruction, then disappearing back into the dark mountains and caverns below the earth. Those that would side with evil are testing us, flexing their strength. The beast that governs a realm of darkness and misery has arisen again. This time in the image and form of a banished follower of the Dark Arts, Lord Maelstrom.'

Again he paused to take a drink.

'He was once a fine practitioner of the natural laws of Magik and helped to heal the land and kingdoms many, many ages ago from the onslaught and ravages of evil. Gradually, he found too much satisfaction with his powers and started to exert them for his own pleasure, and he became cruel and malicious. Finally, in his wickedness he killed his only brother who had tried to stop him from torturing the land and the people. It was then that the Guardians stepped in. Sensing that Lord Maelstrom could shift the balance of influence to the evil ways, they gathered together and stripped him of his powers, banishing him to the confines of the mighty Ice Mountains for eternity. It would appear that something has happened to him during the ages that he has spent there and he has now become a vessel for the darkest of powers.'

The king leaned back as though tired. 'I know this may not make sense to you, but you have the ability to help us overthrow the coming threat. The visions and messages from the Guardians only tell us riddles, but above all we have been told to trust your instinct and listen to your words.'

'Well,' said Chris. 'My instinct is to run and my advice is, leave it to the wizards!'

He looked at their faces, stern and grave. *'Maybe I should have kept that to myself,'* he thought.

Then a smile appeared on the king's face and he laughed. 'You said he had a sense of humour and you were right, Gizmo. You lift my spirits my boy.'

Chris smiled as the room was filled with everyone's laughter. *'I still say, run,'* he thought, but he kept it to himself this time.

'Now that you have been acquainted with us, you must tell us about yourself,' said Sir Dragonslayer.

'I'm afraid that is not a good idea,' said the wizard. 'The less you know about his world the better, there is knowledge that many of you should not be privy to. If you are exposed to it through him while he is in our world then so be it, but do not go looking for insight.'

'One small story cannot harm, surely,' insisted Sir Dragonslayer.

Gizmo moved in front of the fire and his shadow grew large across them all.

'I am not a Guardian in name only, Sir Knight. You would be best to remember how Lord Maelstrom started his descent into the world of lost souls by gathering some small, other-world intelligence.' The fire flared up, crackling and spitting sparks, and it seemed the shadows pressed in on them all for a few seconds. Gizmo made a sign with his hand and the fire settled down again, the shadows receding. 'His influence is spreading,' said the wizard. 'It is weak at the moment but it pushes forwards each day, testing us and flexing its strength.'

Chris could not contain himself and stifled a yawn. He looked at his watch. 21.20. *'My time or their time?'* he wondered.

He caught Sir Dragonslayer staring at his watch so he quickly covered it with his hand. He felt tired; the warmth of the fire was making him drowsy.

'If you don't mind, I think I've had enough for one day and I would like to go to bed now,' he announced, fighting back drooping eyelids.

6

What's in a Name?

As sleep pulled away from his mind, Chris became conscious of water dripping on to his face and he lifted his hand to wipe it away. As his senses became aware of giggling and muffled laughter, he slowly opened his eyes and his vision cleared to reveal that his surroundings had changed. He was in a stable. A smiling, red-haired boy was standing over him with a wooden ladle in his hand with which he was dripping water onto Chris.

'Wake up, sleepy head,' he said cheerfully. 'The sun's risen and is shining on the castle walls, you're well late for your master's breakfast.'

Chris sat up with a jerk. 'Is this a dream?' he asked out loud.

As if to ensure that he was awake, the boy tipped the remaining contents of the ladle on to Chris's head. Splosh! And there was an outburst of laughter.

Chris jumped up, wiping it away furiously.

'Oh, thanks, I really needed that. I don't suppose you've got some soap while you're at it?' he said sarcastically.

'No, but we can arrange to throw you into the moat,' said a gruff voice.

Chris wiped his sleeve across his eyes and took in his surroundings. The stable was a long building with rows of stalls spread out to either side of him, some of which contained horses. There was a small crowd of eight or nine boys standing around him, all about the same age as himself as far as he could make out, but they were all bigger than him (as usual).

'Gerrouta my way,' growled the voice again and a large, round-faced boy with long blonde curly hair pushed his way through the others. He was a good thirty centimetres taller than Chris.

'What have we got here then?' he asked, standing in front of Chris. 'Another little weed that needs watering?'

He gave Chris a shove backwards into the straw as he reached for the wooden bucket of water that the red-haired boy was holding.

'Gimme that, carrot-head,' he snarled to the red-haired boy. Chris could see what was coming and as the boy lifted the bucket, he dived between his legs.

'Why, you!' exclaimed the boy as he twisted around, intent on soaking Chris.

Chris rolled to one side and as he did so he spotted his leather belt and dagger lying in the straw. He grabbed out for it but as he pulled it towards him the belt entangled itself around the boys ankle. The boy tripped and fell, the bucket landing on top of his head, its contents completely soaking him.

There was a gasp from the rest of the boys as his large, chubby hands lifted the bucket from his head. He looked like a drowned rat, his once curly locks now flattened against his head and shoulders.

'I'll pulverise anyone who makes a sound, let alone

laughs,' he hissed through clenched teeth as he glared at them. 'As for you,' he directed at Chris, 'I'm gonna sit on you and stuff horse manure in your mouth.'

He rose menacingly towards Chris who got to his feet and clutched his belt and scabbard, not knowing what to do next.

'Hold it, Maxim,' said the red-haired boy, stepping forward. 'You can't touch him.'

'Who says so?' shouted the thoroughly wet Maxim.

'This says so,' replied the boy, holding up Chris's scabbard for all to see.

'Royal knight's squire, Sir Peacealot's by the look of the crest on it. If you touch him, you'll be in the stocks for a week and there's a lot of us could do with some target practice with some rotten old vegetables.'

There was a murmur of eager agreement from the rest of them.

Maxim's face went bright red and his bottom lip started to quiver. For a moment Chris thought that he was going to cry. But the look that he gave Chris was filled with rage.

'I'll get you,' he snarled, looking Chris up and down, 'You, you, slimy little frog.' Then he pushed his way through the crowd and disappeared out into the courtyard.

Chris turned to the red-haired boy. 'Thanks, I guess I owe you one.'

'Owe me one what?' he asked.

'A return favour,' said Chris. 'For helping me out.'

'You don't owe me anything; we've been waiting for him to get his comeuppance for a long time, haven't we guys?'

The group nodded in one accord.

'I wouldn't have missed it for the world, did you see the colour of his face?' said a really tall boy.

'Yeah, didn't he remind you of something, with his hair hanging down like that?' asked another. 'You know, like the turnip-headed dummy that the knights use for target practice, the one with the old rope stuck on top as hair.'

With that the group collapsed with uncontrollable mirth and Chris joined in, enjoying the laughter and revelling in the attention.

Gradually the laughter subsided and the red-haired boy approached Chris. 'I guess that I'd better introduce everyone,' he said, as they all gathered in a circle around Chris.

'Smithy – his dad is a blacksmith. Speedy – he can run faster than any of us. Fish – he hates water! Smiley – it's not very often than he isn't smiling. Finder – if we need it, he'll get it. Lofty, he's the tallest.' He was nearly twice the height of Chris. 'Snoop – he's our spy when we want to find out information, and finally, this is Fixer – she can put most things back together again, eventually.'

'But you're a girl,' said Chris, and regretted saying it almost instantly. 'I mean, I didn't notice at first,' he said apologetically. 'No offence meant,' he added hastily.

'None taken,' she replied, the smile on her face remaining as proof.

Chris continued to stare at Fixer, mesmerised by her short, cropped brunette hair, freckled face and hazel-brown eyes.

She looked him up and down. 'But you're a boy,' she said jokingly and Chris went bright red as everyone laughed.

'I guess I deserved that,' said Chris.

'And I guess that we're even,' said Fixer, holding out her hand.

Chris shook her hand and knew then that he had made a very good friend.

The red-haired boy offered his hand to Chris, who shook it as well.

'I'm Ginger, no prizes for guessing why,' he grinned, pointing to his hair. 'There's one other thing that you should know,' he continued, 'the boy that you've very quickly made an enemy of is Maxim, his dad's head stable master and so he thinks that he can push us all around. We try to keep out of his way as much as possible as he's always looking for trouble. Don't ever let him catch you alone, he's nothing but a big bully and he'll deny that he was near you if you report him for being nasty. He's just jealous because we're all knight's squires and he's just a stable boy.' He looked Chris up and down. 'Well I guess we all know what you're called.'

'Do you?' said Chris, surprised.

'It's obvious,' continued Ginger. 'You look like one and Maxim guessed it right away.'

'Did he?' asked Chris, totally confused.

'Of course,' continued Ginger. 'You look even more like one with your hood up.' He reached forward and pulled the hood of Chris's jerkin over his head. It was now that Chris looked down at himself and realised that he was in different clothes. Green leggings, cross-strapped to the knees with brown leather boots and a long green-sleeved top which fell just below his hips. He looked back at the others, who were dressed in a similar style but in mostly brown and black colours.

'There you go, I wouldn't say you were slimy, but you definitely look like a little green frog, so Frog it is,' said Ginger. The group nodded in agreement and approval.

'But my name's Chr—' started Chris.

'Your name's Frog,' cut in Ginger. 'We all have our birth names but we don't use them, you don't get your real name back until you eventually become a knight, it's tradition and it's the rules. So forget about your old name, from now on you'll be known as Frog to one and all.' He turned to the others. 'Okay gang, you know what to do.'

All of a sudden the place was a hive of activity. Some of the boys disappeared while the others busied themselves in a corner.

'Let's tidy you up a minute,' said Ginger, brushing straw and dust from Chris's clothing. 'Put your belt and scabbard on, you can put your hood down now if you like.'

Chris reached up and flipped the hood back and as he did so he noticed that he was still wearing his watch. 21.20. It was then that it dawned on him that his watch had stopped. Either the battery had gone or it had become frozen at the time that he had left his own world.

Suddenly the stable doors were flung open and sunshine flooded in along with the noise of a busy castle. The others boys had returned carrying colourful pennants on poles.

'He we go, Frog,' said Ginger. 'Enjoy the ride!'

The boys gathered around him, two of them lifting him onto their shoulders. They all lined up around him and marched out into the sunshine. Even at this time of the day the large courtyard was full of people going about their business. Smells and sounds assaulted his senses. Chris tried to take it all in but for the moment the bright sunshine made him squint. Then the chant started.

'Frog, Frog, Frog,' went the group of squires in unison and Chris watched as Fixer unfurled a green pennant with the image of a leaping green frog sketched out on it. Then they were off, the little group parading around the courtyard as other voices joined in, the sound of the chant getting louder.

'Frog, Frog, Frog,' they went.

High above, staring down on the procession from the king's balcony were the king, Gizmo, Lady Dawnstar, Sir Dragonslayer and Sir Peacealot.

'So it begins,' said Gizmo. 'The future of Castellion and the Four Dimensions is in the hands of one small boy called Frog.'

As they stood, each with their own thoughts and prayers running through their minds, other eyes, unseen, watched the events. Thoughts of a darker nature, planning revenge and turmoil, were waiting in the shadows, waiting for the opportunity to strike.

Over the following days and weeks, Frog had little time for thoughts of the world that he had left behind (every day he told himself that it was all a dream and that he should enjoy it while he could as he might wake up at any time). He learned quickly, not just because he was enjoying the adventure but also because of the help he got from the new friends that he had made. Ginger very quickly became his best friend and reminded him of his other best friend, Billy Smart, back in his home world. Fixer became his other close companion. Frog learned that she was Lady Dawnstar's squire, one of only a handful of girl squires who served a group of lady knights known as the Maids of Steel. Lady Dawnstar was their captain and leader.

Most of his time was spent in the company of the other squires or with Sir Peacealot, who not only instructed Frog in the ways and responsibilities of a squire, but also trained him in the art of swordsmanship and horse riding.

Lady Dawnstar presented him with a small horse of his own, a black colt with a white flash on its forehead. It took Frog a while to decide on a name for his horse but finally he settled on 'Thunder', to the amusement of everyone else.

'Thunder?' said Ginger. 'He's so small he won't even make the ground tremble when he gallops along let alone make it thunder.'

'Well, one day he will, you'll see,' said Frog.

Two disturbing events occurred within the space of a few days. A young squire vanished suddenly, without explanation, followed by the disappearance of Maxim, the stable master's son. Neither were seen leaving the castle and no trace or sighting was reported, despite a full search conducted inside and outside the grounds. Everyone was told to be vigilant and be wary of strangers.

One morning Frog was brushing down Sir Peacealot's horse, which had been given to him by King
Hector as a replacement for his old horse that had been
killed by Belzeera, when a herald wearing the royal
tabard and colours arrived at the stable door.

'Are you Sir Peacealot's squire?' he asked.

'Yes,' replied Frog.

'You are hereby commanded to an audience with the
king.' he announced rather gruffly.

'When?' asked Frog.

'Now. I am to escort you myself,' replied the herald.

Frog patted the horse and led him into his stall,
closing the door behind him. 'Let me just wash the
horse sweat from my hands, and I'll be with you,' he
said, as he made his way to a bucket at the back of the
stable.

Once he had splashed some water on his face,
brushed himself down and put on his belt and
scabbard, he turned and followed the herald across the
dim courtyard. It had been overcast and drizzling with
rain for the last two days and today the sky was even
darker, as though a storm was gathering. The herald
turned down an alley that ran along between the main
castle wall and the outer battlements.

'This isn't the way to the court!' shouted Frog to the
figure scurrying ahead in the shadows.

'Shortcut,' the herald snapped back.

About fifty metres into the passage, Frog sensed
that something wasn't quite right and stopped.

'I'm going back the normal way,' he said and turned,
only to see his path blocked by two more heralds
walking towards him. 'Hey, what's going on? Herald,

tell these two that we're on the king's business!' he shouted.

'Oh, they know what business we're about and it isn't the king's,' sneered the herald, advancing on Frog. The shadows in the alley became darker and Frog noticed that the herald's eyes were now glowing red.

'You're not the king's heralds!' he shouted in alarm.

'Not when we're in the shadows or the dark,' one of them sneered, revealing sharp, fanged teeth. 'Our master wants a word with you, so let's do this quietly, shall we? Hold him, while I tie him up,' he instructed the others.

They grabbed Frog's arms and turned him around roughly.

'Let me get this over his head first,' said the one behind, and Frog looked up to see a piece of sacking being unfolded above him.

Frog remembered his training, not only from his tae kwon do but also the advice that he had been given by his parents, should an adult attack him.

He brought his left heel sharply back into the shin of one of the heralds behind him and then his right heel down on the other's foot. There were two howls of pain as the grip on his arms was released. Quickly, he leaned forwards and whipped his head back as fast and as hard as he could. As he felt the impact with the herald behind him, he heard the crack of a chest bone and then he was free, running along the alley and back to the courtyard, shouting for help. Turning his head as he went, he saw two figures hopping up and down with the third clutching at its chest and coughing wildly.

As he reached the end of the alley, a tall, dark and hooded figure appeared from the shadows. It towered over him and blocked his escape. Frog skidded on the wet cobbles, coming to a halt on his back and staring up at the black-cloaked figure. He rolled onto his stomach in an effort to get to his feet and looked back into the alley.

The three figures had now turned and were facing him.

The faces that once were human were now those of savage-looking wolves.

At once all three reared their heads back and emitted piercing howls. Their hairy, clawed hands began tearing at their clothes, ripping them off in shreds until they stood there, balancing on their hind legs, three man-sized animals covered in black, matted and greasy fur. As one they dropped to all fours and leapt forwards, foam and slather running from their mouths. Frog thought of one more desperate act and turned back to the figure.

'If you help me, I'm sure that the king will reward you,' he pleaded.

'I need no reward from the king,' the figure replied in a deep, rough voice. 'Now get behind me.'

Frog just stared, frozen to the spot.

'Now!' came the command, which shook Frog to his senses. He scampered between the figure and the wall as the man crouched on one knee before the oncoming wolves. He extended an arm from his cloak, his leather-gloved hand taking the shape of a flat palm with extended fingers, pointing towards the oncoming fury.

The first wolf leapt from a distance of three metres,

its red eyes blazing, and clearly intent on sinking its fangs into the figure, who then stood, sidestepping the wolf with a swirl of his cape, and bringing his fattened palm up and across the creature's neck. There was a 'Snap!' as it dropped, lifeless, to the ground. The other two wolves leapt together at the figure, who now ran forwards to meet them head on, both of his hands reaching out and grabbing them in mid-air by their throats, twisting them in to each other and bringing their heads together with a 'thwack!' He let one fall to the ground, dazed, as he grabbed the back legs of the other, bringing it down across his knee. There was a louder snap and the wolf rolled to the ground, lifeless. The other wolf had recovered enough and was readying itself to pounce at Frog, who stared at it helplessly. It leapt with a growl of victory on its lips.

Frog stared into the oncoming snarling mouth, its stench reaching him and making him feel sick. He brought an arm up in futile protection. There was a movement in the background as the man reached inside his cloak. A black coil appeared in his hand. As he pulled back his arm, there was a loud 'crack!' and a length of black shining rope snaked out and wrapped itself around the wolf's throat, jerking it back and away from Frog. The rope tightened and coiled like a snake into the animal's fur, cutting through it until, finally, the wolf's head and body dropped to the ground, separated. With a casual flick, the figure re-coiled the whip and walked towards Frog, who was still trying to take in these events.

A hand came out of the cloak and helped Frog to his feet.

'Has no one ever told you not to go down dark alleyways with strangers?' the deep voice enquired.

'Who are you?' Frog asked.

'Let's get out of this place before we get into introductions,' he replied.

As they left the alleyway, Frog turned to see the steaming bodies slowly melting away and disappearing.

'Who, what, were they?' he asked.

'Servants of Fangmaster, the Hellhound. How they found out about you will be of concern for all and we must now take counsel with the wizard.' They came out into the courtyard and Frog turned to face his rescuer.

'Before we go any further, I need to know who you are,' he said.

A hand swept back the hood to reveal a man with jet black, raven hair and a scar on his face which ran from his forehead, across his left eye, and down his cheek. A black leather patch covered the eye. In the centre of the patch, stencilled in red, was the image of an unblinking eye.

'Those that fear me, or do not know me, call me the Dark Ranger. To you and the Chosen, my name is Logan. I am a freeman of the kingdom.

'What does it mean? Freeman?' asked Frog.

'It means that I can go anywhere I choose in the kingdom, unchallenged. This I was granted by the king many years ago and it was announced across the realm for all to know,' he answered. 'No door bars my way, no entry is denied, no path is blocked. No one can refuse my questions or my enquiries. My allegiance is to the cause of good and should those that are good turn to

103

evil then they become my enemies. My destiny is to trust no one but to be trusted by all. That is the reason why Gizmo asked me to watch over you.'

'How long have you been watching me?' asked Frog.

'From the day that you arrived in the castle,' replied Logan.

'Wow!' exclaimed Frog. 'You are good, I would never have known.'

'That's the whole idea,' said Logan. 'Now let's get a move on before anything else happens.'

7

The Map

Unchallenged, Logan and Frog made their way through the castle. Every guard that they encountered stood back and cleared the way for them. Doors that were unguarded opened as they approached and closed behind them.

'You weren't joking, were you?' said Frog as another pair of guards scrabbled to open some particularly heavy doors ahead of them.

'I never joke,' replied Logan, sternly.

'I bet you enjoy a good laugh, though?' continued Frog.

'Laughter distracts the mind and causes mistakes. Laughter is for fools,' said Logan as he glanced down at Frog.

'I guess you're not known for your sense of humour, then?' replied Frog as they reached the large wooden doors of the royal court.

Logan raised his fist and hammered the doors with three blows. 'Open in the name of a Freeman!' he commanded, and the doors silently swung open.

'Very impressive,' said Frog. 'But I'd like to see you try and open my money box!'

Logan glared down at Frog and they strode forward to a court deserted except for a small group huddled around a large table at the far end of the great room. Frog could see that the group consisted of King Hector, Gizmo, Sir Peacealot, Sir Dragonslayer and Lady Dawnstar, who all turned as he and Logan approached.

Gizmo looked at them, concerned. 'This can only mean one thing. That the boy has been discovered. Is that the case, Logan?'

'The bad news is that his presence has been detected, the good news is that they appear to have limited information as to what the boy looks like or what his name is. Furthermore, at the moment it is a lower rank of enemy that has attempted to take him. Fangmaster sent some of his Hellhounds to kidnap him, they were disguised with an image spell that only Lord Maelstrom could have administered. This may be how the other boys were taken, however on this occasion they panicked and paid for it,' Logan replied with satisfaction.

'Excuse me,' interrupted Frog. 'But I wouldn't say they panicked, one of them tried to bite my head off!'

'Exactly, they were told to capture you and take you to their leader. They panicked and failed,' said Logan.

'How do you know what they were planning?' asked Frog. 'You didn't turn up until I was nearly free of them.'

'I was watching and listening to them long before they approached you. I heard their plans and I knew what they had been sent to do,' explained Logan.

'Then why didn't you deal with them before they

grabbed me? It would have saved me from a nasty few moments,' complained Frog.

'Oh, stop whinging like a child,' interrupted Gizmo.

'Technically, I am a child!' pointed out Frog.

'Yes, well,' glowered the wizard. 'Stop this bickering, the both of you and come over here.'

He reached inside a fold of his cloak, withdrew a fine silver chain and deftly placed it over Frog's head and around his neck.

'Here, take this before you move another step,' he said.

'But there's nothing on it,' said Frog.

'That's exactly what people are supposed to think,' said the wizard, giving Frog a secretive wink. 'Tuck it away for now, all will be revealed sooner or later.'

He indicated the table on which was set a map of the kingdom and far-reaching lands.

'There have been further reports of troubles throughout the lands,' said the king. 'We are trying to see if there is a pattern which might pinpoint a central place of command.'

Frog looked at the map; there were pictures of mountains and rivers, villages and towns, grasslands and forests, all with the various names of the locations written over them. It reminded him of the sort of old map he had seen before in museums, all brown and ancient. However, something was missing; he studied the map a while longer and then it came to him.

'The sea,' he said, looking around at them. 'Where's the sea?'

'What do you mean?' asked Sir Dragonslayer.

'The map must cover hundreds of miles but the land

just stops at the edges,' explained Frog. 'Where's your coastline?' He looked at their faces and they looked back, puzzled.

Gizmo spoke. 'He means the Endless Water.'

'But that's a myth,' said the king. The others nodded their heads in agreement.

'You mean that you don't have oceans?' asked Frog with amazement.

'There is a legend that tells of the Endless Water, but no one has ever found it, or if they have they have never returned to tell of it,' said Gizmo. 'Land is all we know and land is all there is.'

'Have you never followed a river to see where it goes?' asked Frog.

'I have,' said Logan, and they all turned to him, 'I have probably travelled more of this land than anyone. There is not much that I haven't seen.'

'Well then,' continued Frog. 'Surely the rivers make their way to the sea or Endless Water as you call it.'

'If there is such a thing then it is far below us,' said Logan. 'The rivers pour into great cracks, great holes in the earth. Steaming and thundering down, the white foam is swallowed into darkness.'

'But it's got to go somewhere,' persisted Frog.

'I told you, young Frog; there are many things that will not make sense to you in this world, but you must accept them. Now let's get on with business,' instructed Gizmo.

They all turned their attention to the map. There were various little tokens placed on it. Some were small carvings of creatures and some were emblems of elements such as fire, water and ice. Frog noticed that there were several locations where wolf-type figures and flame tokens were placed together. In another area, surrounding what was marked as the Ice Mountains and Frozen Wastes, small white ice figures dominated the landscape.

To the south of what was marked Castellion Stronghold was a gathering of black creatures, some with wings, others with lizard-like tails, which were surrounded by fire and black, cloud-shaped tokens.

'Here,' pointed out Gizmo. 'This is where villages have been attacked by Fangmaster's Hellhounds. They have destroyed every living thing and torched the earth so that the landscape is charred and barren. Fangmaster himself has not been seen and it would appear that these are separate packs of wolves acting as primary attack forces sent to test the ground and pave the way for his legions.' He placed a finger on a white figurine. 'This is another concern. The Frozen Wastes are spreading, moving out in all directions from the Ice Mountains and, as they move, the Hidden People move with them, breathing cold death on every living thing that they encounter. From what my messengers tell me, the strongest movement appears to be on the southern front. They have reached our townships and are creeping slowly towards the great rivers and lakes. They move under cover of night when the warmth of the sun cannot impede their progress and there is little light to make them visible.'

'Moving in our direction?' asked Lady Dawnstar.

'Yes,' acknowledged Gizmo. 'It would appear that the intent is to bring the Frozen Wastes across the kingdom to join with this.' He moved his hand to

FROG

indicate the black clouds and dark creatures at the bottom of the map. 'When the two powers convene, the land will be covered in ice and entombed in darkness, the only living things will be abominations of Lord Maelstrom's design and making.'

Then the king spoke, with a whisper, dreading that he already knew the answer as he asked the question.

'Where are the forces destined to meet and form the catalyst of destruction?'

'Here,' said Gizmo, solemnly opening his arms. 'Castellion Stronghold. Lord Maelstrom knows that this is the centre of the realm's governance. All people look to Castellion Stronghold for guidance and strength, we are the heart of the land in many ways. If we were to fall, all others would lose faith. The armies would collapse and the people would run in fear. Despair and chaos would infect the land.'

He touched the map with his silver cane and the shapes came to life. From the model of Castellion Stronghold poured tiny figures, knights on horseback and ground troops with swords, spears and shields marching out across the map to meet their enemies. Miniature armies formed to face each other as the ice and black clouds descended over the landscape and covered it entirely until there was no movement to be seen. They all stared at the map in silence.

Gizmo passed his hand over the image and the map returned to normal.

'The future has many paths so let us not be distracted by the darkest one. We must prepare and make plans. This war will not be won by Magik alone, the strength and faith of the people will influence its outcome, as will

110

our leadership and courage. We must rally to the land and call our people together. Lord Maelstrom may think he commands the battlefield but let us take control of óur destiny.' He pulled a small golden talisman in the shape of the blazing sun from his plaited beard. 'This is where we will decide our fate.'

He placed the token onto the map directly in the path of the Frozen Wastes and the figurines of the frozen Hidden People. The place was marked with a name – Blackwater Down. The talisman melted into the map and became part of the parchment.

'I don't know about you,' said Frog. 'But I hate the cold, I say you fight ice with fire.'

'Explain yourself,' said Sir Dragonslayer.

'Well, you and your dragon friends would be a great help. I take it they do breathe fire?' asked Frog.

'Yes, of course,' he replied.

'Okay,' continued Frog. 'Send them up to melt these ice creatures and the frozen land. That'll stop them,' he said, looking pleased with his suggestion.

'It's a good idea,' acknowledged Sir Dragonslayer. 'But we would be totally outnumbered. I think on the last count we only have about two hundred trained dragons and dragon masters in the Kingdom. As the Frozen Wastes move forwards, the army of Hidden People increases, made from those poor souls that are overtaken and frozen to death by the ice. Once people of the land, they become transformed into Hidden People. There are thousands upon thousands of them already. More continue to pour from the Ice Mountains. Goodness knows how long Lord Maelstrom has been creating his vile creatures.'

111

'If we can warn our people to evacuate and clear the land, the Hidden People will have no poor souls to convert into their kind and strengthen their numbers,' suggested Gizmo. 'They will end up spreading themselves too thin in their efforts to cover the ground. I have a feeling that the advancement of the dark army to the south is governed by the progress of the Frozen Wastes and the Hidden People in the north. Lord Maelstrom will not be eager to attack Castellion Stronghold without the combined forces of Darkness and Ice. He knows also that the wolf legions are as unruly and as unpredictable as their leader Fangmaster, who I would bargain has his own plans for domination. This may well be the weakness that we need.'

He turned and walked to the blazing fire in the large stone hearth and stood there in silence, staring into the flames.

'What's he doing?' whispered Frog.

'Thinking,' answered Sir Peacealot.

'What about?' asked Frog.

'How should I know?' said Sir Peacealot irritably.

'Sorrreeee,' muttered Frog.

Suddenly, Gizmo turned and the fire roared up, flames licking the wall above the hearth. His eyes were ablaze, as if reflecting the fire's flames.

'Sir Dragonslayer, send out for your dragons and their masters. Lady Dawnstar, gather your Maids of Steel from near and far. Logan, instruct your Rangers to ride out across the realm to bring all those in the paths of Darkness, Fire and Ice to the safety and province of Castellion Stronghold. Sir Peacealot, send

word to every king's knight and squire that they rally
here ready for battle. My Lord King, I beg you bless
these commands and release Castellion's war banners
across the land to instruct all good living things to our
aid. Send out the hornsmen to signal the call to arms.
We will deliver a mighty message to Lord Maelstrom
that we fear him not. The time has come to awaken the
legend.'

The king stepped back and touched the centre of the
band which circled his head. From the image of the
flaming sun, a bright golden light shone out and filled
the room, reaching up and flowing out of the windows
and doors. Frog felt a warmth and strength run
through him, hands gently clasped his. On one side
stood Logan and on the other Lady Dawnstar. They all
joined hands in a circle, the golden glow running
through them, bringing their hearts and senses
together in one accord. All fear was banished from
their minds, pure courage coursed through their veins.

In those few moments, Frog matured. The boy who
was Chris became a second memory, existing just
beneath the surface of his thoughts. His perception of
standards and values took on a worldly-wise status.
His wisdom became that of a travelled and educated
man. However, he still looked the same and the magic
of childhood remained with him; he was still a boy at
heart.

When the golden light subsided, they all looked at
each other. Each one of them had a symbol, a small
mark, on their foreheads. It was the sign of the
burning sun. Frog reached up and examined his
forehead; it felt cool to the touch.

'The Circle of the Chosen is complete,' announced the wizard.

Frog looked around at the others, his eyes falling on Lady Dawnstar.

'She really is beautiful,' he thought to himself.

'Why thank you, young Frog,' she replied, smiling kindly.

Frog went red with embarrassment before realising that he had not spoken out loud. 'I didn't say anything,' he added quickly.

'But I'm sure that you did,' she insisted.

'No need to be coy,' said Logan. 'I heard the compliment you gave the lady.'

'And I,' said Sir Dragonslayer and Sir Peacealot, in unison.

'But I only thought it,' protested Frog, going even redder.

Gizmo chuckled. 'This will take some getting used to; you will all need to sit with me and learn to control your new ability before it drives you insane.'

'What new ability?' asked Logan.

'Our minds are now connected and we have the power to communicate with each other over reasonable distances like this,' he replied smiling.

Their mouths opened in wonder and astonishment as they realised that although Gizmo was not openly talking to them, they could hear him quite clearly.

'What trickery is this?' asked the king.

'No trickery my Lord. It is the Magik of the Dimensions, a gift to aid us, to bind us together. This is how it was foretold to the Guardians,' said Gizmo. 'The boy is the catalyst for all that will now decide our destiny. We are bound by the symbol of light and life. Let us use its power wisely.'

It took them some time that evening to practise and control their new gift of communicating by thoughts. All of them had at least one embarrassing moment when they unwittingly shared a personal thought. With sympathy and understanding they made light of and joked (though not unkindly) about such instances and, in the end, with Gizmo's help and perseverance, they mastered the art of either shielding or sharing their minds and thoughts.

It was another act which brought them closer together and strengthened the bond between them. What they also discovered was that some of them had stronger mental ties than others. For example, none of them, except Gizmo, could communicate with the king, because his thoughts were being shielded from them by the golden band that encircled his head. Frog could easily transmit and pick up thoughts with Lady Dawnstar, Sir Peacealot and Gizmo, but it took him more effort to mentally reach out to Sir Dragonslayer and Logan. In the background of their minds, there was a clear sense of each other, something that made them aware of one another's existence. This was their bond: consciously or unconsciously, they were all connected. As the evening drew to a close, Gizmo hushed them into silence.

'This new ability also brings danger. Lord Maelstrom has the power to probe minds and he will, if the opportunity arises, take great pleasure reaching out and infecting your thoughts with all manner of dreadful images and feelings. Be on your guard at all times.'

8

Through the Telescope

Lady Dawnstar, Logan, Sir Dragonslayer and Sir Peacealot left Castellion Stronghold the very next day to follow Gizmo's instructions and the next two weeks passed in the blink of an eye. Frog had been given orders to gather the other knights' squires together and brief them of the situation, while the royal heralds toured the Stronghold, announcing the call to arms.

A great encampment formed on the open fields outside Castellion Stronghold which grew larger each day with new arrivals. Tents and marquees were erected, flags and banners of all shapes and colours were displayed.

As the sun was setting one evening, Frog gazed out from the battlements on to the scene, watching small camp fires spring to life and amazed at the growing tented city of the many groups and communities that were being brought together for a common cause. He came to the same viewpoint at the end of each day to watch the new arrivals and hoping to sense and finally see the others returning to safety, particularly Lady Dawnstar.

Gizmo had been right, their powers of mental

communication faded into silence as the distance between them grew. Frog had been able to sense the others for the first day of their absence from Castellion Stronghold, then, one by one, he had lost contact with each of them as their journeys took them beyond the reach of their shared thoughts. The only contact in his mind was Gizmo's and more often than not his voice shouted in Frog's head: 'Will you leave me alone? If you're going to search for the others' presence, then channel your mind as I showed you and give me some peace!'

Frog learned the art of control very quickly after the third warning from the wizard which involved promises of having Frog spend the day in the form of a pig amongst the other pigs in the castle's mucky pigsty.

Knights, men and women, visited the king for counsel and his commands. Sometimes the King would present Frog to them and sometimes they were brought to Frog for private introductions. On each occasion they would all bow and swear allegiance to the boy who stood before them, in the same way as they did for their king. People stared at the mark of the burning sun on his forehead and more than once Frog caught a glimpse of someone making the sign of the cross, or some pagan symbol, on themselves while mouthing a silent prayer as they passed by him.

One morning, Frog had a particularly rude awakening. With a yelp, he was shocked out of his slumber as a wet, ice-cold object was thrust down his neck.

His eyes shot open and he gasped for air, as his breath caught in his throat.

'Gotcha!' shouted Ginger with glee as he danced around Frog in excitement.

'Wha! Wha! What's going on?' stammered Frog, his teeth starting to chatter as the cold melted into his neck and ran down the inside of his tunic. He scrabbled at his clothes to remove the lump of what he now guessed was snow or ice.

'Come outside and see,' said Ginger eagerly, and he dragged Frog to his feet towards the stable doors.

Frog managed to loosen his clothes so that what was left of the snowball could slither out from his waist and drop to the floor.

'Ginger! Give me a chance,' he complained as he was pulled towards the courtyard. 'It's only snow.'

'Only snow?' Ginger replied, as they reached the open doors.

Frog stared out on the scene before him. It was the whitest, brightest snow that he had ever seen. So white in fact that the glare was uncomfortable.

Everything was covered in a good layer and the snow was still falling gently from a seemingly clear sky. Children were running around, kicking it and throwing snowballs at each other while older people looked skyward with concerned looks on their upturned faces. The sun was obscured by a single black cloud.

'But the sky is blue. It doesn't make sense,' said Frog.

'Wake up, slowcoach. That's what's so weird,' said Ginger, scooping up another handful and pushing it under Frog's nose. 'The sky is blue, it's summer!'

'Not good. Definitely not good,' said Frog.

'Do you think it's got something to do with the Frozen Wastes and the Hidden People?' asked Ginger.

'More than likely,' replied Frog. 'Look,' he said, pointing towards the castle.

'What?' asked Ginger, shielding his eyes against the glare.

'Up there, on the balcony of the high tower,' said Frog with excitement. 'It's Gizmo, he's waving something at the sky.'

There was a bright orange flash which made Frog, Ginger and the castle inhabitants duck nervously. Then the dark cloud was gone and the snow stopped falling. The sudden return of the sun in the sky increased the air temperature and melted the snow, making it evaporate into clouds of steam. Frog looked back up to the tower but the wizard was already gone from the balcony. His voice, however, appeared calmly in Frog's mind.

'Come to my chambers,' he instructed. 'Take the route via the air lift in the tower behind the tapestries in the royal court. Hold the chain that I gave you in your left hand and no one will see you during your journey.'

Frog felt for the chain around his neck and a small unseen talisman settled between his fingers.

'Come on, Frog,' said Ginger, turning around and looking straight at him. 'This is no time to play hide and seek. Where have you gone now? You can't have gone far, you're not that quick.'

Frog waved his other hand in front of Ginger's face and Ginger didn't react.

'He really can't see me. I'm invisible!' Frog thought to himself with glee as he carefully moved behind Ginger. This was too good an opportunity for him to miss. He

119

reached down, picked up a handful of soggy, ice-cold straw and stuffed it quickly down the back of Ginger's tunic.

'Oh, very funny,' shrieked Ginger, leaping around like a drunken puppet, with one hand down his tunic trying to retrieve the mucky mess and the other lashing out into thin air. 'One day, I'll have some magic tricks of my own and then you're for it.'

'Frog! Will you stop playing around and get up here now!' commanded Gizmo's voice in his head. 'Or do I need to remind you of a vacancy that awaits you in the pigsty?'

Frog didn't need reminding twice and very quickly he made his way to the tower and found himself floating in the air current as he travelled up to the wizard's apartments. Every time he took this journey he told himself not to look down but, uncontrollably, he always did and then wished that he hadn't!

As he stepped out onto the balcony overlooking the wizard's apartments, he could see Gizmo seated in the chair of the giant telescope. He was staring intently with one eye into the lens. There was an enormous lump in his cheek upon which he was sucking vigorously. The laboratory seemed to be working overtime, tubes and bottles burbling and gurgling away. Liquids were mixing and separating in various places within the maze of glass shapes.

Frog made his way down the stairs and was greeted by a large Storm, who sauntered out from behind the staircase, a bloody, chewed bone in his mouth which he promptly dropped at Frog's feet.

'No thanks, I've just eaten,' said Frog nervously.

Storm gave a low growl, rubbed his head affectionately on Frog's leg, picked up the bone in his mouth and sauntered off in the direction of the cushioned area, only to collapse effortlessly amongst the cushions and continue to grind and crack the bone open with his large, gleaming white teeth.

Frog wandered over to the plants, which were bathing in their usual golden glow. Some had definitely increased in size lately and towered over Frog as he walked along the benches. A particularly pretty pink plant not unlike a lily opened its petals in display as Frog approached it. Frog leant forwards and he caught a peculiar smell coming from the flower when it suddenly gave a loud belch and disgorged a collection of tiny bones onto the surrounding earth.

'Oh. paleese!' exclaimed Frog. 'That really is gross.'

The flower turned its head menacingly towards Frog, exposing a circle of needle-sharp teeth amongst its inner petals, and Frog thought it a good time to move away.

Further along the bench his eye caught the glint of something lying on the earth. Looking closer he could see that it was a gold ring and, thinking that the wizard may have mislaid it there, he reached forwards to pick it up. Without warning, from out of the earth on which the ring lay, a large oval shape attached to a long green stem reared up and towered over Frog. The seam around it split open to reveal a blood-red, slavering mouth lined with rows of twisted razor-sharp barbs. Frog stared at it, mesmerised for a moment as the plant prepared to strike. Then his instincts kicked in and he grabbed the talisman around his neck and stepped quickly to one side. In that instant, the plant lunged forwards, its mouth slapping closed as it met nothing but empty air. It pulled quickly back and, if a plant could look confused, this one surely did.

Frog slowly backed away, releasing the chain when he was at a safe distance, and wandered over to the wizard.

'What bit of *don't touch*, don't you understand?' he asked Frog without turning around.

'Sorry,' murmured Frog guiltily.

'I'm just going to have to take precautions with you until I've finished,' said the wizard. 'This won't hurt but it will keep you out of mischief for a while.'

As Frog stood there he felt his hands drawn together as if magnetised and looking down watched in fascination as the ends of his tunic sleeves knitted themselves together, trapping his hands inside.

'Now, be a good boy and sit down by Storm until I'm ready to join you,' said Gizmo. 'Or would you rather that I ask Storm to come and get you?'

'Okay. Okay. I get the message,' said Frog a little embarrassed as he made his way over to the cat and plonked himself down amongst the cushions. As if to take Gizmo's lead, Storm rolled across Frog's lap, giving his half growl, half purr, content that Frog was not going anywhere.

Frog leaned back and stared up at the ceiling, his eyes immediately falling on the brown leathery material stretched across the hang-glider style wings that hung above the telescope.

'Now, that's definitely a hang-glider,' he thought to himself. 'Where on earth did he get a hang-glider?'

Frog's mind drifted back to his own world and the times when he would visit an area on the edge of the chalk downs with his parents as they picnicked and watched the hang-gliders soar and swoop over the fields and meadows below. Homesickness struck his stomach like a hammer and he felt tears starting to well up in his eyes. He really needed his home, he needed to see his mum, he wanted his dad back.

He wasn't sure any more that he was really enjoying this adventure. A tear rolled down his cheek and he felt very much alone. He closed his eyes and a vision appeared in his mind of his home burning, his parents were trapped inside, calling out his name.

'Chris! Chris! Help us, help us! Come home, come home, we need you.' It was as though he was ensnared in a nightmare and then a voice whispered in his head.

'Go home, boy. Go home. You are needed there. Even your father has returned. Who is more important to you? These strangers who are just using you for their own ends, or your family? Use the dagger and open the Slipstream. Do it, do it now!' the voice added with urgency.

'Yes, yes,' Frog murmured to himself. 'Open the Slipstream, use the dagger, I must go home.'

His eyes remained closed, the vision of his burning home flickering before him. He struggled to reach the dagger on his belt, but he couldn't free his hands.

'See how they hold you prisoner?' whispered the voice. 'Don't trust them, you must escape and open the Slipstream.'

'Yes, yes,' agreed Frog as he continued to struggle.

Another voice called to him. A gentle voice this time,

cutting through the awful image and dissolving it along with the sickly feeling in his stomach.

'Do not be afraid, my dear Frog. It is trickery, your mother is safe, nothing has changed in your time. All is as you left it.'

Then, there she was. Lady Dawnstar, fierce and beautiful, her face clear in his mind, smiling, lighting up the darkness and giving courage and clarity to his thoughts.

'He's mine,' whispered the voice, now poisonous and angry. 'Interfere at your peril, you fool of a woman.'

'Be gone, you false lord, for I am no ordinary woman and I will be there at your day of reckoning,' she replied sternly. Touching the sun on her forehead, she flooded Frog's thoughts with a golden, warm glow, which cleared all sense of doubt and concern from his mind. The threat of the whispering voice was gone and he opened his eyes. Storm, now in the shape of a normal-size cat, lay on his lap, purring and preening at Frog's chest. He brought up his hand and absently stroked the cat, accepting without surprise that his hands were now free.

'She's coming back, Storm. She's on her way back to us, I can feel it,' he said with a smile on his face.

He looked up to Gizmo who was offering him a drink.

'That was the first real test of your courage,' he said. 'Do you know whose voice that was?'

'Lord Maelstrom, I presume?' replied Frog, taking the wooden cup and gratefully drinking the cool contents. 'Mmm! Very refreshing. More magic?' he asked.

'No, just home-made pear cordial,' said the wizard.

'The Dark Lord found a weakness in your memories and was testing you. In fact, as you saw earlier, he is testing his strength and his influence across the land.'

'You mean the snow?' enquired Frog.

'The very same,' said Gizmo. 'He is trying to put doubts in the people's minds, but it has just confirmed to me that he is only capable at present of producing annoying illusions. Come here, I want you to see something.' He led Frog over to the giant telescope and instructed him to sit in the chair.

'Do I get a gobstopper too?' asked Frog hopefully.

'Only if it serves to keep you quiet for a while.' Gizmo touched the jar which proceeded to rattle. A hole appeared in the top and a bright blue ball shot into the air.

'If you want it, you'd better catch it yourself,' said Gizmo.

As before, the ball arced downward but this time Frog was ready. He caught it firmly in his hand and then quickly popped it into his mouth.

'Happy now?' asked the wizard.

'Yepth phanku,' said Frog, surprised at how big the gobstopper was in his mouth. 'Naw I no hy they cawed gostophers.'

'Enough!' reproached the wizard. 'Now, look into the eyepiece.'

Frog leant forward and did as he was told, the gobstopper rattling against his teeth. What he saw nearly made him cough it out.

The scene was as clear as if it was only a few metres in front of him, a view of the land from the air as if he were in a helicopter (or on a hang-glider), but this

125

landscape was frozen with shining, black ice. No sun shone, only the light of a full moon gave the scene clarity and detail. Jagged frozen figures in their thousands were swarming forwards and with every step, they made the land and vegetation blacken and wither underfoot. Anything living that got in their path was immediately crystallised into solid ice-covered beings which joined and added to the advancing army.

'Hold tight,' announced Gizmo, pulling a lever and turning the chair a little.

There was a slight blurring and then a new scene was spread out in Frog's view. The land was bathed in twilight, but far on the horizon glistened the shining black ice, rippling with the advancing army of the Hidden People. There was a township in the foreground with people hurriedly leaving their homes, some with large bundles strapped to their backs, some leading loaded carts pulled by whatever livestock was able. Men, women and children with tearful and angry expressions were looking anxiously to the north and the advancing menace.

This was by no means a scene of panic but a well-organised evacuation, for there, amongst the people, was the familiar figure of Logan, astride a large black horse, his cloak swirling around him. He was shouting and encouraging the people not to panic, his voice clear and spreading courage into the hearts of young and old alike. Frog had the feeling that, if need be, all of these people would turn, stand and fight alongside Logan if he asked, such was the trust on their faces when they looked towards him.

'Now you really must hold on,' said the wizard as he pulled and pushed various levers. The whole contraption rotated and began to rise up, the long barrel of the telescope levelling out and pointing in the opposite direction.

'Prepare yourself to see some of the horrors that Lord Maelstrom has in store for us,' said the wizard.

Again the image blurred, then a grainy-greyish hue gave way to flares of fire lighting up what was left of the burning countryside. The air was polluted with acrid smoke drifting across the landscape, a landscape that was black and desolate. Burnt and stunted trees clung to the ashen soil, and thick plumes of smoke rose up to feed the dark menacing clouds that blotted out the sky.

The creatures that scrambled, crawled and slithered over the desolate land were scrawny, blackened and twisted. Their eyes were filled with a sickly green light, their expressions were vicious and evil. Frog could feel the despair and hopelessness that accompanied these advancing legions.

There was a slight movement and the view moved to the front line of the destruction. Here there were groups of the black wolves, their matted, oily fur hanging lankly from their bodies. They were in the process of burning a village and terrorising the occupants. Some of the wolves were on all fours, rounding up their victims into groups while others were up on their hind legs carrying flaming torches with which they set light to the buildings and vegetation.

Frog stared in disbelief as the villagers that had not been killed by the wolves in their attack were tied up and staked to the ground, left to become helpless prey for the army of advancing creatures to feed on. A gathering dark cloud above them was signalling their doom. Frog pulled his head away from the viewfinder and turned to Gizmo. He spat the gobstopper out into his hand, his face now red with anger.

'Why aren't we saving those people? Where's the help that you sent out?' he cried.

'Help is at hand, but at the moment it cannot be everywhere that it is needed,' replied Gizmo. 'We are gathering in as many of the people as we can, but we must also bring our forces together, here at Castellion Stronghold, so that we may deploy our armies and strike back with accuracy and surprise at Lord Maelstrom and his wicked cohorts.'

'But what about *those* people? They need our help *now!*' pleaded Frog as he climbed down from the telescope in frustration.

The wizard put his hands on Frog's shoulders and looked him squarely in the eyes. 'One thing that you will have to accept, as painful as it may be, is that we cannot save everyone. There will be casualties, some close to our hearts. But you must focus on winning the war and not just the battle. Evil will have its triumphs, it has always been that way. It is up to us to lessen that triumph and give ourselves the greater victory.'

'But I need to do something,' said Frog. 'I feel so helpless. What's the point of me being here if I can't make a difference?'

'Don't be too eager to put yourself in jeopardy, young Frog. Danger will find you soon enough. Maybe sooner than you think. Now, go and gather the squires together, make sure that they are well prepared for their masters. Tomorrow morning there will be a gathering of the commanders and the Chosen. You can chose one squire to join you and be your companion in the forthcoming perilous venture. Pick wisely, for they may have more of a part to play than either you or I know.'

Frog left the wizard and made his way back to the stables to pass on the message to the rest of the squires. Along the way he discarded the gobstopper; he had quite lost his appetite.

As the first of the stars twinkled in the late evening sky, Frog stood once again on the battlements, this time accompanied by Gizmo and the king. They had all sensed some time earlier that Logan, Sir Peacealot, Sir Dragonslayer and Lady Dawnstar were returning, having completed the missions that they were sent on.

The first to arrive, amongst great excitement, was Sir Dragonslayer and his dragon masters. They appeared in the sky to the west, the sun sinking below the horizon, now bathing the clouds red and reflecting on the jewelled underbellies of the great dragons. They flew in formation, two hundred of them, the hues and colours of the dragons adding to the spectacle and wonder. As they grew nearer, more and more people thronged onto the battlements and out of their tents and pavilions to watch the great beasts land on an area of the plains cleared and prepared for them, their arrival being accompanied by loud cheering and applause. Most people kept their distance, but a few brave souls rushed forwards for a closer look, not only at the majestic animals, but also at their legendary riders. Their eagerness was brought short by one of the beasts living up to its temperamental nature and exhibiting disapproval at so many humans advancing at it.

It let out a tremendous roar and emitted a large stream of flame above the cowering heads. Many left with singed hair which they would later display to others as a trophy of the occasion.

Frog watched in wonder as the rider remonstrated with his mount in the strange guttural language of dragons. A rare event to hear it openly spoken.

No sooner had Sir Dragonslayer joined Frog, the king and Gizmo in their place on the battlements, when all three felt the presence of Lady Dawnstar in their minds and, looking out, they saw her banners flying amongst the galloping white steeds carrying her and her Maids of Steel. It was in that moment that Frog saw the glory that was in the name of her army. He could not even estimate their number, the suits of bright, polished steel armour blended together into an advancing shining cloud. Helmet-less, their golden hair flew around their heads like flaxen halos. They turned towards the east and circled to the rear of the castle where there was clear grazing land and space for their encampment.

'Welcome home, my lady, I've missed you,' channelled Frog in his mind.

'You have been in my thoughts also,' she replied. 'Has the Dark Lord bothered you since our last encounter?'

'No,' answered Frog. 'But I get the feeling that he's

listening to and watching us when he gets the opportunity.'

'Fear not, my friend, for we have safety in numbers. I'll be with you as soon as we've made camp and tended to our steeds,' she replied.

Frog turned his attention to Sir Dragonslayer, who he had not yet had the chance to welcome back.

'I never realised that dragons could be so beautiful, do you think that I could actually meet one?' he enquired.

Sir Dragonslayer looked at Gizmo and the king. 'I take it that you haven't told him yet?' he said.

'We thought that we would leave that pleasure to you,' replied the king.

Sir Dragonslayer turned back to Frog. 'Meet one? You're going to ride one.'

'You're having me on!' exclaimed Frog.

Sir Dragonslayer looked quizzically at Gizmo.

'An expression of surprise and acceptance,' explained the wizard.

Frog stood there open mouthed until Sir Dragonslayer leaned forwards and lifted his chin to shut it, prompting laughter from everyone.

That evening there was a banquet in the central hall. Great quantities of food and drink were displayed, with serving staff to-ing and fro-ing carrying dishes of hot cooked meats and vegetables.

Frog was seated at the high table between King Hector and Lady Dawnstar, along with Sir Dragonslayer and Gizmo. There were two empty seats which awaited the arrival of Logan and Sir Peacealot. Gizmo had told everyone that he knew they were safe and that their arrival was imminent. Just after the first dishes were served the great wooden doors of the hall were opened to a fanfare and Logan and Sir Peacealot strode in. They marched side by side to the king's table and bowed graciously.

'My Lord King,' announced Logan. 'The surviving peoples of the northern territories have been removed from the path of the Frozen Wastes and are journeying to Castellion Stronghold to join our stand against our adversaries. Sadly, those villages and their populations living in the outer lands could not be reached in time and they have fallen prey to the Hidden People and have joined the ranks of the frozen, walking dead. There is nothing now between us and the coming threat in the north except for empty lands. They'll take no more souls from us to feed their army.'

Sir Peacealot stepped forward.

'My Lord King, I have gathered every knight and war-worthy man to our cause. Those that have not yet made camp continue to arrive and join the throng. They come in their thousands, by horse, foot or by whatever fashion will transport them, for all pledge allegiance to the king, Castellion and the Chosen. The Legend has inspired the land.'

'So be it,' announced the king. 'Let us all now be seated and take our sustenance, as it may well be some time before we have again the pleasure of such luxury. Tomorrow, we set in motion the events to shape our future and embark on perilous journeys. Let us also take great comfort that we share each other's company, trust and loyalty.' He stood and the room fell silent, no one moved, all eyes were on the king. He spoke clearly and effortlessly for all to hear.

'For Castellion. Let the Light free us from evil.'

As one, all of the representative knights, squires, Maids of Steel, Rangers, dragon masters and free people stood and raised their arms in salute, touching the centre of their foreheads and repeating the words. The chorus of their voices sounded around the hall, resonating and building in volume to a great crescendo and in the seconds that followed they heard the words echoed, flooding out through the tall windows to the castle grounds, and surrounding fields and plains, vibrating through every stone of the building. Every voice of the gathered armies spoke as one.

'For Castellion. Let the Light free us from evil.'

The rest of the banquet passed with Frog listening to stories of past adventures being exchanged by those around him. Now and again Gizmo would point out a particular character from one of the tables and share a tale concerning bravery or battle. Frog noticed that nearly all of the individuals had a wound of some description, a missing ear or eye, the odd scar etched across their face or in a couple of extreme cases an absent limb.

'And they're your best fighters?' he remarked to Gizmo. 'I'd hate to see your worst!'

'Would you like me to introduce you to some of our brave warriors?' Gizmo asked. 'We could start with Sir Firebrand over there.' He pointed to a huge man with a great red beard and mop of tussled hair. A patch covered one eye and part of his nose was missing. He turned and grinned in Frog's direction, showing a mouth of broken and missing teeth.

'On second thoughts,' said Frog nervously. 'They all

look as though they're pretty tough. I'll pass by that offer if you don't mind.'

At that moment, Sir Dragonslayer appeared at his side.

'Come, my young friend. I've something to show you,' he beckoned.

Frog looked at Gizmo, who nodded in agreement. Sir Dragonslayer led Frog out through a side entrance and up a narrow, winding stone staircase. Eventually, they reached an open doorway and stepped out onto a wide, flat roof. Frog caught his breath, for there, crouched before him, was an enormous dragon. Sir Dragonslayer approached the creature and placed his head against the great beast's muzzle. Frog could sense that something was passing between them, then suddenly Sir Dragonslayer and the dragon's conversation was in his head.

'*Allow the boy to ride me?*' said a soft, almost musical voice. '*Do you know what that means?*'

'*That he will be the first ever to have been given the honour without enduring the Ritual,*' replied Sir Dragonslayer's voice.

'*But we have no meld, he will not know what to do,*' the voice came again, concerned.

'*He is special, he melds through me, he will feel and know through me,*' assured Sir Dragonslayer's voice.

'*How can this be so? What magic allows this?*' questioned the dragon.

Sir Dragonslayer explained. '*He has been brought to us through the Slipstream, the Guardians know of his coming. He is one of the Chosen.*'

'*The Guardians? One of the Chosen? Bring him to me*

then. I need to smell his presence,' instructed the dragon.

Sir Dragonslayer turned but Frog was already approaching. By now he had made up his mind that this was too good an opportunity to miss. Besides, the voice enchanted and intrigued him, it was as if he had heard it in a dream a long time ago. Meeting the dragon felt like meeting a long-lost friend.

He stood before it, staring into its large, emerald green eyes, feeling the hot breath wash over him. His knees suddenly felt weak, not from fear, but from excitement, and he had to use all of his strength to stop them from trembling. Then, the musical voice was in his head, stronger and more vibrant than before.

'A Chosen One, ay? Tell me, small one. Does my company make you want to scream and run?'

It leaned closer, the snout of its nose touching Frog's chin.

Frog relaxed and opened his mind, letting his memories and thoughts escape, his head growing dizzy with the experience.

The dragon stepped back, bowing its head to the floor and Frog's feet.

'Truly, you are a Chosen One, I feel your essence, I share your hopes, dreams and fears and I am honoured. Climb my foreleg, take my reins and ride with me.'

For Frog, what followed was in recollection a blur, it all passed so quickly. Climbing onto the dragon's shoulders and taking off into the night, watching the moonlit earth float beneath them and feeling so close to the endless stars above. The dragon shared many things with Frog during the flight, visions of its past and precious secrets, inner fears and glimpses of dragon dreams. A bond and great respect passed between them. Now and again they were joined by other, riderless dragons who fleetingly spoke to him as they passed by.

'All my brethren can touch your mind and you theirs, call to them and they will answer, they will forever sense your presence wherever you are in this world, never before has a mortal been given such a gift,' said the dragon.

The experience did not cause some great life change in Frog, but it gave him further understanding of how mysterious life could be. One visible transformation was apparent – his eyes were forever the greenest emerald eyes that you would come across.

In his sleep that night, he dreamt comfortably about his mother and father. Of the past, the present, and of flying dragons. It was the deepest and most peaceful, restful sleep that he had ever had.

9

Secrets of the Scrolls

The next morning, in the royal court, Frog stood on the royal dais along with the other members of the Chosen. Ginger stood nervously but proudly to one side along with the other young companion of the Chosen, Fixer, Lady Dawnstar's squire.

The commanders and knights, representing the combined armies of the kingdom, were gathered in a great semicircle around the royal dais. None were dressed in their battle armour, but in comfortable travelling attire, as they all knew that there would be many days' journey until they reached the various fields of engagement. Their squires and servants were in the process of preparing and packing the various forms of armour, along with the food and supplies which would be needed to feed and equip the vast armies and militia as they travelled to face their enemies.

The gathered throng looked none the less resplendent and fierce in their subtle browns and greens, dark blues and reds. Many had swords hanging from their belts, some with double axes strapped to their backs. Archers leant on their longbows and the dark-skinned Rangers wore leather chest bands holding rows of short daggers, with their long bull whips coiled over their shoulders. All stood ready in expectant silence, all eyes were on the king.

King Hector rose from his throne and stepped to the edge of the dais, and as one, all who faced him dropped to one knee and bowed their heads.

'Look to me,' he commanded, and three hundred faces rose to meet his gaze.

'From this day forth you will bow and kneel to no one, not even me. I ask only that you follow the guidance and command of those called the Chosen, we seven who now stand before you. Now rise, and attend to the wizard's instructions.'

Gizmo stepped from the raised stone platform and into the centre of the floor, the gold and silver runes of his midnight blue cloak shifting and shimmering in the material as it billowed around him as if caught by a constant breeze. He carried the rolled up map and unfurled it on the floor. He then brought forward the silver cane in his hand and tapped the map with its tip. The material stretched and grew until the map was now at least three meters square, spread out for all to see.

'Here lies the present and the future, I have consulted with the highest of Magik and the laws of nature, balance, cause and effect,' he announced. 'The fate of kingdoms and worlds beyond ours depends on the defence of Castellion. The future hangs on our victory over the wickedness that designs to conquer and destroy us. Take these orders as your destiny and do not stray from their direction, lest you put us all in peril.'

SECRETS OF THE SCROLLS

Once again he touched the map with his cane. The parchment started to segment into small scrolls and each scroll sealed itself with a gold ribbon and rose into the air until there were as many of them as there were commanders, knights and the Chosen. Three hundred and seven in all. The scrolls floated around the hall until each one hovered above its selected individual.

Gizmo continued. 'The contents are guarded against the prying eyes of our enemies. Read them well and only share them with those that you can truly trust. Some of you may find that you are bound by the same instructions and path, others may find that they do not comprehend the reason in their orders. Have patience, see the task and passage through, do not doubt its motives. Now, return to your camps, consult the scrolls and make your preparations to leave. May the Light be with you.'

He lowered his cane and the scrolls dropped into waiting hands.

There was no cheering, reverie or loud camaraderie. Instead, farewells and good wishes, along with heartfelt embraces were exchanged and as the Chosen watched from the dais, the hall emptied quietly and in an orderly fashion.

Ginger appeared at Frog's side.

'Remind me how I ended up here?' he asked Frog.

'Because you've become someone who I can trust and rely on,' replied Frog.

'Am I going to regret this?' asked Ginger.

'Probably,' smiled Frog.

'Then I wouldn't miss it for anything,' Ginger grinned back.

The others were opening their scrolls and Frog did likewise with Ginger and Fixer leaning over his shoulder.

The lettering on the scroll was plain and the instructions were simple:

> *You will leave immediately*
> *and accompany Lady Dawnstar,*
> *Logan and Sir Peacealot into the*
> *Labyrinth and solve its secret,*
> *seek out the Earth Sage*
> *and release the Blackwater.*

'What about us?' asked Ginger, indicating to himself and Fixer.

'I go where Lady Dawnstar goes,' said Fixer.

'So, what about me?' emphasised Ginger.

'You go where I go,' answered Frog.

'The Labyrinth. Not really my favourite idea of an adventure,' said Ginger worriedly.

'Labyrinths are just mazes, puzzles,' said Frog. 'It'll be fun. I like puzzles.'

'Well I hope you're good at solving them,' said Fixer. 'Of all who have gone into the Labyrinth, no one has ever returned or been seen again. Ever.'

'Thanks for reminding me,' said Ginger gloomily.

The king turned. 'Let us compare our instructions.'

They gathered in a circle and the king continued.

'I am to take my army of royal knights and fighting men and women of Castellion Stronghold to the south and face Lord Maelstrom and his despicable creatures.

No doubt I shall enjoy cutting into Fangmaster's stinking wolves and with a bit of luck I'll separate his head from his body once and for all. Dealing with Lord Maelstrom, if he puts in an appearance will, I'm sure, be a different matter.'

'I am to accompany King Hector,' said Gizmo. 'I must take myself where the threat of Lord Maelstrom is the strongest. These will be testing times for my Magik.'

'I go north, to the Frozen Wastes with my dragon masters, Logan's Rangers, the bowmen of Dinham and the Maids of Steel,' said Sir Dragonslayer.

'My Rangers go without my leadership?' questioned Logan.

'My Maids also,' added Lady Dawnstar. 'Who will they follow?'

'They will follow your most trusted commanders,' said Gizmo. 'They have their instructions also and this is how it must be. You have trained your people well. Now it is time to let them show you what they can do and, if necessary, carry it out without you. Your challenges lie in a separate direction, the Labyrinth awaits.'

'I cannot help you on your task for you go into the domain of the Earth Sage where my Magik has no authority. You must use your own strengths and the powers as given to you. Fail and we are all in peril.'

'No pressure then,' said Frog.

'Hold on to your sense of humour, young Frog, you may need to call upon it many times in the coming days,' said Gizmo sternly. 'Now, you must all take leave on your quest. Logan will lead you to the Labyrinth. He is the only one who has knowledge of its location apart from myself.'

None of them could stop themselves bowing to the king as they left, it just seemed the right thing to do no matter what his command. Gizmo and the king watched the party disappear through the great doors.

'There lies our future, how it plays out is now out of my hands,' said Gizmo to the king. 'Last eve I consulted the Guardians and the news is not good. There has been a breech in the Dimensions and the missing Rune Stone has returned. It would appear that the Stones are drawn back to their own Dimension after one phase of the moon. They return to the last holder and in this circumstance, as the witch Belzeera was cast out into the Dimensions, the Stone has returned from the Slipstream with new Magik and into Lord Maelstrom's hand.'

'All he needs now is the boy and by covering the Stone in the boy's blood, he will gain the ability to take his malevolence through the Slipstream and into the next Dimension.'

The king placed his hand on the wizard's arm. 'I will be guided by your wisdom and loyalty, my friend, but I will not let Castellion become the first of the Dimensions to fall and be used as a catalyst of destruction.'

'It will need the strength of man and the force of Magik to work in harmony. Should one overpower the other, then there will be chaos,' warned Gizmo.

'Then let us to battle and play out our parts, Lord Wizard. My sword arm is stiff and needs some exercise, let's prod the wasps' nest that is Lord Maelstrom and distract his attention for a while.'

'I've always been very good at swatting wasps,'

replied Gizmo, and they allowed themselves a chuckle as they too made their way across the now deserted hall and out through its towering doors.

In the courtyard by the main stables, Frog, Ginger and Fixer were making sure that Lady Dawnstar, Logan and Sir Peacealot's horses were ready and that all they needed was packed and secured on the accompanying mules. The three of them also had leather backpacks and had prepared their own horses ready to ride. Frog took particular pride in making sure that Thunder was well brushed, his hooves polished and that his bridle gleamed.

So it was on that warm but overcast morning, the party of six horses, three mules and six riders made their way through the throng of the castle grounds and out amongst the various groups of Castellion's defenders, who were making their own preparations for the parts that they would play in the coming confrontations.

As the little party moved in single file, with Logan leading the way, the occasional captain or commander gave recognition to them with a nod or a touch of their foreheads in formal salute before they turned back to encourage their groups with a sense of urgency and purpose. Such was the vastness of the assembled forces that it took the group over an hour to pass by the outermost sentries and travel westward, out across the open landscape of grass plains, the green horizon appearing endless to Frog's eyes.

An hour later, Sir Dragonslayer met with his dragon masters and the commanders of Logan's Rangers,

Lady Dawnstar's Maids of Steel and the bowmen of Dinham.

He had shared most of what was written in his scroll, only keeping back some small detail which he was instructed to reveal closer to the time of battle. As Gizmo had predicted, there had been no question or lack of loyalty from Lady Dawnstar's or Logan's commanders towards Sir Dragonslayer's leadership. He was accepted without exception, along with the orders that he passed on.

Their army was to advance in three waves in as much daylight as possible to the north, towards the Frozen Wastes and the Hidden People. Firstly, Logan's Rangers were to scout across the region and relay messages back to the groups on any strengths and weaknesses that they observed in the enemy's lines. Then the Maids of Steel on their white steeds, moving forwards in gleaming rows, would be ready to cut through whatever resistance came their way. Finally the bowmen of Dinham were to follow through at a distance, well within the range of any target that they needed to reach with their arrows and awesome accuracy. Supporting and protecting them all from the air would be Sir Dragonslayer and his dragon masters.

The night time would be the most treacherous, as this would be when the effect of the Hidden People's powers would be at its strongest. As they advanced, the sub-zero temperatures would blacken and freeze everything in their tracks. This was the moment at which Sir Dragonslayer would need to be most resourceful if he were to hold back and defeat the deadly menace that took no prisoners and threatened to overwhelm the land.

In the late afternoon, King Hector and Gizmo were the last to depart Castellion Stronghold, leaving behind a token force of landsmen and soldiers to defend the castle from any small groups of Lord Maelstrom's allies that might find their way through the outer defences.

The knights and fighting men and women, gathered under King Hector's banners, were spread out across the southern borders. Their numbers were so great that more than a mile separated the outermost captains. Their ranks were a hundred deep. King Hector rode along the front lines, spending time in view of all of his people, riding along back and forth, sometimes speaking words of calm encouragement and other times shouting rallying cries of support. During encampments he would walk amongst the camp fires sharing warmth, nourishment and conversation with as many of his people as he could.

Gizmo would disappear during the nights, only to reappear each morning at sunrise with Storm by his side. The animal retained its panther size for most of the time but occasionally it would be found, sleeping in the back of one of the supply wagons, curled up cat-size, with a contented look on its face and fresh blood on its whiskers.

Despite the size of the force, they progressed with a good pace forward towards the ever growing blackness that filled the southern horizon and the rising sound of thunder that each day could be felt vibrating through the ground beneath them. Forked lightning stabbed at the ground in the distance and could be seen during both the days and nights. At the end of each day, blood-red fingers of cloud would streak out through the far-off blackened sky and across the horizon.

10

Going Down

Frog's party had been travelling for three days when the grassland stopped and a landscape of misshapen, grey rocks spread out before them in all directions. It seemed to him that some giant had attempted to lay his own grey, stone crazy-paving. Only this really was crazy, with enormous blocks of rock tilted this way and that, some rising and some falling. Laid out before them was a flat stone platform inserted into three rough, grey stone walls, two or three metres in height. The rock barrier extended into the distance on either side.

'Is there no way around?' questioned Lady Dawnstar.

'We're not going around,' answered Logan. 'We're going in.'

'But we'll never get the horses across, the sides are too sheer, and even if we did manage to get them onto the ledges their hooves will just slide on some of the rocks and they'll fall and be injured,' she replied.

'Just follow me,' instructed Logan stepping on to the first large flat rock. Frog shrugged and followed, leading his horse slowly and carefully. One by one, the rest

147

gently encouraged their horses and the mules to step up and on to the rock, until there was just Sir Peacealot and his horse left standing on the grass verge.

'There's no room,' he said. 'We'll never all fit on there.'

'You've got to,' shouted back Logan. 'Or none of us is going anywhere.'

Sir Peacealot climbed the step and pulled gently at his horse's reins, softly encouraging the animal. The horse placed both front legs on to the rock but couldn't move further.

'I told you, there isn't enough room,' repeated Sir Peacealot.

'Hang on a minute,' said Frog. 'We can make room, everyone get on their horses, that should do it.'

One by one they followed Frog's lead until they were all mounted and were able to move close to each other. Sure enough, the space that was made enabled Sir Peacealot to get his horse on to the platform.

'Now what?' he asked as he mounted his horse. 'We're all stuck here with nowhere to go, the rocks are too high around us, we're blocked in, the only way is back.'

Logan reached forwards and put his hand inside a small oval recess in the rock. The rock gave a loud shudder and with a grinding, crunching sound tilted away and lowered its surface until it was level with the one that they were all occupying. As it settled, it seemed that a chain reaction had started and a zig-zag pathway of rocks lowered, righted and levelled themselves out into the distance before them, forming an even corridor through the other towering crags.

'Well. I'm glad that worked,' said Logan with a sigh of relief. 'Now follow me.'

The party followed in single file at a steady pace, giving the horses and mules time to find their footing on the smooth surface of the rock, the sound of their hooves eerily echoing against the sides of the now towering rocks on either side of their passage.

Frog made his way forwards to walk beside Logan.

'Have you been here before?' he asked.

'Once,' replied Logan. 'Many, many years ago.'

'So you know where we're going?' asked Ginger.

'To the Labyrinth,' replied Logan.

'What's in the Labyrinth?' asked Frog.

Logan turned. His face was deadly serious. 'Our destiny.' He nodded back over their shoulders. 'Now I would suggest that one of you keeps an eye on the mules before we lose our supplies.'

Ginger and Frog turned to see that two of the mules were just standing still and were gradually being left behind.

'I'll get them,' said Ginger, handing the reins of his horse to Frog. 'You keep going, I'll catch up.'

'I don't think that there's much chance of us losing you,' said Fixer as Ginger scampered past her. 'But I'll wait here for you just in case.'

Ginger spent at least five minutes trying to coax the mules to move. He pushed, pulled, pleaded, begged and threatened, but they remained stubbornly still. Meanwhile, the rest of the party were becoming small figures in the distance and Frog's voice could be heard.

'Come on you two, we haven't got all day!'

'Okay Ginger,' called Fixer. 'You obviously haven't got the touch.'

Ginger's red face appeared from behind one of the mules. 'All right then, Miss clever pants, you get down here and shift them.'

Fixer smiled. 'I don't need too,' she said and, raising two fingers to her lips, she gave a sharp whistle.

The two mules immediately sprang into a trot and headed down the passageway after the others while Ginger stood there open-mouthed.

Fixer rode down the passage to the bewildered Ginger. 'Come on then!' she said, reaching down her hand. 'Don't just stand there catching flies, get on up here, or have I got to whistle at you too?'

Ginger grabbed her hand and swung himself up onto the back of the horse.

'Why didn't you do that in the first place?' he asked.

'I was bored and needed a little amusement,' she said with a mischievous giggle. 'Now hold tight, because if you fall off you can walk the rest of the way.'

With that, she spurred her horse and they were off at a speedy trot after the mules and the rest of the group.

When they rejoined the others, Fixer regaled them with the story and poor Ginger had to endure the laughter that followed, including comments relating to how many 'asses' they had actually brought along. However, he took it all in good spirit, as the humour was well natured and not intended to belittle him.

Sometimes the passage narrowed, leaving just enough room for them to travel in single file, and at other times it widened so that they could ride two or three abreast. None of them could fail to notice that they were on a gradual slope, taking them deeper into the rocks that towered menacingly above them, causing a claustrophobic atmosphere. The air was also getting warmer, becoming thick and heavy. The horses behaved nervously, pulling at their reins and snorting in short bursts. Gradually the light began to dim and a fine mist crept down the dark stone walls and collected on the ground, swirling around the horses' and mules' legs.

For some time, Lady Dawnstar and Sir Peacealot had been riding at the front with Logan, their conversations a whisper to the ears of Frog, Ginger and Fixer, who had been kept busy encouraging the mules to keep moving.

Suddenly Logan stopped.

'Here we dismount and continue on foot. Ginger, organise some torches before we lose the last of the light.'

Ginger untied three torch staves from one of the mule's packs and handed them to Frog and Fixer. He then pulled a stone flask from one of the bundles and poured a thick, sour-smelling liquid over the torch heads.

'Phew!' exclaimed Frog. 'What's that smell?'

'Some mixture of the wizard's,' replied Ginger. 'I think it's better that we don't know what's in it. Let's just get them alight. Fixer, can you make a spark?' he asked.

Fixer produced a tinderbox from inside her tunic and with the first strike ignited Ginger's torch, which flared with a brightness that illuminated the stone corridor, pushing the descending darkness well away from them.

'Well done. Now light the other two,' instructed Logan. 'You keep one at the back, I'll take one for the front and Sir Peacealot can carry the other.'

They moved forwards, the light of the torches giving them more confidence; even the mist seemed to melt back and recede from the light.

'Is this your first adventure?' Frog asked Fixer as they moved on.

'Depends what you call an adventure,' she answered.

'Well I guess trudging through a dark crevasse and heading into a dangerous Labyrinth qualifies for one,' said Frog.

'Lady Dawnstar has taken me into spookier places,' she replied proudly.

'Like what?' asked Ginger.

'Like into a Madbagger's lair, to rescue some little children.'

'A Madbagger? You've been into a Madbagger's lair?' said Ginger, his eyes wide with surprise. 'You're crazier than I ever thought.'

'What's a Madbagger when it's at home?' enquired Frog.

Ginger and Fixer exchanged a look, half smile and half fear.

'You'd best wait until we're in daylight before we describe it to you,' said Fixer.

'Yes, in these surroundings, just talking about one gives me the spooks,' added Ginger.

'Oh, come on, you guys, nothing could be that scary,' announced Frog.

'Okay, you asked for it,' said Fixer. 'I'll start and Ginger can fill in the other details.'

Smiling mischievously, Ginger nodded in agreement. Fixer opened her mouth, when suddenly there was a whooshing noise. Ginger let out a yelp as his torch was snatched from his grasp and flew rapidly skyward. Its flame was extinguished many feet above them. The wooden stake clattered to the ground next to him.

'What the ...?' he cried, rubbing his hand as he felt the splinters left in it from the wooden stave.

There was another whoosh and Frog caught site of a dark object moving at head height towards Sir Peacealot. As the knight turned to see what the shouting was about the object slammed into his chest and he fell sideways to land under his horse. The horse reared up in surprise, its hooves raised over him, ready to crash down on his head. He rolled and came out from under the horse, drawing his sword as he did so. The creature that had hit him had already picked up the torch which he'd dropped and carried it skyward. They watched as its flame was extinguished. The horses were panicking and the mules were braying in terror as several dark shapes landed on their backs, scrabbling to get to their necks.

'What are they?' cried Fixer.

'Bat-rats!' shouted Frog. 'Don't let them bite you,' he warned.

Logan grabbed a half dozen stakes and threw them on the ground. He pulled a flask from one of the bundles and threw it towards Ginger.

'Light as many torches as you can!' he ordered. 'The darkness is their ally, if we lose the light, we're defenceless.'

153

Ginger and Frog crouched down, dousing the torches with the liquid, while Fixer readied her tinderbox. Logan had his whip in hand. He expertly flicked the long leather lash around the necks of those that were threatening to bite into the flesh of the horses and mules, each crack signalling the end of a creature as the twisting coil separated the vicious little heads from their bodies.

At the same time, Lady Dawnstar and Sir Peacealot were scything their swords through the air above them, which resulted in sliced portions of the black creatures dropping lifeless to the ground around them.

With a sudden flare everything was bathed in a bright blue light from the torches. Ginger and Frog had laid them out in a row on the ground, their liquid-soaked heads touching so that when Fixer made a spark they ignited as one. Quickly grabbing one each they passed them to Logan and Sir Peacealot, returning to pick up the rest and raise them high into the darkness. Ear-splitting screeches ricocheted around them as the remaining creatures retreated into the night, high above the towering stone walls.

'Has anyone been bitten or scratched?' asked Lady Dawnstar urgently.

There was a brief panic by Ginger, who wasn't sure if the blood on his hand was caused by a bat-rat bite or a splinter cut. But much to the relief of all it turned out to be the latter. Ginger let Lady Dawnstar remove the splinter and tend the wound, grinning as she fussed over him while Fixer gave him a jealous look.

Logan surveyed the scene in the steady light. The remains of at least two dozen of the creatures lay strewn around them, their dark blood creating black liquid pools underfoot.

'Touch every one of them with a torch and burn them, else you would be surprised at what evil can put back together,' he said as he lowered his torch to the headless body at his feet. At once it burst into sickly green flames, the long black tail thrashing, its legs still clawing to reach him. A feeble screech emitted from the separated head nearby and Logan touched this also, to the same effect.

'Don't forget the heads and don't get any blood on your skin,' he warned.

Logan thought that there would be no repeat attack, but they all kept one eye skyward while they completed the grizzly task of burning the remains of their assailants.

'He knows we're here, we must double our speed if we're to reach the Labyrinth before he sends some other, more persistent, vile creatures to assault us,' said Logan after he had finished inspecting the horses and mules for injuries.

'I suppose he means Lord Maelstrom,' said Ginger.

'Well I don't think he means Father Christmas,' said Frog.

'Who?' asked Fixer.

Frog looked at Ginger and Fixer. 'It's a long story,' he explained.

'That's Okay,' replied Fixer. 'I think we've got plenty of time at the moment.'

As they resumed their journey, Frog told them the legend of Saint Nicholas and related the magic of Christmas, which stirred memories of his home and family. Ginger and Fixer found comparisons with the Festival of Winter in Castellion and the custom of exchanging gifts was not too dissimilar. They sang songs and decorated their homes to celebrate the season. The Festival was based on friendship and sharing so that no one would go without food and warmth during the coldest time of the year.

They had been making steady progress along a corridor that had now widened out for them to walk comfortably in pairs when Logan raised his hand to halt their advance. In the light of his burning torch they could see that the rock walls ended on either side and disappeared into blackness, as did the ground before them. He lowered his torch to his feet to reveal the top of some stone steps, also descending into the dark.

'No horses from now on,' he said. 'Everything we need, we carry. Change into whatever battle gear you prefer. Take only what is necessary but remember, if you take too much and can't carry it, no one else will carry it for you.'

They stood in silence for a few moments until Frog spoke up.

'Nothing has made sense to me since I arrived in this crazy world of yours so I guess one more weird decision won't make any difference.' He walked up to the Ranger. 'But if anything happens to my horse, I'm not sure if I could forgive you.'

Logan looked down at Frog. 'As long as your horse does what he's told, then he won't come to any harm. Now lets move, we've got to be in the Labyrinth by sunrise and we've still got quite a way to go.'

When they had changed and agreed what provisions they needed to take with them, Logan instructed them to secure a fresh burning torch to each of the animals' saddle packs and then went up to each horse and mule in turn. He stood cheek to cheek with them for a moment and whispered gently in their ears. Finally he turned them to face back down the long black corridor. He lightly touched the hind quarters of Lady Dawnstar's white steed and it trotted off into the darkness, the others following in turn.

'What did you say to them?' asked Frog.

'I told them not to be afraid,' said Logan. 'You best take the same advice young Frog, as much depends on your courage.' Picking up his backpack and blanket roll, Logan gripped his torch and took the first step down into the stairwell.

After only what seemed a few minutes, they could see an amber glimmer appearing below them and as they made steady progress down the remainder of the steps they could see that they were approaching a semicircular flagstone floor at the foot of the steps. Facing them on floor level was a stone arch set in a block stone wall, the two burning braziers either side being the source of the amber light.

Logan stepped forward and dipped his torch into one of the braziers. As he withdrew it, they could see that the torch was extinguished. He indicated for the others to follow suit. They did so and were surprised that their torches were cold, as if they had never been lit.

Now in the flickering orange light they turned their attention to the inscription carved above the entrance.

157

The way shall be lit if you stay in view.
Up may be down, but what's left is true.
My corridors are long,
my passages unforgiving.
If you have the courage and the knowledge
You will return to the land of the living.

'I hate puzzles,' complained Ginger.

'It's no problem,' said Frog. 'Our Ranger friend has been here before.' He looked at Logan.

'That's true,' Logan agreed. 'But never into the Labyrinth.'

'Not good,' stated Frog. 'No chance of Plan B, then?' he enquired.

'Plan B? What's Plan B?' asked Fixer.

'I'm working on it,' replied Frog.

11

Into the Labyrinth

As they approached the entrance arch, they could see two things. Firstly, an eerie glow emitted from the floor, walls and ceiling, lighting the way along the corridor. Secondly, there were no joins in the stonework – it was as if the passage had been hewn out of solid rock.

'I don't trust this light,' said Logan. 'We'll still take our torches, just in case. Ginger, bundle them up and strap them across your backpack. Frog, you carry the lighting fuel, a couple of flasks should do.'

After a brief discussion, they decided to enter with Lady Dawnstar taking the lead, Frog next, then Sir Peacealot, Ginger, Fixer and Logan bringing up the rear. They were about ten metres into the passage when they were faced with their first decision, a choice to follow a right- or left-hand passage. In the end they chose to take the right one because, as Fixer pointed out, 'We don't know if we're trying to get to the centre of the Labyrinth or find a way through it, so at this stage it doesn't make much difference.'

'I'm sure that I was told a solution to mazes,' said Frog. ' But I can't remember it at the moment.'

'Thanks for sharing that with us,' said Ginger sarcastically. 'That's really helped.'

'One thing that we do need to do,' interrupted Fixer, 'is to mark where we've been in case we happen to double back on ourselves.'

'How are we going to do that?' asked Sir Peacealot.

'Scratch the walls at each junction,' said Fixer. 'So if we put a cross on the wall here and we end up back in the same place, we'll see it and know not to follow the same path.'

'Good idea,' said Logan. He removed one of the daggers from his chest belt and scraped a cross onto the stone wall, but no matter how hard he tried, he could leave no mark, not even a scuff.

'I know,' said Frog. 'Write on it.'

'What with?' asked Ginger.

'Crayon, felt marker, chalk,' said Frog, forgetting himself.

They all looked at him blankly.

'Perhaps not,' he said resignedly.

'Just a minute,' said Fixer, her face lighting up with a smile. 'Ginger, turn around.'

'What for?' complained Ginger.

'Just do it,' she insisted.

Ginger did as he was told and Fixer stuck two fingers into the end of one of the torches.

'This do?' she said, grinning and holding up her hand.

Everyone looked at her blackened, sooty fingers.

'Brilliant,' said Frog. 'Fixer by name and Fixer by nature.'

Fixer walked forwards and smudged a black arrow

on the wall in the direction of the passage they were taking.

'That should do it,' she said. 'We'll use this at every intersection.'

They continued on, the strange light emanating around them and illuminating their way. After a while they entered a large, square room. There were three open doorways: one to the right, one to the left and one straight ahead. There was also a square shaft in the centre of the ceiling with another below it in the middle of the floor. Logan looked into the shaft in the floor and was surprised to see that the bottom was only a couple of metres down.

'I think that it's time that we rested,' said Lady Dawnstar, looking at Frog, Ginger and Fixer, who had already sat themselves down against a wall. 'Our little friends are nearly asleep on their feet. I must admit that I'm tired myself. I think that we've travelled well into the night and we should take advantage of the space here and get some rest.'

They set up camp as best they could, lighting a small fire and cooking themselves a simple stew from their provisions. No sooner had Frog, Ginger and Fixer consumed their portions than their eyelids slowly closed and all three were fast asleep, bundled up together in a corner of the room.

'I'll take first watch,' announced Sir Peacealot.

'After our encounter with those bat-rats I think we should expect anything,' added Lady Dawnstar. 'So I'll take second watch if you don't mind taking third, Logan.'

Logan nodded in agreement and set his bedroll out

across the opening where they had entered the chamber, while Sir Peacealot sat himself against the opposite wall. Lady Dawnstar positioned herself at the foot of the now softly sleeping trio.

Something teased Frog awake and he opened his eyes to find that he was staring at the open mouth (and into the nostrils) of a softly snoring Ginger. The room looked strange in its self illuminating blue-grey light. He pulled himself up onto one elbow, rubbing an eye and taking in the scene. Everyone else was asleep. He had no idea if he had been asleep a few minutes or a few hours, but he felt a presence, a movement.

He looked around. Next to him, Fixer slept quietly, her arm draped across his waist. He removed it gently, feeling embarrassed should someone see. Lady Dawnstar lay on her side at his feet. Logan, his cloak wrapped around him, was stretched out by a doorway and Sir Peacealot, his back against a wall and his arms hanging limply by his sides, slept with his chin slumped against his chest. This was where Frog had to rub both of his eyes, for there, perched on Sir Peacealot's lap, was a small white mouse, busily cleaning its whiskers. The mouse looked exactly like Merv, his own pet mouse back in his home across the timeless Dimension. Merv had a striking black streak running up from behind his head, between his ears and down to his nose. This mouse had the exact same markings.

'Merv?' Frog heard himself say, and then realised how daft he was being. He looked around again to make sure that no one had woken to see him trying to talk to a mouse.

The mouse stopped its cleaning, gave itself a little scratch with its hind leg and stared at Frog.

'It's all right,' it announced. 'They won't wake up until I allow them to.'

'Merv?' Frog heard himself repeat involuntarily.

'Well I hope that the resemblance is accurate, after all I've picked the image up from your subconscious,' said the mouse. 'However, I can change myself into some other form if you like, maybe a parent figure would be more comfortable for you?'

'No. No,' stammered Frog, quickly deciding that an image of one of his parents would be too much to deal with in the present circumstances. 'You'll do just fine.'

'Good,' said the mouse, sounding satisfied with itself. 'I knew that this would be a pleasing likeness.'

'You mean that you can read my memories?' asked Frog.

'I can take any image as long as it is represented in the mind,' replied the mouse. 'A mouse, a horse, a bird, even a tree. Or one of the more unpleasant creatures that exist in nightmares or the dark recesses of the psyche.'

'Then what are you really?' asked Frog as he built up the courage to move closer.

'I am the Earth Sage.'

'Really? But what do you actually look like? said Frog.

'Patience, young Frog. All will be revealed. You must prove your worth to me. And I must judge the strengths of those that accompany you,' the mouse replied.

'Can't you just show us the way out of here?' Frog pleaded.

163

'I do not control the Labyrinth. Only you have the solution, the answer is in your will to survive,' the mouse explained.

'I just knew it wasn't going to be that easy,' Frog said resignedly. 'What have I got to do now?'

'You have to convince the others to follow you, let you go in front. At the moment they still feel that it is their destiny to lead and protect you. They will not believe your story of our encounter. This is their world and they think that they know better, their vanity makes them vulnerable to disappointment and self-doubt. Those that have self-doubts are destined to wander the Labyrinth's corridors forever. Your will is strong because of your desire to return to your home, your world.'

'Tell me about it,' said Frog. 'So what you're saying is that if they don't let me make the decisions and take the lead, we'll be stuck in here forever?'

'The Labyrinth has not yet shown you all of its secrets, it has not yet challenged you, my young friend. It will try to mislead you and separate you. If you allow this then you will fail and you and I will not meet again to enable the release of the Blackwater.'

'So what is this Blackwater?' quizzed Frog.

'It is the turning point, your moment of glory and Castellion's salvation. But only if you figure out its use.'

'I am so fed up with riddles,' confessed Frog. 'Nobody talks in plain language around here. No wonder there's so much trouble.'

The mouse jumped down from Sir Peacealot's lap and ran across the floor to the edge of the square pit. It turned and addressed Frog.

164

'Let us hope that we meet again in this world and not the next,' it said. Then it jumped into the hole and was gone.

Frog crawled to the edge, looked down and shouted after the animal, 'That's *exactly* what I mean!'

'Frog, why are you shouting into the hole?' said Logan.

Frog turned to see everyone awake and staring at him.

'A mouse,' he answered. 'What?' asked Ginger.

Frog sat down and told the group what had happened. They listened intently until he had finished. 'Well?' he asked.

'It's obvious,' said Ginger. 'You've been dreaming.'

'Either that or it's one of the Labyrinth's tricks,' added Logan. 'If the Earth Sage were to appear, it would be to fulfil his task, not to play games as a talking mouse. The situation is much too serious for such a frivolous encounter.'

'I'm afraid that I have to agree,' said Lady Dawnstar.

'And I can only say what I saw,' said Sir Peacealot. 'I've never been known to fall asleep on watch. I firmly remember seeing you crawl across the floor and start shouting into the hole. There was no mouse here and certainly not one on my lap. You've been having a dream.'

'He said that you wouldn't believe me. But I don't care what you think. I know what happened. You've got to trust me or we're all going to be stuck in here,' pleaded Frog.

'We do trust you, Frog,' said Lady Dawnstar. 'But you must understand, we have experience of these things, our duty is to protect you and make sure that we complete this task and that's why Logan and Sir Peacealot and I have to make the decisions.'

'I would have thought that *you* would believe me,' said Frog, disappointed in her.

She knelt, face to face with him. 'There are many things that you do not yet know, things that we can only share with you when we feel the time is right. I'm sorry but that's how it must be. Please understand.'

'You need to understand that I don't want to be here. I want to go home, to my own world, to my family. I didn't ask for this to happen to me,' he said angrily. 'Just because some mad magician thinks that I can save your world, you're treating me like an object, not a person. Well it's not fair!' He turned away and felt hot tears beginning to run down his cheeks. There was an awkward silence as he went to his bedding and started to pack it. But his anger had spurred him into action. Already he had a plan.

Lady Dawnstar went to Logan and Sir Peacealot and there was a brief, hushed discussion. Ginger gave a shrug to Fixer and they both started to pack their gear.

Before any of them had realised, Frog had packed his belongings, shouldered his bag and was standing over the edge of the pit in the floor.

'I don't know about you lot,' he announced, 'but I'm following my mouse.'

With that, he slid himself over the side until he was hanging by his fingertips and then let himself drop the rest of the way. It was only a matter of a metre or so and he landed squarely on the solid floor, the eerie light showing him that in fact there was only one way that he could go. He looked up and five worried faces stared down at him.

'The passage only goes one way, I'll wait for you at the next junction,' he announced, and strode off before anyone could argue.

Logan, Lady Dawnstar and Sir Peacealot exchanged surprised looks and then turned to assemble their bed rolls and packs.

'That's done it,' said Ginger to Fixer as they collected their belongings.

'What do you think we should do?' asked Fixer.

'Well, I don't know about you,' Ginger replied, hoisting his pack and the torches onto his back. 'But right now, I'm following him.' He moved towards the pit but Fixer grabbed his arm.

'Don't you go disappearing as well, that'll only make things worse,' she hissed.

'You know, he's right. They've got to learn to trust him,' said Ginger. 'Now let me go unless you're coming with me.'

'Why don't you just wait until the others are ready?' asked Fixer.

'Because he trusts me – and I trust him. Now are you coming or are you going to wait to be told what to do?' Ginger replied.

Fixer bit her lip. 'Lady Dawnstar is going to be mad at me,' she said. 'Okay, let's do it.'

She quickly grabbed her pack. They both ran to the edge of the hole, swung their legs over and slipped down into the passage. As they touched the bottom they heard Lady Dawnstar's voice.

167

'Hey, you two! Come back here!' And then, 'I'm going to have words with you, my girl.'

The walk seemed long. It was a straight passage, dimly lit at ground level, and a fine mist started to swirl around their legs.

'He can't have gone much further,' complained Ginger.

'Perhaps he's got lost,' said Fixer, concerned.

'No, there haven't been any turn-offs. He said that he'd wait at the next junction and I don't think that he'd let us down,' said Ginger.

As he spoke, the passage started to curve to the right and they could hear voices echoing down the walls from ahead of them.

'That's Lady Dawnstar's voice,' said Fixer.

'And Sir Peacealot's,' added Ginger.

'But it's coming from ahead of us,' she said.

'No, it's a trick of the passage,' said Ginger, breaking into a jog. 'They're definitely behind us, it would have taken them a few minutes to pack up and follow us into the hole. Anyway, there's been nowhere that they could have passed us without us knowing.'

They turned the bend and were astonished to see, at a junction ahead and seated on the ground, Logan, Lady Dawnstar and Sir Peacealot, in conversation with Frog.

'Ah. Here they are at last, what kept you?' asked Frog.

'What kept us?' asked Fixer. 'We left *before* them. How did they get here ahead of us?'

'Never mind that, my girl,' said Lady Dawnstar sternly. 'I want a word with you.'

'Now who's for it?' said Ginger, grinning at Fixer.

'And I want a word with you, Ginger,' said Sir Peacealot.

'Looks like you are,' said Fixer.

Ginger and Fixer didn't exchange what was said to them when they were taken to one side by their respective knights, but suffice to say they would be more cautious with their actions in future. In the group discussion which followed, it was discovered that after dropping into the pit, Lady Dawnstar, Sir Peacealot and Logan had followed the same single route along the passage. They had not encountered any other junctions and had followed the straight passage until it had curved, where they had found Frog patiently waiting. Mysteriously they had not seen or remembered passing Ginger and Fixer although by rights they should have.

'It would appear,' said Logan, 'that the Labyrinth has the ability to cloud our senses. We must keep our wits about us at all times.'

'Another good reason for us all to keep together,' added Sir Peacealot, looking sternly at Ginger and Fixer.

While they had been waiting for Ginger and Fixer to arrive, the others had given Frog the opportunity to voice his concerns and had agreed that he would lead the party from now on as long as they were all content with the direction they were going. Frog had also suggested that, to ensure that they did not lose anyone, they connect themselves together with the coils of rope they had brought. Everyone thought that this was a good idea and so it was, having chosen to take the next right-hand passage, they continued on their way.

At various intervals they would come across a hole

in the floor which dropped down to another passage but each time they decided to ignore the option and press on forwards.

They continued to move cautiously until the passage opened out into a small, circular room. There was another pit in the floor and the wall opposite had a metre-square opening at its centre. There were also similar square openings in the walls on either side and one above them in the ceiling.

As they gathered together to look at the situation, there was a sound of rumbling and Sir Peacealot, who was at the back of the group, shouted over the echoing noise.

'The passage! The passage has sealed behind us!'

They looked past him to see that the corridor that should have led back to where they had come from was now a solid stone wall.

'Looks like decisions are being made for us,' said Logan, and as he spoke another rumbling, grinding sound started. The ground beneath them began vibrating. Slowly at first, the whole passage tilted to the right and they all slid against the wall. Next, it jerked and tilted to the left, throwing them against the other wall. Then with a grating sound the passage started to rotate back to the right.

'Make sure that your ropes are secure and try to hang on to each other!' shouted Logan.

The passage continued to turn and rumble, rolling them around from floor to ceiling to wall and floor. Round and round.

'Now I know what it's like to be in a tumble dryer,' muttered Frog to himself.

Amidst the rumbling and shouting, Logan had managed to get himself turned upside down. Frog lost his grip and slid towards one of the gaps, the slack in the rope taking him right up to its edge. As he scrabbled to grip on to the ledge he could see Logan grasping for the rope, but he was slipping towards Frog. Frog could also see that Fixer was desperately trying to get a foothold to prevent herself from being dragged forwards with Logan. A vision of them all tumbling into the hole, each one dragged in by the previous, flashed through his mind. Things however, were about to get even more complicated. The Labyrinth took another turn but this time it rotated forwards (or what Frog thought was forwards!). He saw Fixer slide sideways and disappear into a hole.

Dust had begun to fill the air and none of them could see clearly, but Frog, who was now hanging by his rope and suspended in a hole, saw Logan's grey shape pass above him. As he questioned how gravity could be pulling him down, but also taking Logan in another direction, the Labyrinth turned again and Frog was pulled across the passage only to find himself hanging in the opposite hole. The rope swung him into a wall, where, with a crack, he hit his elbow and the nerve-tingling sensation of his funny bone shot down his arm. Frog's temper was up and he'd had enough.

'Right, that's it!' he shouted, kicking out at the walls. 'It wasn't funny in the first place and it's not funny now so, pack – it – in!' He emphasised the last three words with three good kicks at the stonework. He reflected after the event that he could have broken his foot, but amazingly it wasn't even bruised, which was even more astonishing as his backside and arm were black and blue for a week afterwards.

Abruptly, the noise and the movement stopped, the silence only broken by the creaking of his rope as he hung there listening to coughs and splutters from the others as the dust settled.

'Is everyone all right?' came Lady Dawnstar's voice.

'I think, I am,' replied Frog.

'Ginger, Fixer. How are you?' she asked.

'I'm okay,' moaned Ginger, his voice slightly muffled.

'Fixer? Fixer, answer me!' shouted Lady Dawnstar.

'I've got her,' said Sir Peacealot, coughing dust from his throat. 'But she's been knocked unconscious. We've been thrown into one of the passages.'

'Tell me about it,' complained Ginger.

'Logan!' shouted Frog. 'Where's Logan?'

They all shouted for Logan, but there was no reply.

'He's got to be close,' said Frog. 'He's attached to the other end of my rope and stopping me from falling. Actually, I'd be a lot happier if someone could give me a hand out of here.'

The dust was clearing and Lady Dawnstar, who had ended up in a corner, was the only one who had not been thrown into one of the passages. One end of the rope attached to her was taut and the other was slack. She pulled on the slack end, which disappeared into what was now a side passage.

'Ow!' came Ginger's voice. 'Steady, it's wrapped around my leg.'

'Unwrap it and find yourself back to me,' said Lady Dawnstar. 'But be careful when you come out as there's a bit of a drop.'

172

She looked to where the other end was going and saw that it was a tangled knot tightly pulled down onto the floor with one end disappearing into a hole. Two other lengths snaked out to separate holes in the other walls.

'Frog, you'll have to hold on while we get the others out from the side passages,' she warned. 'Then we can all help to pull you up.'

'Okay.' came a nervous reply, 'But don't let me drop.'

'Don't worry, I won't,' she promised.

Sir Peacealot clambered out of the opposite passage and reached back in to retrieve the unconscious Fixer. He laid her on the floor and tended to a gash on her forehead. Ginger emerged from his passage looking pale and shaken but with no broken bones or cuts.

'Logan!' Lady Dawnstar shouted once again, but no answer came. 'Ginger, I need you to help me pull up Frog. Grab this rope and take as much of the strain as you can.'

Slowly they eased the rope up until eventually a pair of hands gripped the ledge and Frog's dusty face appeared. They grabbed his arms and he scrabbled up and out of the hole.

'That, I do not want to do again. Where's Logan?'

Lady Dawnstar pointed at the wall opposite.'He should be down that passage where the other rope leads.'

Frog shuffled around to peer into the hole. 'Logan!' he shouted hopefully, but the only answer was silence. 'I can't hear him in my head,' Frog said to Lady Dawnstar. 'I'm trying to reach him with my mind but I can't get any response.'

'Haven't you noticed that since we've been down here, none of us can transfer thoughts?' she replied.

'I haven't been trying until now,' said Frog. He pulled at the rope but it was slack. He pulled it more urgently until the end of the rope slid out of the hole and on to the floor. He turned, white-faced, to the others just as Fixer opened her eyes.

His voice was almost a whisper. 'We've lost him, we've lost Logan.'

12

Pebbles

'What happened?' groaned Fixer.

'Take it easy, young lady,' instructed Sir Peacealot. 'You've had a nasty bump on the head.'

Fixer reached up to feel the large lump that had formed on her forehead. 'Ow! Is that really my head?' she groaned.

'Steady,' warned Sir Peacealot as Fixer tried to get up. 'You look very pale, you need to rest a while.'

'Here, sip this,' said Lady Dawnstar, offering Fixer a drinking bottle as the others gathered around.

'Is everyone else okay?' she continued.

Apart from a couple of grazes and several bruises between them, they had been considerably lucky, although they would have various aches and pains to contend with for a few days. Lady Dawnstar produced a small leather pouch from which she handed out a little yellow leaf to each of them.

'Take these,' she instructed. 'Rub them on any grazes or cuts that you may have, like this,' she leant over and demonstrated on Fixer's bump, apologising that it would hurt a little to start with. Fixer closed her eyes as the leaf was rubbed on her forehead and then gradually her face relaxed and she opened them again.

'Wow! That's amazing. It feels all warm and numb, even the horrible headache has gone,' she said in surprise.

'It will speed up the healing and take the swelling down but you will need to keep still and rest for a while to get the best benefit,' said Lady Dawnstar.

Ginger applied a leaf to his badly grazed elbows.

'That's stopped my elbows from stinging already. What is it, some of Gizmo's magic?'

'It's a plant that only grows in certain parts of the forest. It's not easy to find and you need to know where to look for it,' Lady Dawnstar explained. 'I managed to find time to collect some before we left. I suggest that we take some time to refresh ourselves with food and water while we decide on what to do next, but first let's free ourselves of these ropes for a while.'

They untied their ropes and opened their packs while being very careful to keep clear of the hole in the floor.

'What about Logan?' Frog asked anxiously. 'Aren't we going to look for him?'

Sir Peacealot looked up from tending one of his bruises. 'I hate to think the worst, but it was bad enough for us being spun around and you were lucky that your rope didn't give way, otherwise you might have met the same fate as him. The Labyrinth turned so many times that I've lost all sense of direction. Who knows which passage we entered by and which way up or down used to be?'

'Wait a minute,' said Frog. 'That's it!'

'What's it?' said Ginger.

'I was hanging in a deep hole which means it must have been one of the side passages, because all of the other holes in the floors have been *short* drops.' He looked up. 'See, there's no hole in the ceiling, so that must have been the way that we came in and which was sealed shut behind us. I bet that, that hole, used to be the floor. If it's the same as the other floor passages it will be a shallow drop with just one corridor leading off it.'

'So why did Logan disappear?' asked Ginger.

'Probably because his rope came loose when the Labyrinth turned and he had no choice but to take his chances and slide down the passage he was in,' said Frog hopefully.

'So you're saying that if we want to find Logan, that's the way we need to go?' asked Lady Dawnstar.

'I guess so,' replied Frog as he made his way around to the opposite passage and peered in again.

'I can't see anything but shadow,' he said. 'So let's see if I'm right.' He climbed up and into the hole and disappeared into the unlit passage.

'Frog, get back here, you haven't got a rope on!' shouted Lady Dawnstar.

But there was no answer. Ginger made as if to go after Frog but Sir Peacealot grabbed him.

'Oh, no. We're not losing the two of you. We all wait,' he said anxiously.

They sat in silence. The time seemed endless until finally, with a shuffling sound, Frog appeared in the gap.

'It's just one passage all right,' he announced. 'And

look what I found.' He held out a short dagger. 'It's one of Logan's.'

All sense of time had been lost during their journey into the Labyrinth, but after checking that Fixer was all right, they decided to press on.

The group tied themselves together again, but this time shortened the rope. It was felt that they would rather remain within arm's length of each other than risk finding themselves hanging on the end of a long rope. None of them wanted to go through the experience that Frog had.

One by one they climbed into the passage: first Frog, then Sir Peacealot, Ginger, Fixer and lastly Lady Dawnstar. Once out of the initial shadow, the passage was bathed in the same eerie light, which again seemed to radiate from the stone around them. As they moved forward, they found that the passage floor sloped at a sharp angle downwards.

'How much deeper can we go?' questioned Fixer.

'It's going to be a heck of a climb back up,' said Frog.

'Thanks for pointing that out,' said Ginger.

'Shush!' said Sir Peacealot, suddenly bringing the others to a halt. 'What's that noise?'

It was a low hum, a sort of whirring drone. *Drum – Whoosh – Drum – Whoosh – Drum – Whoosh*, it went.

'What now?' said Ginger.

'Let's go and see,' said Frog. 'We haven't got anything else to do!'

As they slowly progressed downwards the sound became louder until the whole passage thrummed and droned around them.

'It looks like there's a room up ahead!' shouted Frog. 'The passage is widening out.'

The last few feet of the passage declined rapidly and they spilled out into a chamber. Clutching at each other to keep their footing they finally stood in a group surveying what they were confronted with.

The whole of the opposite wall was a turning, spinning wheel like a large millstone. It had four door-sized openings in it, each one, in turn, passing a raised stone step on the floor with a stone door frame set on it. The sound as it revolved clockwise was not as loud now that they were in the room and they only needed to raise their voices slightly to be heard. Set around the room were small piles of pebbles, bleached white and of all shapes and sizes.

They stood there, mesmerised by the revolving wheel, each one trying to think of the next steps to take.

'You took your time,' came a voice.

They turned as one. There, propped up against a wall to the right of them, was Logan, a bloodied cloth wrapped around his head.

Frog could not contain himself and rushed over to him.

'Did you fall? Are you okay? Does it hurt?' he asked in quick succession.

'Yes. Yes and yes,' Logan replied.

Lady Dawnstar was quick to unwrap the makeshift bandage and administer some of her leaves. In the process, Frog noticed that there was a long red gash across Logan's forehead.

'That's gotta hurt,' he declared to Ginger and Fixer, who were also watching with concern.

Logan confirmed that what had happened to him was just as Frog had guessed, except that he had deliberately released himself from the rope as the Labyrinth had turned, for fear of it becoming wrapped around his neck and turning into a noose. What he hadn't bargained for was such a rapid descent. On the last turn of the Labyrinth, the force had catapulted him downwards on his back. When he was ejected into the room, he was travelling at such a pace that he hit the stone door frame and literally bounced back onto the floor. The last thing he remembered was the turning of the wheel and the spinning of his head.

'It could have been worse,' Logan added. 'I might have been thrown straight into one of the wheel's openings. I dread to think what would have happened to me after that.'

As they rested, Frog surveyed the scene. There were, in fact, two wheels, one behind the other with a stone platform between them. The rear wheel was turning anti-clockwise and also had doorways which revolved past the platform. Frog stood on the raised stone step and realised that the wheels weren't really turning all that fast. The eerie light flickered and strobed, creating the illusion that the wheels turned quicker than they really did. He could see that if he timed it right, he could step through one of the passing openings and then onto the central platform without too much trouble, as long as he concentrated on what he was doing. He could then repeat the process to step through the second wheel. However, it wasn't possible to see what he was stepping *into*; for all he knew there could be a sheer drop into oblivion waiting for him.

He turned his attention to the piles of pebbles. They looked as though they had been deliberately placed where they were, but why? They had not seen so much as a loose rock or stone so far, so why the pebbles? He picked one up. It was smooth and shiny and reminded him of the pebbles that he used to gather from the seaside back home. He used to collect the flat ones so that he could skim them out across the water, seeing how many times he could get one to skip over the surface. Then he would look for others that were nicely rounded and were good for target practice on an old piece of driftwood. Sometimes he would lob them into the potholes, high up in the cliffs, then wait and listen for the echoing clatter as they ricocheted off the walls, falling down into an unseen cave. The vision and memory filled his mind until he was aware of someone's voice calling him back from his daydream.

'Frog? Frog!'

He slowly roused himself, reluctant to let the images go.

'Frog? Are you all right?' asked Fixer, standing beside him.

'Yeah, sure, just thinking, that's all,' he replied.

'Thinking of home?' she asked.

'Something like that,' he said.

'If you get to feeling lonely and homesick, you can always talk to me,' she said, putting a kind hand on his shoulder.

'Thanks, Fixer,' he replied.

'What's going on, you two?' asked Ginger, joining them.

Frog looked at Fixer, who had suddenly gone red in

181

the face. She quickly pulled her hand away as he too felt his cheeks going warm.

'Oh, just a bit of puzzle-solving,' he said, looking away.

Fixer picked up a pebble and Ginger followed suit.

'What's with the pebbles then?' he asked.

'That's the puzzle,' replied Frog as he walked up to the raised stone and studied the revolving wheel.

'One, two, three, four. One two, three, four,' he counted as the doorways passed him. He stuck his hand out into the passing gaps, pulling it back each time, just before it could become trapped by the stone block that followed and swished by.

'That's a dangerous game you're playing,' warned Logan from behind him. 'I've been watching that wheel and there's no doubt in my mind that if you got caught between the blocks, it would spin you around and crush you to death.' He picked up a large pebble. 'Watch this.' He threw it at the wheel and it caught between the door frame and the revolving stone as the gap closed. There was a loud *crack!* as the pebble exploded into dust. The wheel didn't even judder, it just continued turning .

'Look, I've been timing it and I think that you can step through, as long as you focus,' said Frog.

'I'm all out of focus,' complained Ginger.

'But what's on the other side?' asked Sir Peacealot.

'I'm not sure at the moment,' replied Frog. 'But I think that the pebbles may help us.'

He picked up four pebbles and walked to the raised area. Counting out loud, he waited until a gap opened and then threw a pebble in. It immediately struck the second stone wheel, bounced back and was crushed into a ball of dust, just like the previous one.

'Don't do that!' complained Ginger.

'Oh, do shut up Ginger, or I'll throw you in,' said Fixer.

'What are you trying to do, Frog?' asked Lady Dawnstar.

'If I can get a pebble through, we'll find out if there's a drop, or solid ground behind the second wheel,' explained Frog as he threw another pebble which, much to Ginger's dismay, met the same fate as the others.

'I need to get onto the central platform,' said Frog. 'Then, all I've got to do is get a pebble through the next wheel to find out.'

'You're crazy!' exclaimed Ginger.

'Are you volunteering to do it, Ginger?' asked Fixer, giving him a dig in the ribs.

'I think we need to talk about this,' said Logan.

'What's there to talk about?' said Frog, picking up some more pebbles. 'We can't go back.'

'You mean that we'll all have to go through that thing?' squawked Ginger.

'Of course not,' said Fixer, putting her arm around Ginger's shoulders.

'Oh, good,' said Ginger, raising a smile.

'We'll just sit in this room and live happily ever after,' she continued.

Ginger's face dropped again.

Frog looked at Logan. 'I'm doing this, one way or another,' he said as he looked at the others. 'Does anyone else want to go first?'

'I think that I should do it,' said Sir Peacealot.

'Okay,' said Frog. 'How long does it take the first wheel to turn, how long does it take the second wheel to turn and when should you throw the pebble?'

'I'll work that out,' said Sir Peacealot.

'I've already worked it out,' said Frog. 'That's why I'm the one who's going to do it.' He looked at Logan and after a few seconds the Ranger nodded in agreement.

'Right,' said Frog, 'Let's get this show on the road.'

He walked back up on to the raised stone and began counting. 'One – two – three – four. One – two – three – four.' On the second *four* he stepped through the gap and was momentarily out of view to the others as the stone section swished by. He stood on the central platform and saw that there was more room than he had first thought. The second wheel turned in front of him, but in the opposite direction. Even though he knew that he was not going to try and step through it on this occasion, it was still unnerving.

Steadying his thoughts, he watched the gaps in the wheel pass him and began to count again. 'One – two – three – four.' He went to throw a pebble but this time the gap was closed. He counted again. 'One – two – three – aha!' This wheel was slightly quicker. A gap appeared after three seconds, and he counted twice more just to make sure. When he was confident that he had the rhythm right, he counted again and on *three*, he dropped a pebble through the gap. It disappeared into the darkness without a sound. Nothing. The pebble had fallen into thin air and for all he knew it was still falling.

'I don't think I'll share that with Ginger,' he breathed to himself.

He counted again and dropped another pebble. This time there was a clatter as it landed on a stone floor and rolled to a stop. Three seconds later the gap was closed again by the turning wheel.

The next pebble disappeared as noiselessly as the first did. He threw a fourth and it also dropped without a sound.

'*So, on every fourth gap a floor appears. Let's take a closer look,*' he said to himself.

The strobing shadows impaired his vision so he waited for the next gap to pass him and crouched down for a better view. He leant forward as close as he dared to the revolving stone in front of him. He watched three gaps pass in succession and then, when the fourth gap appeared he saw a stone bridge slide out from his platform and connect with a passage on the opposite side. Then, as the wheel closed the gap he could just see the bridge slide back to reveal a black abyss.

'*Three seconds, we're going to have to be quick,*' he said to himself.

He stood, turned, counted *four* and stepped back into the chamber where five relieved faces greeted him.

'Well?' asked Ginger. 'What happened?'

'The good news,' said Frog, 'is that we can get out of here.'

'Brilliant!' exclaimed Ginger.

'The bad news is that it's not going to be easy,' he warned.

'I just knew there would be a catch,' said Ginger.

Frog explained what he had worked out in his mind;

the second wheel had four gaps. Three just dropped you into a seemingly bottomless hole, the fourth allowed you to continue down the next passage. A stone bridge connected the exit passage to the central platform, but only when a particular opening in the wheel came around to line up with the platform. So, in effect, they had a one in four chance of getting it right.

'Do you know which one it is?' asked Lady Dawnstar.

'Not yet,' said Frog. 'But I'm working on it.'

'That's not the right answer,' said Ginger.

'*GINGER!*' they all shouted in unison.

Ginger got the message and was quiet for quite a while.

'Fixer, can you light me one of those torches?' asked Frog. 'I've got an idea.'

Fixer pulled a torch from her pack and sparked it alight. Frog picked up a few more pebbles.

'Back in a minute,' he said, and before anyone could say anything he had stepped through the first wheel.

Five minutes later he was back, the torch no longer alight.

'Just as I thought,' he announced, looking pleased with himself. 'As one of the gaps gets to the bottom of the wheel, a small stone bridge slides out so you can walk across. You do have to be quick though.'

'How quick?' asked Logan.

'The count of three,' replied Frog.

Ginger went very pale.

'How do we know which gap to go through?' asked Logan.

'The one following a big black cross on the wheel,'

replied Frog, holding up a soot-blackened hand and grinning with satisfaction.

After checking on Logan's wound, which the application of the leaves had reduced to a red line on his forehead, they packed up their kit and made ready for the dangerous ordeal.

Frog demonstrated what they needed to do, showing them how to count for the first and second wheels. He checked that they all understood what they had to do (especially Ginger). Then they agreed in what order they would go through. It was decided that Frog would go first, and would take a burning torch so that the others would have a steady light to show the way across the small stone bridge. Once he had gone, each one in turn would count to twenty before following the previous person. Ginger would follow Frog, then Sir Peacealot, Fixer, Logan and finally Lady Dawnstar.

'Do *not* look down. Keep your eyes focused on the wheel in front of you and step forward on the right count,' encouraged Frog. 'Right?'

'Right,' they replied.

'Right, Ginger?' asked Frog.

'Right,' said Ginger, swallowing hard.

Once again Frog stepped up to the stone step and counted aloud. 'One – two – three – *four*,' and then he was gone.

He stood on the central platform and waited for the marked stone to appear. 'One – two – *three*.' He stepped out, his foot landed on solid stone and he took two steps forward and into the safety of the new passage. As he turned and looked back the gap in the wheel had gone and so had the stone bridge. A dense black chasm was all that remained between where he stood and the turning wheel. He propped the torch against the wall and watched as the gaps went past, then the stone bridge slid out, quickly and silently into the gap. To his surprise, already standing in the gap was Ginger, blinking in the flame light.

'Now?' he asked. Half stepping forwards.

'No!' shouted Frog hastily. 'Wait for the cross.'

It seemed to Frog that the wheel suddenly turned in slow motion. He counted the gaps as they passed, shouting at Ginger to stay still each time. Then the fourth gap appeared.

'Now! Now! Now!' shouted Frog.

Instead of stepping across, Ginger threw himself out at Frog, his arms flailing, his feet leaving the ground with a leap. Frog had no time to sidestep Ginger who tumbled into his arms, tripping him up so that they both fell in a heap on the floor. Ginger finally came to a rest on top of Frog, their noses touching.

'Thanks, mate,' said Ginger.

'No problem,' breathed Frog. 'Now will you do me a favour?'

'What's that?' asked Ginger.

'Gerroff!' shouted Frog, and pushed Ginger to one side. He stood up, gathering his thoughts and instructing Ginger to stay where he was, 'or else!'

No sooner had he taken up his position again when Sir Peacealot appeared in the passing gap. Frog readied himself to guide him across, but at the next opening and without hesitation, the knight stepped out quickly and with two steps was across the bridge and beside Frog.

'You don't hang about, do you?' said Frog.

'Not where there's bottomless pits involved,' he said, and, seeing Ginger he added, 'Get up and stop mucking about Ginger, you make the place look untidy.'

The next to cross was Fixer, who took a while longer to appear on the platform.

'Take it easy, Fixer!' shouted Frog as the wheel rotated. 'Remember to count when you see the black cross.'

Another gap appeared, Fixer stepped forwards, looked down and stepped back as it closed.

'I can't do it, there's nothing there!' she shouted to Frog through the next opening.

'I told you *not* to look down,' he replied. 'You've got your timing wrong, but don't worry, it'll be all right, I'll tell you when to move.' He watched the wheel turn and as the bridge slid out he shouted, 'Now! Move it, Fixer. *NOW!!*'

Fixer hesitated a moment too long and then stepped on to the stone bridge as it began to slide back into the rock. The wheel turned behind her, caught her backpack and knocked her off balance. The momentum brought her out into the dark chasm and for a moment she seemed to hover in mid-air. Then she fell forwards, scrabbling for the ledge and Frog.

'NOoooooooo!' screamed Frog as he reached to grab her outstretched hands. He gripped her wrists, but her weight pulled him forwards onto his stomach and he felt himself sliding over the edge. The pain ripped into his arms as Fixer swung below him. The edge of the rock bit into his chest and squeezed the breath out of him. His head began to swim, he squeezed his eyes

189

shut and gritted his teeth as the pain brought a black shroud over his senses.

'Hang on,' he gasped. 'You're not going anywhere without me.'

The last thing that he heard himself saying was, 'I'll never let you go, I'll never let you go.'

And then he passed out.

13

Fire and Ice

Sir Dragonslayer looked down from the plateau where he stood and surveyed the scene. The plain below glistened and twinkled with ice and frost, the full moon reflecting its pale light on the desolate landscape. He had brought his army many miles north with little resistance. A few foolhardy packs of Rock Bears had attacked them on a couple of occasions, suddenly appearing out of caves in ambush but the Rangers had scouted the path ahead well and each time had reported back the lie of the land. Every time any attack came, they were alert and well prepared, with the Maids of Steel dismounting quickly and engaging the rock bears face to face.

Normally, the sight of a two- or three-metre tall, snarling bear with unnaturally large fangs and razor sharp claws bounding towards you would be enough to make anyone run for safety. But not the Maids of Steel.

Standing resplendent in their mirror-polished armour, they drew their swords and stood their ground, meeting the bears head on, cutting them down with one or two passes of their swords until the

191

attacking creatures lay dead, red blood seeping through the matted fur of their bodies.

Each time the Maids had remounted their steeds, Sir Dragonslayer noticed that none of them was even breathing hard, such was their strength and skill.

Eventually they had reached the great dirt plain that pushed its way through the northern hills and signalled the gateway to the heart of the kingdom of Castellion. They had set up camp earlier that evening, the great beacon fires built and lit along the whole length of their front line, bringing light and warmth and to warn of any attack by the Hidden People. The night was when they were at their most dangerous, the moonlight making them hard to see, almost transparent. Flames and firelight helped to give them some reflective form, but it was still a sharp pair of eyes that could spot them before they were within touching distance. The touch that, when connected to any living thing, froze it inside out. Fauna and flora withered and blackened. Humans and animals crystallised within seconds and became one of them, an ice-encased zombie with no memory or feeling, its only purpose to freeze and crush everything in its path. Such was the curse placed on them by Lord Maelstrom.

Sir Dragonslayer put his fingers up to his mouth and gave a high-pitched whistle which pierced the quiet sky. A few seconds later and high above, silhouetted by the moon, the majestic shapes of two mighty dragons hovered, their wings beating effortlessly. Suddenly they moved apart and streaked down to either side of the valley, curving inwards as they reached no more than a few metres above the ground, their riders now visible, pulling back on the great leather reins. At once, streams of flame jetted from the dragons' nostrils, flaring at the ground before them as they swept across it. As the yellow fire licked out, the frozen ground steamed and the ice melted, shrinking back a short distance and in the same light, distorted, frozen figures could momentarily be seen, their mouths open in silent screams as they dissolved into oblivion. In that same light, Sir Dragonslayer also caught sight of the endless frozen army of Hidden People stretching out for what seemed over a mile into the distance. He breathed in and a chill passed through his body.

He gave another whistle to signal for the riders to return to camp, satisfied that he had seen all he needed. The enormity of their task impressed upon him as he pushed the consequences of failure to the back of his mind. Tonight would be long, cold and not without incident. He turned and hurriedly made his way back to brief the commanders.

When the attack came, they were in their positions, but if it hadn't been for the Rangers and their sharp eyes, they could still have been taken by surprise. The rows of Hidden People were reflected suddenly in the light of the fires, only a metre or so from the front line of the Maids. With lightning reaction the Maids of Steel struck out with their swords, not cold steel, but this time red hot and glowing metal blades. They had been resting their swords in the burning braziers which had been placed between them along the line. The hot metal sliced through the frozen figures on contact, shattering them on to the ground, the pieces melting and steaming as they fell. Behind the Maids, the Rangers fired up their swords, ready to change over with the Maids when their swords grew cold. Acting in relay, they allowed each other the opportunity to reheat their weapons and then stepped forward to fight off the oncoming figures, chopping and cutting, chopping and cutting.

Behind them, another row of fires had been prepared and it was from these that the lines of bowmen lit their arrows and fired them into the sky, where they rained down and found the advancing ranks of the Hidden People, ice turning to fire, then turning to steam and turning back to ice under the advancing feet of the next frozen figure.

They battled on for hour after hour and still the Hidden People came.

Occasionally a Maid, or Ranger, was unfortunate to have their bare skin come into contact with one of the Hidden People. Their faces would instantly turn white as the frost coursed through them, turning them into one of the dangerous enemy. This was when their brothers and sisters in arms had to be at their most courageous and cut them down without a second thought, lest they be the next victims.

Sir Dragonslayer knew that his army could not keep up the resistance forever and they would eventually tire. He also knew that as soon as their defence was breached, the frozen figures would touch as many of his people as possible, as quickly as they could, turning Ranger, Maid and bowman alike into one of their frozen army to add to their numbers and strengthen the assault. He realised that it was time for the dragons and dragon masters to enter the battle.

He walked quickly to where he had left his mount. The dragon was crouched in a clearing, waiting patiently and as Sir Dragonslayer approached, it lifted its head and gave a welcoming grunt, a slight wisp of smoke escaping its nostrils. No audible words or commands were exchanged as he climbed up and positioned himself between the dragon's wings and its scaled neck. Seating himself in the hollow of the creature's shoulder blades, he gripped the thick leather reins and the dragon extended its wings. With effortless strokes, they rose into the air, Sir Dragonslayer using the fingers of one hand to whistle out a piercing signal into the night sky.

The telepathic bond each dragon rider had with their dragon was hard-earned through trust and dedication from the moment that the dragon chose to let its rider climb onto their great shoulders for the first time. Unless you were a dragon rider, you did not know the ritual. It was known as *melding* and was carried out in a secret location, high in the mountains. It was also reported to be very painful for a human; some had actually been struck blind during the rite although this was a penalty paid by those who were trying to use the power for evil rather than good. Once the process was completed, which could take two or three days and nights, dragon and rider were inseparable. Their thoughts were joined, as were their feelings, each one experiencing the other's emotions and senses. A dragon would die for its rider and a rider would without question die for their dragon.

As they rose higher and higher, the other dragons and their riders swept up out of the surrounding landscape to join in formation above the battle spread out below them. In the distance, the ice figures were pouring out of the frozen forests and wasted land, their numbers pushing forwards from a hundred or so deep. At the front line, he could see the well organised army of Castellion, the Maids of Steel and the Rangers, all working in relays to step forwards with red, glowing swords, cutting and scything into the advancing deathly shapes, keeping them at arm's length whilst the bowmen of Dinham loosed their flaming arrows, which when they fell to earth created momentary gaps in the relentless, glacier-like mass.

Sir Dragonslayer's plan was to give his people some respite and create a break in the onslaught by attacking the source of the frozen army. Again, his piercing signals rang through the air and the dragons fanned out along the length of the valley in two rows. The first row dipped their heads, tucked in their great membrane wings and plummeted down at the enemy. When impact seemed imminent, they opened their wings, almost stalling in the air, and released great streams of liquid flame at the clamouring figures below them. There they hovered and beat their wings together to fan the flames into an intense crystal-blue. Anything within a hundred metres instantly melted, the ice turning to boiling water and then clouds of steam exposing the black earth beneath, which then burst into flames. The gnarled stumps of the forest ignited and a firestorm of searing flames rose up. The first row of dragons swept away, exhausted, their flames depleted, and their places were filled with a second row of majestic sky lords who breathed down another furnace. But this time they were moving forwards, using their wings to force the firestorm back over the land until they reached the foot of the ice-covered mountain range. All land behind them was now a blackened, hot desert, any moisture scorched away, all evidence of any frozen army destroyed. Their task completed, they turned and flew away. As they returned to the battle front, they joined in with what flame they had left and melted as much of the remaining attack as they could. Finally the Maids, Rangers and bowmen were left to destroy the enduring ranks that were left, still trying to press forward in a futile attempt to break through the line.

Sir Dragonslayer circled back and out to the north, looking for any signs of an advancing army. The dark earth still smoked and flared, charred and lifeless right up to the stony outcrops at the base of the mountains which still glistened with frost in the moonlight.

'It's not over,' he thought to himself. 'They will come again when the land has cooled.' He knew that this had only bought them a couple of days at the most. But at least they could rest and strengthen their defences. It was written in his scroll to hold the line and wait for the coming of the Blackwater. If this arrived then all would be well; if not, the orders were to turn back with whatever people he could muster and rally to the defence of Castellion Stronghold.

Two things bothered him: he had no idea *when* the Blackwater would come or how it would help, and he had never turned and run from any battle or fight before in his life.

For the rest of the night there was an uneasy peace.

Sentries were posted and they slept along the line of battle, ready for any unexpected attack. The next morning, in the comfort of blue skies and warm sunshine, Sir Dragonslayer called a meeting of the commanders and explained their situation.

They knew that the next attack would be relentless, there was no telling what numbers the Hidden People's army had grown to but, as they had covered the northern territories for several months and Lord Maelstrom had been preparing for this moment for many years, there would no doubt be thousands, if not tens of thousands, pouring out of the Frozen Wastes at the next opportunity. His dragons could not repeat the same effective actions again. They needed time to recover and replenish the chemical that was produced in their throats which enabled them to breathe flames. Never before had they been called upon to deliver their fire with such ferocity and with such prolonged effect. They needed weeks, rather than days, to regain their normal ability. The dragons had played their part, and their flames now spent they could only wait and be used as a last fighting reserve.

It was decided to strengthen the fortifications by making it as hard as possible for the Hidden People to approach them, and so trenches were dug along the line of defence. There was not a man or woman who did not spend time shovelling the hard earth to create two rows of deep pits that ran about twenty metres apart, parallel to their main battle line. They realised that the tactic wouldn't kill the enemy, but it would slow down their progress. They made full use of the natural resources in the land around their encampments, and trees were harvested to make thousands more arrows, the heads of which were bound with moss and soaked in the flammable sap from fir trees. Cloth from sacking and bedding was fashioned into thick gloves and balaclavas to cover as much human flesh as possible, to make it hard for the Hidden People to touch anyone's bare skin.

For two days and nights they toiled, taking it in shifts so that everyone slept and replenished their strength. As the sun went down on the third day a feeling of unease grew through the camp. Sir Dragonslayer and his commanders looked skyward. No moon appeared in the sky: the night would be black.

Before the last of the sun's rays had melted over the horizon, the fires and braziers had been lit and were well stocked. All were in position, the Maids, Rangers and bowmen, all stood proud and ready, their faces masked and their hands covered by either armour or cloth. Behind them all, the dragons and their riders waited uneasily as a last line of defence to either rescue what souls they could or cause as much damage as possible in the event of being overrun.

With a blink, the sunlight was gone and a thick, dark blanket of fog crept out and spread over the land, so that even with the burning fires it was impossible for anyone to see more than a metre in front of their eyes. The silence was complete except for the crackling and fizzing of the fires, swords already glowing red in the flames.

Sir Dragonslayer gave an order for the bowmen to fire a volley of flaming arrows as far as they could and with a *whoosh*, a hundred or so streaming lights flew

out and over the landscape to fall and embed themselves into the ground, half a mile from the waiting
army. All eyes watched as the arrows burnt in the
distance and were then extinguished as a black carpet
rolled over them.

Under cover of darkness, the assault of the Hidden
People had returned.

Sir Dragonslayer shouted his first command of the
battle.

'Rangers! We depend on the sharpness of your eyes,
look well for us.'

When the time came, the trenches not only slowed
down the advance, but they also served as an early
warning system as the Hidden People noisily clambered
into and out of them. By the time they had reached the
battle line, the Rangers had no trouble in picking up
their movements and drew their swords from the fires
in readiness, as did the Maids of Steel.

Sir Dragonslayer looked along the ranks of
unwavering, brave and loyal allies. He drew his sword
from the fire, sparks flashing from the orange-white
blade. His voice was clear and heard by all.

'For Castellion. Let the Light free us from evil.'

A resounding cheer let loose into the night air as the
last battle for the northern territory began.

14

The Earth Sage

Frog was aware of a rubbing and squeezing of his chest and then of the same sensation on his arms. He opened his eyes to see Lady Dawnstar leaning over him, her hands gently massaging his bare chest with yellow leaves, while on either side, Sir Peacealot and Logan were applying the same treatment to his arms. He felt something in his mouth and spat it out, then a sore aching feeling coursed through his limbs and across his body.

He gasped and caught his breath.

'Just breathe slowly,' Lady Dawnstar said softly. 'The pain will subside, just breathe slowly,' she repeated.

Frog lay there, clenching his teeth and balling his fists against the pain. It seemed that it would never end, until finally a warmth spread across his skin and numbed the hurt. His head began to clear and his memory started to return.

'Fixer?' he gasped, trying to sit up but gently restrained by Lady Dawnstar. 'Where's Fixer?'

'All in good time, my friend,' said Sir Peacealot. 'Let's tend to your needs first.'

'No!' replied Frog as he struggled again. 'Where's Fixer?'

Logan, Sir Peacealot and Lady Dawnstar exchanged worried looks.

'Your injuries aren't dangerous, but if you are to recover properly we need to care for them. Tell us that you'll calm down first,' said Logan.

'Okay, okay. But tell me about Fixer,' insisted Frog.

Lady Dawnstar leant back, revealing Fixer standing at Frog's feet, her tear-stained face staring back at him. Ginger stood at her side holding her hand, his face as white as a sheet.

'I'm sorry, Frog,' Fixer cried. 'I'm really sorry.'

Frog smiled and rested back. 'No problem, Fixer. I told you that you weren't going anywhere without me.' The effects of the leaves coursed through him and he drifted off into a deep sleep.

When he awoke, he was laid out, wrapped in his blanket, his head resting on a soft pillow which, when he opened his eyes, turned out to be Fixer's leg.

'Hi sleepy, how are you doing?' she asked, looking down at him.

Frog gathered his thoughts and looked around him. They were all in what appeared to be another large chamber. There was a small fire burning and the smell of something cooking. He slowly raised himself up on to one elbow, a slight stiffness pulling across his chest.

'Where are we?' he asked.

'A new chamber, we decided to rest and have some food,' replied Fixer.

'What? How did I get here?' asked Frog.

'They took it in turns to carry you.' Fixer indicated to the others. 'Even Ginger had a go. He also insisted on carrying your pack and all of your belongings.'

'How long have I been asleep?'

'I'm not sure, time doesn't have any meaning any more but the passage leading from the stone wheels was straight and long, and by the time we got here we all needed to sleep. We've only just woken up ourselves.'

'What happened, Fixer? How did I, we, not fall into the opening?'

'It was Sir Peacealot, his quick thinking saved us both. As soon as he heard you shout, he knew there was trouble. He all but threw himself halfway over the edge to grab my arm with one hand and you with the other. I think all three of us would have gone if Logan hadn't appeared through the wheel and leapt across the gap. The first I knew was his long whip was coiled around my waist, then he was pulling me up while Sir Peacealot managed to scrabble back with you.

'We could see that you had trouble breathing, you'd gone deathly pale. Then Lady Dawnstar came through the wheel and as soon as she joined us she asked what had happened. It was your chest, the weight of me and my backpack had crushed it against the stone ledge.' She paused and a tear ran down her cheek. 'I'm so sorry, Frog, if I had listened to you it wouldn't have happened. I thought that I'd killed you.'

'Hey,' said Frog. 'Everything's okay now, so stop worrying. Tell me what happened next.'

Fixer wiped away the tear with her sleeve, smiled and continued.

'Lady Dawnstar pulled up your clothes and we all saw the red and black marks across your chest, it was awful. Logan made Ginger and I move away and told us not to look. But I had to, I watched Lady Dawnstar put one of those leaves under your tongue and then she kissed you – on the lips!'

Frog opened his mouth to speak, but no words came out, except he went bright red and his cheeks burnt.

'Anyhow,' continued Fixer. 'She explained afterwards that it was to breathe the healing into your body because it was damaged on the inside, but she had to be careful not to let you swallow the leaf as they can be poisonous. Next, they all started to rub more leaves on you. It was ages until you opened your eyes.'

'I guess we were really lucky,' said Frog.

'I was lucky that you were there,' said Fixer. 'But Logan says you could have saved yourself a lot of pain.'

'What do you mean?' said Frog.

Fixer reached behind her. 'You forgot to wear this.' She dropped the dragon-skin waistcoat onto his lap. 'He was really worried about you and he's told me to tell you that you must wear it at all times from now on, or he'll personally feed you to a Madbagger.'

'Point taken,' said Frog. 'In fact, will you help me on with it now?'

'Yes, but one more thing. Lady Dawnstar says that you're to have these, you might need to use a few more if your chest still hurts.' She gave him some of the leaves which he put into the cloth pouch that he had tied to his belt.

Fixer helped Frog on with the garment. He found that apart from some small stiffness in his chest, and a

204

little unsteadiness when he first stood up, he was generally okay. When he was ready they both went and sat with the others. Each, in turn, asked Frog how he felt. He assured them for the umpteenth time that he was all right, but it would be very nice thank you if someone wanted to volunteer to carry him for the rest of the journey. That was when they all laughed and agreed that he was getting back to his old self.

The meal was some dried rabbit, stewed up with vegetables, which prompted them to discuss how much food and water they had left. Each of them had half a canteen of water, maybe two or three days' worth. The food consisted of more dried rabbit, corn cakes and some root vegetables that, if chewed slowly, would fight off the pains of hunger for a couple of days.

'So,' said Logan. 'We've got to get out of this place in three days or find more water and food.'

'I don't know about you, but I can't tell which is day or night any more,' said Ginger.

'That's our biggest problem, so we need to find the Earth Sage and a way out as soon as we can,' said Logan.

'It looks as if we've been saved from making decisions this time,' said Frog, pointing to the only exit. 'Has anyone had a look to see where it goes?'

'I had a wander down earlier,' said Sir Peacealot. 'It turns left then right and then gives you three options again. Just one small problem, this weird light stops and all of the passages are in darkness from there on.'

'How many torches do we have and how much fuel's left?' asked Logan.

'Six torches,' said Ginger. 'I checked them when we made camp here.'

Fixer looked in Frog's pack and pulled out the two fuel flasks.

'One's full and I think the other is about half empty,' she said, shaking the flasks.

'We'll light three torches as we did before and see how long they last,' said Logan. 'When they burn down, we'll use the other three.'

'What happens when they burn out?' asked Ginger.

'We start singing happy birthday,' answered Frog, but no one laughed.

When they were ready, they roped themselves together again. Frog insisted that he felt much better and convinced them to let him lead the way. Sir Peacealot insisted that he follow him with Ginger and Fixer between him and Logan, and lastly Lady Dawnstar. However, they all noticed that Frog didn't hurry along with the same urgency as before.

'Are you sure he'll be all right?' Logan asked Lady Dawnstar.

'He's a tough lad,' she answered. 'His spirit is strong and his body will heal quickly.'

'I'm surprised that he survived back there, I've seen grown men die of such an injury,' said Logan.

'I think he may well surprise us even further,' said Lady Dawnstar.

'Let us hope so my lady, let us hope so,' said Logan.

They reached the first intersection and decided to carry straight on. Just as they were about to move, Fixer reminded them that they needed to mark the wall with a sign to show that they had passed that way.

Sir Peacealot doused his torch and let it cool a little before he blackened his hand with soot and marked an arrow on the wall.

'Here,' he said to Fixer, unwrapping a piece of the cloth bound around the torch's handle and rubbing it in the sooty head of the torch. 'Take this for now in case we need to make any more marks.'

The passage continued for a short walk, then Frog brought them to a halt.

'What's the problem?' asked Lady Dawnstar from the back.

'It's a dead end,' said Frog. 'We'll have to go back.'

Lady Dawnstar turned and led them back to the intersection where they next decided to take the right-hand passage. Again, Frog led the way until they reached a left-hand turn which led them to another left-hand turn and they emerged at another junction.

'Which way now?' asked Logan.

'We've run out of choices,' said Fixer.

'What do you mean?' asked Ginger.

'Look,' she pointed. 'We're back where we started.'

On the wall in front of them was indeed the sign that Sir Peacealot had made only a short while earlier.

'What now?' said Fixer.

'I know it sounds daft,' said Frog. 'But the only passage that we haven't entered is the one that we just came out of.'

They all looked at him in the flickering light of the torches.

'Well?' he said. 'Has anyone got any better ideas?'

'What if we end up back here?' asked Lady Dawnstar.

'We phone a friend!' said Frog, and although no one

understood what he meant, he chuckled to himself and enjoyed his joke. They continued to stare at him, waiting for an explanation.

'Look, if we end up back here, we'll just have to think of something else. But until that happens, let's go,' he said.

They followed him silently until they came to a junction, where they had a choice to take a passage leading off to the right or to carry straight on.

'How did we miss this turn?' asked Ginger.

'We missed it because it wasn't there the first time,' said Fixer. 'Frog was right, the passages change when you approach them a different way.'

'We're never going to get out of here,' complained Ginger.

'Oh, yes we are,' said Sir Peacealot. 'Even if it's just to stop you from moaning.'

They continued down the passage until they reached another intersection with three choices. One right, one left and the other straight ahead.

'If we go down any of these, there's no guarantee that we won't end up back here,' said Lady Dawnstar. 'We could be going around in circles at every junction until we choose the correct passage and find the right way. We'll run out of torchlight at this rate.'

'I think that I've got the answer,' announced Frog. 'I've just remembered what I read in a book about mazes.'

'Well, what is it?' asked Logan.

'You have to keep your hand on the left wall, if you do that, even though it may be the long way, you'll eventually find the centre of the maze.'

'If I could just say something,' said Ginger, nervously.

'Go on,' said Sir Peacealot. 'But don't complain.'

'Well,' continued Ginger. 'First, this isn't a maze, it's the Labyrinth. Second, how do we know we need to get to the middle? I mean, I thought that we were trying to get out. And third, what if the whole thing starts spinning and turning like it did before?'

'Good points,' said Frog. 'But if you ask me, a maze and a labyrinth are the same and how do we know that the middle isn't the way out? If we have a repeat of being rolled around, remembering which is left and right will be the least of our problems.'

'Just checking,' said Ginger.

'I say we use our hands,' said Logan decisively, and they all agreed to follow Frog's idea.

The group turned left and walked purposefully on, all touching the left-hand wall as they went. This continued for some time as they negotiated various junctions and cul-de-sacs, marking the walls with a sooty smudge as they went. Eventually, the flickering torches warned that they needed replacing and the last three were soaked in the liquid and lit just as the others guttered out.

'How long do you think they'll last?' asked Frog.

'I'm not sure,' said Logan. 'We might get some extra time if we wrap some strips of cloth around them and soak them in the last of the liquid.'

'Time to get a move on then,' said Frog, and off he went. The rest had no choice but to follow him as they were all still linked together.

The passages continued to eat up their footsteps and

the torches burned down once again. Logan tore up some strips of cloth that some of their food had been wrapped in and the others did the same. They soaked the cloth in what was left of the liquid, quickly twisting the material around each torch head and relighting them.

'If we ever needed to find light again, now is the time,' said Lady Dawnstar as they set off down another left-hand passage.

More turns, more dead ends and with no end in sight. Frog stopped.

'Have you noticed,' he asked, 'that the floor has been steadily sloping down for quite a while now?'

'You're right, I thought it was just me and my tired legs,' agreed Logan.

'Is that a good or a bad sign?' said Ginger.

Before anyone could reply, the torches gave one last flare and then went out. They were in absolute and total blackness.

Frog brought his hand up to his face. He touched his nose with his index finger and could see nothing.

'That's done it,' he said, his voice sounding flat and lost in the dark.

'Everyone check your ropes, we don't want to lose anyone now,' said Lady Dawnstar.

After they had all made quite sure that they were safely attached to each other, Frog continued to lead the way. He shuffled his feet forwards slowly, just in case the floor should give way or disappear in the dark. They moved with their right hands on each other's shoulders and their left hands continued to touch the wall. Their progress was now painfully slow and they had no idea how far they had travelled, when Frog called out for them to stop.

'We've reached an opening,' he said. 'I'm going to take us around to the left, if you keep your hands on the wall you'll feel the corner when you get to it.'

He moved around the corner slowly, his hand feeling the texture of the stone change – a new, smooth surface slipped under his fingers.

'I'm not sure, but I think there's a curve in the wall,' he observed.

As he moved on, the sounds of the others' movements started to echo, as did Fixer's voice.

'It feels different, where do you think we are?' she asked.

'I think that we're in a room of some sort,' said Logan, his words sounding hollow.

'There's definitely a curve in the wall, I think that we're going around in a circle,' said Frog. 'We'll find out when we reach the doorway again.'

The moments passed as they stepped slowly on, trying not to trip over each other's feet, but the doorway never came. Frog stopped again.

'That's funny. We should have reached the entrance by now. I hate to say this, but I think that we've been sealed in,' he said.

'If we've been sealed in, are we all still together?' asked Lady Dawnstar. She urgently called out their names and to her relief they all answered one by one.

'Just a minute,' Frog said to her. 'You're in front of me.'

'So I am,' replied Lady Dawnstar. 'If I put my hand

out, can you reach it?' Frog extended his arm in the dark, his hand brushing past and then finally clasping Lady Dawnstar's.

'You're right,' she said. 'We must be standing in a circle. If only we just had a glimpse of our surroundings, then we might be able to know what to do next.'

For a few moments there was silence as they all searched their thoughts for an answer. Then, out of the darkness came Fixer's voice.

'I've got an idea. We've still got one of the flasks, even if it's just got a small drop of the liquid in it, I'm sure that if I can get a spark to it, we might have some light for a few seconds.'

'Well done, Fixer, it's worth a try,' said Logan. 'Right, who's got the flask?'

'I think I have,' said Ginger.

As Fixer was standing next to Ginger she managed to feel her way into his pack and retrieve the flask . She carefully placed it on the floor at her feet, found her flint and released the stopper.

'Everyone needs to be ready to take in as much as they can, I'm not sure how much light we'll have or for how long,' she warned.

She struck the flint. A small spark flashed out and was swallowed by the darkness. It was, however, just enough for her to see that she needed to hold the flint closer to the neck of the flask. She could smell the foul reek of the liquid as she crouched closer to her target. Another spark sailed out and was extinguished. She held her breath and struck the flint again. Two diamond-white embers struck the neck of the flask and fell in. For a moment there was nothing. Then, slowly, a glow emanated up from the neck and formed a delicate orange flame which flickered and teased around the rim.

Shadows danced on the walls which, as Frog had guessed, were curved. In the unsteady light their eyes made out the shape of the room. It was circular, with a domed ceiling. In the centre of the floor, no more than half a metre from where they all stood in a circle, was a large round hole, big enough to swallow every one of them. The stone floor around its rim was carved with lettering.

'Quickly!' shouted Logan. 'The lettering, try to make out what it says.'

They craned their necks and strained their eyes as the tiny flame shifted shadows across the letters, distorting their shape and form. They could tell at once that the light was dying; the dim glow began melting back into the flask until it was gone.

'Keep thinking about the letters, try to make sense of what they mean,' said Logan.

'I thought that I saw the words, *Step forward as one*,' said Fixer.

'Part of it said, *Be bound only by the hand of Trust*,' said Logan.

'I saw the bit about, *All others fall into Darkness*,' said Ginger.

'Thanks Ginger,' said Sir Peacealot, sarcastically.

'Did anyone see something like, *Trust the sword of Faith*?' asked Frog.

'I saw, *Trust the* word *of Faith*, but then everything got blurred,' added Sir Peacealot.

'I definitely read, *Step forward as one, all others fall*

into Darkness,' said Lady Dawnstar. 'We need to put this together.'

'Did you see the size of that hole?' said Fixer.

'All the more reason to keep our backs against the wall,' warned Logan. 'Right, let's try and work this out.'

After numerous variations, they couldn't decide where the writing started. It was then that Ginger came up with a daring suggestion.

'If we all kneel down and lean forwards we can carefully feel for the letters that are in front of us, then we could call them out and put the words together in the right order.'

'Ginger, you never cease to surprise me,' said Sir Peacealot. 'What an excellent idea.'

In the complete darkness they all cautiously sat down, placed their hands on the floor and slid them forwards until they felt the carving beneath their fingers, each tracing the pattern and calling it out. Logan found the words *'into darkness'* and then a strange pattern which he felt signalled the end of the writing, and Ginger, next to him, managed to spell out, *'Be bound only'*, which was decided to be the beginning of the verse. After a few minutes and starting with Ginger, they in turn read out the lettering under their hands.

Be bound only by the hand of Trust
and the Word of Faith
Step forward as one
All others fall into Darkness

'Another puzzle!' said Ginger, trying not to sound despondent.

'One thing's for sure, we can't go back and the only way out is through this opening. Whether we like it or not, it's telling us that we have to step into it,' voiced Frog.

'It's *how* we do it,' said Fixer. 'It's telling us *how* to do it.'

'Go on. Explain,' said Lady Dawnstar.

They could hear Fixer breathe in nervously before she translated her thoughts.

'*Be bound only by the hand of trust.* I think that means that we untie ourselves and hold hands, that we trust in each other. *The word of faith.* We have to say the word "faith". Then we have to *Step forward as one.* Well, that's obvious. *All others fall into Darkness.* I think that means if someone breaks their hold or loses faith ...' Her voice trailed away.

'We have to commit to this together,' said Sir Peacealot. 'But what happens once we step out? Could be the end for us should anyone waver or panic.'

'Only one way to find out,' said Frog, standing up.

Lady Dawnstar felt his movement. 'What are you doing?' she said.

'I'm untying my rope and getting ready to trust Fixer and step out. If we don't do this together, then everything else has been a waste of time. We will fail.'

In that moment, they all knew that he was right.

When they had checked that they were all free of the ropes, they held hands and felt for the edge of the hole with their feet. Standing there, some of them had tears in their eyes, some were trembling, but all of them felt their hearts in their mouths.

215

They listened to Frog, his voice growing from a whisper.

'Faith. Faith. Faith. Faith.'

They joined him, the chant growing stronger. 'Faith. Faith. Faith. Faith,' more determined until as one they stepped out into the void as a wind rushed upwards, billowing their hair and clothes around them.

Frog closed his eyes, squeezing them until a couple of tears escaped. Blood pumped through his temples, he waited for the falling sensation, his stomach ready to turn somersaults.

But the fall never came. Instead, a light started to penetrate his eyelids and he cautiously opened them. He looked around the circle to see the others, their eyes wide open in awe. They were all holding hands, the rushing air suspending them in the air above a beam of light, flaring up and out of the hole. Below them, from out of the light, a stone circle was rising, a platform that eventually met their feet and took their weight until they were standing on it. The platform continued to rise, lifting them towards the domed ceiling which gradually peeled open, allowing them to pass through it and into another chamber. A floor sealed around the circular stone base and the light went out. The billowing wind dropped away to stillness. They stood there in silence, each catching their thoughts, trying to make sense of what had just happened.

Above them, the night sky was clear and bright. Stars and constellations twinkled and glinted against a deep-blue backdrop of infinity. A comet streaked overhead, majestic in its silence.

'Look,' said Frog, letting go of the others' hands

and pointing to the heavens. 'Right there, it's Orion's Belt!'

All eyes followed the direction of his finger. The row of three blue-white stars seemed to magnify themselves in the sky.

'Orion – the Hunter. He exists in many worlds, many dimensions,' came a voice from the shadows.

Instinct took over. Lady Dawnstar and Sir Peacealot drew their swords. Logan uncoiled his whip and weighed a throwing knife in his hand as they formed a barrier in front of Frog, Fixer and Ginger.

'Your bravery is admirable,' said the voice, its form still hidden. 'But your weapons have no use in this place.'

Their eyes widened in disbelief as their weapons turned into harmless leaf-covered branches which they dropped to the ground.

'Then we will fight with flesh and bone,' said Sir Peacealot, stepping forward in defiance.

'I see your sleep in the earth has not dulled your wits, Sir Peacealot,' said the voice.

'How do you know my name? Who are you? Show yourself or so help me, I'll come and get you,' he replied.

'There's a thin line between bravery and foolishness, Sir Knight. If you approach me before invited, you wouldn't like what you see.'

'Just a minute,' said Frog, as he pushed his way through and stood beside Sir Peacealot. 'I know that voice.' He walked forward to the shadow, crouched down and put his hand out.

The mouse scuttled onto Frog's palm and looked up at him. 'Greetings young Frog, we meet again.'

217

Frog turned to the others and presented his out-stretched hand. The white mouse sat comfortably on its haunches, staring back at them.

'I would like to present,' said Frog, smiling at the others, 'the Earth Sage.'

'But he really is a mouse!' blurted out Ginger.

'My true image, or any other that you might imagine, is hidden from you for this moment. In my domain, all is not what it seems.'

'Now, where have I heard that before?' said Frog, knowingly.

'Put away your armaments, they will be needed soon enough, but not here,' said the mouse.

They looked at where the branches had fallen and there lay their weapons, restored. Logan retrieved his whip, inspected it suspiciously and coiled it over his shoulder. Sir Peacealot and Lady Dawnstar tested the weight of their swords before sheathing them.

'I will adopt a form more reasonable to you all,' said the mouse. 'Put me down please, Frog.'

No sooner had Frog placed the mouse on to the ground than the little form began to shimmer, its shape billowing like a ball of fine, white cotton wool, growing in size until it reached human form. Details began to appear and as they watched a sky-blue robe enveloped the figure of a slender woman, her face dark, her black hair cascading over her shoulders. She reminded Frog of a mysterious, beautiful Egyptian queen.

Her voice came as a surprise to them all. In contrast with the mouse's high-pitched tones hers was soft and clear.

'Now you may take counsel with me and rest a while,' she said, waving her arm. Suddenly they were bathed in clear, bright moonlight, revealing a woodland clearing, a small brook gently flowing to their left. She indicated to a burning log fire with two rabbits cooking over it on a spit.

'Come, rest yourselves. Eat, drink and prepare for the journey ahead,' she said.

'This magic will only fill our heads, not our stomachs,' said Logan.

'This is no magic, my Ranger friend. Everything is real. You are back on the surface of Castellion. These are my woods, my domain, and I share their goodness with you willingly.'

The Earth Sage seated herself on a fallen tree trunk, her gaze, when it fell upon each of them, chased away their fears and suspicions.

They took their places around the fire, gradually relaxing. Each took it in turns to wash their faces and drink the stream's cool water. As they ate the Earth Sage explained the reason for their journey through the Labyrinth. It was simple (she said). They had to prove that they cared about others more than themselves, to show that they needed each other and would leave no one behind. In the end, the final test was for them to show that they would choose to either live, or die, together. The Labyrinth was created by the elements, the earth itself, not man. In conquering its riddles and passages they had earned the right to summon help from the earth in their moment of need. The earth's gift would be the release of the Blackwater.

The Earth Sage addressed Frog. 'When it comes, you

will be the one to let loose its fury, only you can bring the catalyst that ignites its final destructive power.'

They all wanted to know much more, but the Earth Sage told them that she would give them nothing other than the knowledge that they had one mission, and that was to join Sir Dragonslayer and the army of the north. She would leave a guide to help them on their journey, but now they must sleep and replenish their energy and strength.

'How can we sleep knowing that we're needed?' asked Logan.

'I'm too excited,' said Fixer.

'Me too,' added Ginger and Frog.

'All we need is a short rest,' said Lady Dawnstar.

'I agree. Just a little longer and then we depart,' said Sir Peacealot.

'As you wish,' said the Earth Sage, smiling. 'I'll say my goodbyes. You have proved your worth to each other, now save this world from the evils that would cross the Dimensions. Be brave, young Chris.'

To their amazement, she stepped forward and dissolved into the flames of the camp fire. Red embers and blue sparks rose and disappeared into the night. As they sat there transfixed, their eyelids growing heavy, each one of them succumbing to a peaceful slumber, Frog realised one thing as the warmth of sleep took him. *'She called me Chris.'*

15

Let the Light Free us from Evil

The land was scorched, blackened and dry. Smoke leaked from withered and burning stumps that at one time had stood as a green and leafy forest. King Hector and Gizmo surveyed the endless scene of destruction. They had been travelling through the same terrain for a number of days now, their army picking their way through the desolation which grew worse each day. Now there weren't even patches of grass or an odd tree or piece of shrubbery that had escaped the wicked torching by Fangmaster's wolves. Nothing had been spared. The closer their journey had taken them to their confrontation with Lord Maelstrom the more complete the devastation had become.

A mood had settled over the army. Not one of despair, but one of determined revenge, and it was that revenge that they exacted on any of Fangmaster's wolves or Lord Maelstrom's wicked creatures that they came across as they advanced into the growing darkness and burning skyline. They moved forwards in a great V-shaped swathe, spreading out across the territory for many miles, outriders ensuring all the while that not one of the enemy escaped or passed through their ranks. At the head of this great throng rode King Hector and the wizard, and alongside them padded the dark and silent shape of Storm.

'Your pet appears to have doubled his size of late,' observed King Hector.

'He's been starving himself in eagerness of the coming battle, he knows that most of the meat from his kills will be foul and inedible, so it will make the tough and bitter taste of wolf flesh all the more satisfying,' explained Gizmo.

'When do we draw the line of battle, my friend?' asked King Hector.

'Soon,' replied Gizmo. 'Lord Maelstrom's bravado will get the better of him and he will send an envoy to mock us and to give us the opportunity to surrender. That is where we will make our stand. I'll ensure that his envoy takes a message back to him that will draw his legions to us, on *our* terms.'

'You sound so confident, my friend, but I cannot forget that we are dealing with a force that could spell the end of this world for all free and good peoples,' said King Hector.

The sky in the distance flared up and from the orange glow came burning suns of flame, soaring through the sky towards their position.

'And so it begins,' said Gizmo.

The first ball of flame arced its way down towards the king and Gizmo and a shout went out from the king's commanders.

'To shields! To shields!' echoed along the ranks.

With a well-rehearsed swiftness, the king and Gizmo were surrounded by horse guards, bringing up their steel shields and creating a barrier over their heads. The same practice was carried out along the line, with foot soldiers taking shelter between their comrades' horses, sheltered by the canopies of shields. The first missile struck above the king and Gizmo. It bounced off into any poor, unprotected souls further back in the throng. Then came a dozen or so more, each one hitting the protective shields and ricocheting away, only to find other unfortunate victims. Then, as quickly as the attack had started, it stopped.

'We have visitors approaching, tell your commanders to take their positions,' said Gizmo. 'No one is to charge or fire a weapon, at least not yet.'

The shields were withdrawn and the soldiers stood in their lines, waiting for the moment of command as they felt the ground begin to tremble. A storm cloud was gathering in the distance, but this storm cloud was at ground level and moving towards them at great speed.

'What now?' asked the king.

'As I predicted,' said Gizmo. 'Lord Maelstrom sends his messengers to taunt us. Let's hear what they have to say, shall we?'

The cloud thundered towards them, showing no sign of stopping, and above the roar came Gizmo's voice. 'Hold firm and steady, do not break ranks! Hold firm!'

With less than a few metres left, the cloud abruptly stopped and evaporated to reveal an enormous creature nearly eight metres high. Its image was grotesque, the long snout resembling a sickly grey tentacle which reached out menacingly, searching for prey. At the centre of its broad forehead a single red eye stared out, its pupil as black as coal; from the slash of a mouth, sickly drool spilled over rows of pointed teeth as it breathed the stench of decay upon the wizard and the king. Its body was reptilian, almost dinosaur-like and covered in sharp metallic scales, the tips of which curved outwards from its body, ready to cut anything to shreds that came in contact with it. It crouched on stout legs which ended in clawed feet, and these dug viciously into the charred ground as its long tail, a spearhead end to it, swished to and fro in the air behind it.

'I have heard of these creatures,' whispered the king. 'But never thought that I would have the misfortune to come face to face with one.'

'Steel yourself, My Lord, I fear that Lord Maelstrom will have enlisted even worse creations than Madbaggers to fight his evil cause,' said Gizmo.

In a harness, strapped to the Madbagger's long neck, sat a lank-haired wolf, a dirty white streak running across its otherwise grey chest. In its clawed paw it held a long, studded whip. It raised itself on its hind legs.

'Lord Maelstrom sends a message to all those puny and insignificant beings who dare oppose him,' it announced. 'Join his mighty legions now and be spared a torturous end. Now is the time to save yourselves, your leaders are weak, their powers are useless against the forces that will soon be loosed upon you. Join us in the new age of Castellion, fight with us and you shall be rewarded. Refuse and you will die feeling your bones being crushed to dust.'

Storm padded forward and growled.

Gizmo dismounted and patted the panther on the shoulders. 'Plenty of time for wolf flesh, my friend, all in good time.' He looked up at the wolf. 'Why does Lord Maelstrom send Fangmaster's second in command to be his messenger boy? You are nothing but a coward that hides behind the strength of others, you are only capable of attacking the weak, the small and the defenceless. I have heard of your spineless activities and your day of reckoning is at hand.'

'Ha! And I shall enjoy gnawing on your flesh, this day, old man,' spat the wolf, raising his whip.

In the following moments, the wizard's response was an awesome display of vengeance to all who witnessed it. They had never before seen the wrath of a Guardian wizard unleashed and stood in fear and wonder as he brought down the Magik and despatched it through his hands in the direction of the open-mouthed wolf. Before the Madbagger had time to react, the wizard had, with unseen strength, grabbed its tentacle and pulled the creature to its knees. As its tail had scythed around towards the wizard he had reached inside his cloak and produced his silver cane which he used as a sword. It cut through the end of the tail and then sliced into the base of the tentacle, separating if from the creature's head. He held the tip of the cane in front of the Maddbagger's unblinking eye and it collapsed to its knees, powerless.

King Hector and his commanders now watched the seared and smoking remains of the wolf, strapped to the side of the Madbagger, as it receded into the distance. Satisfied, Gizmo mounted his horse and now faced the king and his commanders.

'Prepare your men, ready your weapons, for this day will be the time of decision. We will be faced with similar and greater foes than you have just seen but they can be defeated, both by Magik and by mortal hand. Our friends and kindred face their ordeal in the north, we must together end this threat to Castellion and our freedom. For Castellion. Let the Light free us from evil.'

The arrow, when it came, was without warning, indeed its coming was even unforeseen by Gizmo who could only raise his arm in an attempt to stop it. The twisted arrowhead and its blackened shaft struck his hand and passed straight through his palm before embedding itself in the shoulder of the surprised and stunned king whose eyes gazed skyward at the giant bird that had silently descended from its cover in the storm clouds overhead. Its grinning rider was already loading a second arrow onto his bow.

Gizmo turned and followed the king's gaze. 'Archers, to the sky, to the sky!'

As a thousand steel-shafted arrows found their target and brought both rider and bird crashing to the ground, Gizmo touched the head of his cane to the arrow in the king's shoulder. It disintegrated with a puff of sickly smoke, but King Hector's face was as white as death.

'Prepare a pavilion for the king. Quickly!' ordered Gizmo as he brought the king's cloak over the wound. He escorted him to where a clearing had been made and men at arms were already busy, erecting the king's marquee. Gizmo could see worried looks on some of the men's faces and words were being exchanged in hushed voices. He had to stop any negative message of the king's injury being spread as this was something that would affect the army's morale and courage.

'Spread the word,' he announced as he helped the king from his horse. 'That the king has received an injury, but I will administer the healing Magik needed to revive him.' He saw the expression on their faces change and relax, the exchange of words becoming more positive.

'Let's get you inside and inspect the damage, shall we, old friend?' He helped the king into the tent and onto the soft bedding that had been strewn on the floor.

'Bring me only pure water and nothing else,' he ordered the servants. 'Now, my friend, let's see what poison has been inflicted on you.'

When he had helped the king off with his armour, tunic and vest, at first sight the wound seemed nothing more than a small cut; the force of the arrow had been slowed down by the king's chain mail and layers of clothing but, as Gizmo watched, the wound began to blister and bubble, the red gash turning dark green and black. A servant boy arrived with a jug of water and a bowl and the wizard covered the wound as the boy set the objects down. Gizmo dismissed him from duty with a smile, telling him that the king needed to rest for a while.

He turned back to the king who was looking worriedly at him.

'How is your hand?' he said.

'My hand has never been better,' said Gizmo, holding it up for the king to see. 'It will take more than a poisonous piece of wood and metal to affect me, however, I didn't think for one moment that a passing spell would have been placed upon it. It would seem that the spell was put on it so that it would pass through any object to get to you. You were its target and only you. Lord Maelstrom has excelled in his deviousness.'

The king looked into Gizmo's eyes. 'I feel a coldness in my body, the like I have never felt before. How bad is this wound?'

'It's very bad magic, I'm afraid.' He turned away to soak a cloth and bathe the wound. 'I'll have to use all my knowledge and powers to fight its effects.'

King Hector placed his hand on Gizmo's. 'You didn't say you could cure me and you didn't say you could stop its effects. Look me in the eyes and tell me the truth.'

The wizard sighed and looked at the king. 'This isn't just bad magic, it's foul magic. Magic that has been corrupted and polluted. This is Magic of Lord Maelstrom's making. I can delay its final result, but even I cannot cure it.'

'And what is that final result?' asked the king.

With moist eyes, the wizard could only answer with one word. 'Death.'

They sat together in silence for a while, until King Hector spoke up. 'How much time can you buy me?'

Gizmo inspected the wound; the red and green sores had grown angry and putrid.

'Two days at the most. I can administer a saviour spell which will allow you to fight until the end. You will appear normal to those around you until you suddenly collapse, it will end in a blink of an eye.'

'Can you stop his evil from taking my soul?' pleaded the king.

'Fear not, Lord Maelstrom will not claim your soul to reincarnate you as one of his minions, that I will certainly prevent.'

'Then do your work and quickly. I have my people to lead into battle and a sword that demands I avenge this wicked deed before my time is taken,' said the king.

Those around the king's pavilion heard a painful scream followed by a golden flash which lit up its interior. The king's men at arms quickly drew their swords and rushed into the pavilion only to be met by King Hector, standing strong before them, his sword raised, held by a steady arm.

'Let it be known that every man and woman must now take food and rest while they can. In a few hours we make our stand. Let us be ready and steadfast in our endeavours,' he announced.

They gave their salutes and left to inform the commanders while the king and Gizmo put together the plans which would determine victory or defeat. The last rim of the sun caught the horizon and streaked out its broad rays of light across the landscape, bathing the armour of King Hector's army in a crimson red sheen as they stood in silence, their pennants hanging loosely in the still evening air. Dark, bruised and brooding clouds bore down on them from the south, a roll of deafening thunder rattled through the heavens followed by sharp, jagged lines of lightning, piercing the ground and exploding into showers of flame and rock. Then they came, a multitude of evil creatures and creations, rising out of the earth, howling and screeching, swarming forward, ready to engulf and destroy any other living thing that blocked their path.

As the final glint of natural light faded from the west, Gizmo placed the handle of his cane against King Hector's forehead, the golden sun on his crown burst open and released a blinding blaze of light, out and into the eyes of the advancing hoards. For one final time King Hector's voice gave the command.

'For Castellion. Let the Light free us from evil!'

At once his archers responded and the sky above darkened with a hail of arrows, flying ahead as Castellion's southern army charged forward to meet its blinded and confused enemies.

As the battle raged on, there in the midst of the hacking, fighting figures the wizard could be seen, arcing his silver cane back and forth, bringing down and destroying all evil in his path. Beside him was the dark lithe figure of the giant cat, clawing and tearing apart any foe that came within striking distance.

For a day and a half, the bloody conflict continued, strength enduring from the need to survive, men and women throwing themselves forwards to meet a never-ending enemy. King Hector led the way, upright and proud on his horse, a beacon of light pouring out from his crown, blinding their foes, pushing back the evil darkness, giving courage and hope to all those that fought alongside him.

When the moment came, Gizmo was the first to see the sword fall from the king's hand as his body slouched forwards onto his horse's neck. His golden crown slipped from his head and as it struck the ground all light was extinguished and a cloying darkness enveloped them all.

16

A Dragon's Revenge

Frog woke with a start and looked around him. It was daylight, just after dawn. Lady Dawnstar, Sir Peacealot and Logan were sitting bolt upright as if also woken suddenly.

'What is it?' asked Frog. 'Why do I feel so strange? It's like I've lost a precious memory and a sadness is pulling in my stomach. Something's missing?'

'I feel it too,' said Logan.

'And I,' acknowledged Sir Peacealot

Lady Dawnstar turned to them, a tear running down her cheek. 'A light has gone out in the Chosen.'

'One of us has been lost? But who?' asked Logan.

'I can't tell,' she replied, rising. All I know is that someone has fallen into the shadows and we must hurry. The darkness has turned against us, we are needed now more than ever.'

They roused Ginger and Fixer, leaving them only time to wash their faces in the stream and drink a little water.

'What's the hurry?' asked Ginger.

'We have to go. Now!' said Frog.

'Have to go where? Our guide hasn't turned up yet,'

replied Ginger, turning to pack his bedroll. An acorn struck him on the shoulder.

'Well that won't help,' he muttered.

Another landed on the blanket in front of him and he brushed it away.

'Cut it out,' he said irritably. 'I'm going as fast as I can.'

A third hit him on the head.

'Right, that's it.'

He stood and turned to see the others staring, not at him, but above him. He followed their gaze to see a large black and white bird, perched on a branch. It cocked its head to one side, giving them all a stare with a black, beady eye. With a flutter it drifted down and landed by Fixer.

'What's it doing?' asked Fixer.

The bird picked up a stick in its beak and hopped across to Frog, placing it on the ground in front of him. It then hopped back and repeated the process twice more.

'Well, I'll be ...!' exclaimed Logan.

'Look!' said Frog. 'He's made an arrow, it's pointing towards that path. He's our guide!'

'Excuse me,' said Fixer. 'But why do you assume that it's a he?'

'Because he looks like a he,' replied Frog.

Lady Dawnstar smiled. 'She's right, Frog, it could be a she-bird.'

As if to confirm Fixer's statement, the bird fluttered up and onto her shoulder.

'See,' she said, grinning. 'She knows.'

'That doesn't prove anything,' said Ginger.

The bird flew from Fixer's shoulder and back on to the branch above Ginger where it pulled an acorn loose and dropped it onto him. Their laughter was nervous and full of melancholy. Lady Dawnstar broke the following silence.

'Now, let's get packed, we've a guide to follow.'

They followed the path out of the clearing and into the forest, the bird flying off down trails, indicating which was the correct way to go when they got to forks in the pathways. The rest of the time it happily perched on Fixer's shoulder, occasionally rubbing the side of its head affectionately against her hair.

When the sun was high over them, shining down through the leafy canopy and onto the green undergrowth, they stopped briefly to eat a meal made up of some cold meat left over from the night before. Then they were on their way again, following the bird this way and that. Finally, when the shadows had grown long through the trees, they reached the edge of the forest and a view through the thinning tree trunks showed them an expanse of dry, dusty plain. They moved out into the open and away from the borderline of trees. In the distance they could see a line of hills and towering behind them a range of mountains, their peaks and slopes white with ice and snow, dark clouds hovering above them menacingly.

'I don't believe it,' said Logan. 'The northern mountains, the edge of the Frozen Wastes. I never knew that a forest of this size existed so close to them.'

'So that's where we're headed?' asked Frog.

'Over those hills are the north downs, that's where we should be meeting Sir Dragonslayer and the gathered army,' said Logan. 'Let's hope that we're not too late.'

'Too late for what?' asked Ginger.

'Haven't you noticed how the temperature has dropped since we stepped out of the forest?' asked Logan.

'He's right,' said Fixer. 'I'm going to put my cloak on.' She turned to the bird on her shoulder. 'I guess this is where we say goodbye,' she said.

The bird stroked its head against her cheek and flew up into a tree. It studied them for a moment, then suddenly it was gone, back into the forest.

As the sun reflected on the overhead clouds, painting them blues and pinks and mackerel grey, the party moved forwards across the plain, their breath suddenly appearing from their mouths in fine plumes of mist.

'Not good. I hate the cold,' commented Frog as he tugged his cloak around him.

The walk seemed to take forever, the hills at first refusing to grow in size as they approached them. The air was turning frosty as dusk descended and they finally reached the foot of the rising ground. Unexpectedly, the twilight faded and gloom surrounded them. The sudden loss of light revealed a red glow, rising up from the other side of the hills.

'What's that?' asked Frog.

'I'm not sure,' replied Logan.

It was at that moment that they heard it, a resounding roar of many voices, a battle cry. This was the moment that Sir Dragonslayer and the northern army faced the immense and fierce attack of the Hidden People.

'The battle,' said Logan. 'It's begun!'

Without consultation, they scrabbled forwards and upwards, clambering over the rocky, uneven ground, pushing themselves to reach the brow of the hill, some hundred or so metres above them. As they ascended, they heard the clamour of fighting growing louder, the shouting, the clash of weapons, the cries of warning, of fear and pain.

Drawing in breaths against the frantic efforts of the climb, Frog turned to Ginger. 'Have you ever been in a battle before?'

'Not like this,' Ginger replied.

'How about you?' Frog asked Fixer.

'Not to where any fighting was happening,' she answered.

Frog paused to catch his breath. 'Are you two scared?'

They both looked at him and nodded.

'Then at least we can all be scared together. And I bet they are as well,' he said, indicating the other three ahead of them.

On the other side of the hill, fate played a dark card as Sir Dragonslayer found himself surrounded by ice figures. He had been hacking his way forwards, trying to make a space for others to follow, when the gap had closed behind him.

Several of the Maids of Steel had seen his plight and were trying to forge a path to him but as he stood there, lashing out with his sword, he could see the heat of the blade fading. Each time it contacted with one of the Hidden People, a cold ice blue spread into the steel. He thrust the sword into the figure that faced him but this time the weapon had no effect and glanced off the solid ice-cold body. An arm reached forward and grabbed Sir Dragonslayer roughly by the throat. Another hand tore away the cloth wrapped around his face, his skin exposed for the icy fingers that touched his cheek, and then they were upon him.

Those close to him saw that he tried valiantly to take his own life before he was turned into one of the frozen dead, but moments later he rose from the mass of ice figures, his own body covered in blue-white frost, his eyes lifeless and black as he turned to face his comrades, no longer a friend, no longer an ally. His sole intent was to touch them and make them become as he now was, a frozen zombie and a servant of evil.

On the other side of the hill behind the battle, four figures stumbled, clutching at their heads while two other figures looked on with worried faces.

'What's happening to them, Ginger?' cried Fixer.

'I don't know,' he replied. 'I wish I knew.'

Lady Dawnstar gritted her teeth and pulled herself upright.

'Another of the Chosen has fallen!' she shouted. 'Make haste lest we all fail.' She grasped Frog's cloak and pulled him on, encouraging the others to follow as Sir Peacealot and Logan regained their senses and scrambled forwards.

As they reached the brow of the hill, the scene of conflict was spread out before them. A glacier of transparent figures, their shapes fading in and out as the fires reflected on them, reached out across the valley floor and away towards the mountain skyline. A line of fires glowed amongst the army of fighting Maids, Rangers and bowmen, all desperately struggling to hold back the onslaught.

A deafening roar filled the air, the ground itself seemed to tremble from its intensity as a winged beast appeared from behind their lines.

It was Sir Dragonslayer's dragon, enraged and filled with the pain of its companion's death. In its fury, it swooped down amongst the bowmen, scattering bodies aside as it scooped up and devoured some of the burning braziers. It arced up into the sky, beating its wings as it hovered high overhead.

'I know that dragon,' said Frog. 'What's it doing?'

'Exacting a terrible revenge,' said Logan.

It was then that Frog felt the overwhelming sense of sadness and rage. He buckled to his knees as fury and grief spilled from the dragon's mind and washed into his.

Logan knelt by him and tried his best to comfort him.

The dragon's wings slowed, rhythmically fanning the air, and with each stroke its great exposed chest and belly began to glow a golden colour. 'Is it going to breathe fire on them?' asked Ginger.

'More than that,' explained Logan. 'This is the final and ultimate sacrifice any dragon can make. It is about to reclaim its companion and take them both to oblivion.'

'I still don't understand,' said Ginger.

'Watch and you will. I would advise that you shield your eyes when the moment comes,' he warned them.

The dragon was now blazing white-hot as it dropped

its head and dived for the ground, heading for the shape that used to be Sir Dragonslayer. It plucked him from the frozen throng and rose into the sky with the figure clenched in its great jaws. Higher and higher it flew until, finally, it closed its great wings and fell, its shape lost in the furnace of flames that it had become, plummeting head first towards the foot of the mountains where the Hidden People spilled out in their thousands.

The impact, even though it was miles from where they stood, shook all of them, human and frozen, off their feet.

A ball of light exploded outwards and across the plain towards them and a great, dark mushroom-shaped cloud rose up in the distance. Then a rush of warm air passed over them only to be quickly followed by a return of the freezing temperatures.

Frog raised himself up, a steely look on his face.

Fixer and Ginger stepped back in awe as they saw his eyes flare emerald green.

As the rumbling faded into the distance, there was an uneasy silence as even the frozen figures seemed distracted and confused by what had just happened. In that moment, Lady Dawnstar realised the effect that the loss of Sir Dragonslayer could have on morale. Drawing her sword and throwing off her cloak so that even at this distance her suit of armour reflected the braziers' flames, she raised her voice in command.

'Maids of Steel. To arms! To arms!'

Beside her, Logan and Sir Peacealot raised their voices.

'Rangers of Castellion. To arms! To arms!'

'Bowmen of Dinham. To arms! To arms!'

Faces turned towards them as they charged down the hill, alarm turning to welcome recognition. As the three of them plunged their swords into a burning brazier, the army was galvanised into action with renewed vigour and determination, and before the frozen figures could react, burning steel was once again raining down upon them.

'I guess that we'd better stay up here out of the way,' said Ginger.

'We have our part to play Ginger, I for one have a friend to avenge,' said Frog. 'You can make yourselves useful by helping those bowmen to light up their arrows, for a start.'And he was off, scampering down the hillside, all thoughts for his own safety recklessly left behind.

Fixer smiled at Ginger. 'We can't let him have all the fun!' Then she was running down the hill after Frog.

'You call this fun?' said Ginger. Then, looking around and finding himself alone, he shouted, 'Wait for me!'

He stepped forward, tripped over the edge of his cloak and barrel-rolled down the hill past Frog and Fixer, finally coming to a rest in a crumpled but unharmed heap at the feet of a startled bowman.

'Stop messing about Ginger, there's work to do,' said Fixer.

The devastation caused by the dragon's sacrifice stopped the source of the onslaught and after a short while the rows of advancing frozen figures thinned out and ceased appearing out of the dark frost.

Castellion's men and women stood breathing heavily, their tired bodies exhaling white clouds of breath into the air.

'Is it over?' asked Sir Peacealot.

Logan looked across the valley. To the east, a pale light was breaking on the horizon.

'Dawn is coming, what there may be of it. This is but a pause, they'll not advance again until night descends. Now is the time for us to get these brave souls to fill their stomachs and take rest. Lady Dawnstar, your Maids await your leadership and Sir Peacealot, I would suggest you give counsel and command to the bowmen of Dinham and all others who bear arms. I'll take charge of my Rangers.'

Frog, Ginger and Fixer had gathered themselves together, their faces and hands blackened by smoke from readying the burning arrows.

'What about us?' asked Frog. 'Surely there is more for us to do?'

'Fixer, you belong in the service of Lady Dawnstar. Ginger, you shall now accompany me and Frog should take his place with Sir Peacealot.'

'But we'd rather stay together,' complained Ginger.

'The time will come when we will be at each other's side, have patience,' instructed Logan.

A dragon rider approached the group, his face grave and solemn.

'We wish to avenge our commander with the same sacrifice should the need arise,' he announced. 'It would be a fitting and glorious end to the race of dragons and their riders.'

Logan stepped forward and placed his hands on the man's bowed shoulders.

'Sir Dragonslayer would not want his loyal kinsmen to be so downcast, to make a sacrifice so great, not on this battlefield. He would want to see the fire in your eyes and the flames in your dragons rekindled and taken to the defence of Castellion Stronghold. For should we fail here, that is where the final stand shall be. Would you grant him that wish?'

'You spoke to him of this?' asked the rider.

'It was written in his scroll and he was pledged to follow the order,' answered Logan.

'Then, so it shall be,' said the rider, his back stiffening, his shoulders broadening and a fresh determination filling his face. 'May the Light of Castellion be with you.' He gave the royal salute and turned back to join his fellow riders.

A few moments later as Frog followed Sir Peacealot to meet with the bowmen's commanders, all heads were turned upwards to watch the host of dragons circle in the slate-grey sky in a farewell salute and turn over the hills southwards towards Castellion Stronghold.

Frog spent much of the morning helping to prepare bundles of arrows and replenish stacks of wood for the fires, then at around midday he helped to serve the tired fighters bowls of steaming hot broth that had been cooked in large iron cauldrons over the open fires. Many of the fighters wrapped themselves up as best they could and claimed a few hours' sleep, others dozed uneasily, seated around the burning braziers. In the cold light of an overcast day, the frost refused to leave the ground and a layer of thin ice formed on bowls and buckets of unattended water.

After they had both taken the opportunity to eat, Sir Peacealot instructed Frog to take refuge in one of the small canvas pavilions, erected well behind the battle line, and urged him to get what sleep that he could, assuring him that he would be woken when the time came. Frog suddenly realised how tired he felt and gladly rolled himself in some thick blankets and drifted into a deep slumber.

The shouting roused him with a start and he blinked once or twice while he reminded himself where he was. The light was fading, he had slept into the late afternoon. Throwing back the blankets and leaving the warmth that had cocooned him, the cold air shocked him fully awake. Gathering himself up, he pulled back the flap and peered out from the tent. In the gloom, the ground reflected back at him, white and frozen, clouds of sleet blurring his vision. A wind had risen and was driving the swirling, frozen rain in all directions.

'Not good, definitely not good,' was all he could allow himself to say.

He caught an almost recognisable smell mixed with the gusts of wind and wrinkled his nose, his mind searching to identify it while he pulled the hood of his cloak over him and went in search of the others. More by luck than judgement he bumped into Logan who was frantically trying to make a windbreak out of some shields in order to protect a spluttering brazier.

'What's happening?' shouted Frog.

'The wind and the frozen snow is putting the fires out. We will be defenceless against the next attack.'

'What's that smell, where's it coming from?' Frog's voice struggled to be heard above the wind.

Logan shouted back. 'It's coming from the plain. It's the Blackwater. The Blackwater has risen.'

He signalled for Frog to hold one of the shields while he attempted to drive a lance into the cold, rock-hard ground as a support. With a gust of bitingly cold wind, the flames in the brazier were snuffed out.

'It's no use, we'll be overrun without the fires to heat our weapons. This weather has been sent by Maelstrom himself. The Blackwater has not helped us. There's nothing left to do but to gather ourselves together and retreat to Castellion Stronghold.' he grabbed Frog's hand. 'Quick, onto my back, we need to find the others.'

Sharp fragments of frozen snow stung Frog's cheeks and he clasped his hood across his face and hung on to Logan's broad shoulders. They worked their way to where the front line of defence stood. Men and women had their backs against the worst of the wind, their eyes peering above the cloth scarves pulled up over their faces. Lady Dawnstar and Fixer were among them, their cloaks flapping viciously around their bodies. Frog slid off Logan's back and as he pulled down his scarf to speak, the odour, now even stronger, caught him in the back of his throat and he coughed at its sour dryness.

'That smell,' he rasped to Lady Dawnstar. 'Show me where it's coming from.'

She put her arm around his shoulders and turned them both into the full force of the wind, their bodies bending over in an effort to push themselves, step by step, forwards. After a few metres the smell was so strong that he could hardly breathe. She pulled her face close to his.

'Look at the ground,' she said. 'The Blackwater has come out of the land.'

He looked down at his feet. Instead of snow-covered ice, the ground was a carpet of thick, dark slime, the pellets of sleet turning black on contact with it. He reached down and dipped his frozen fingers into it and as he did so fumes welled up into his head and dizzied his senses, his knees buckled and he passed out.

He came to with the taste of a bitter, burning liquid on his lips and in his throat and he rasped a cough, blinking tears from his eyes. Looking around he saw that he was in a small pavilion with Fixer, Ginger, Sir Peacealot, Lady Dawnstar and Logan standing around him. Logan was replacing the cap of a small leather bottle in his hand.

'You like to live dangerously,' he said. 'That's just a drop of Ranger's elixir, it'll put you right in no time.'

'What happened?' asked Frog.

'You breathed in the Blackwater, you got too close to it,' said Lady Dawnstar. 'That's why these plains are uninhabited. No one can tell when the Blackwater will rise, but when it does it turns the air foul and the ground black. Even when it seeps back into the earth, the soil remains like black, coarse sand, but at least the stench fades after a while.'

Frog sat up. His footwear was black, stained by what he had walked in. He brought his hand up and saw that his fingers were discoloured. He lifted them tentatively to his nose and sniffed.

'That's it!' he said. 'Oil! Filthy black, smelly oil. The Blackwater is oil!'

'Which means?' asked Ginger.

'Stand back, light it up and watch the whole place go up in flames,' he announced. 'If this floods the valley, right across the plain to the mountains, once it's been lit, it'll burn for days and take every frozen thing with it. Nothing will be left.'

'Just one problem,' said Logan. 'We have no flame. Nothing will light in this weather. The air is too cold and the wind is too strong. The frozen snow has smothered all of our fires.'

'Gunpowder! We need some gunpowder. That should do it,' said Frog.

Not for the first time did five faces look blankly back at him.

'Let me guess,' said Frog. 'You don't know what gunpowder is, let alone have any in this world, do you?'

'Never heard of it,' confirmed Ginger.

'You'd think that silly old wizard would have invented gunpowder by now,' said Frog.

The others stared back at him, easing themselves away.

'What? What is it? Have I got something catching all of a sudden?' said Frog.

Sir Peacealot pointed at Frog's cloak. All eyes were now fixed on the bluish glow that escaped from it. Frog pulled the material back, exposing his short sword, and saw that its handle was pulsing with light.

'What does it mean?' he asked, getting to his feet and pulling the sword from its sheath.

'More of the wizard's magic?' questioned Logan.

Frog became very anxious as the radiance from the sword spread across his hand, turning it transparent.

'I don't like it,' he complained, and in an effort to discard the sword, he thrust it into the ground.

'I, I can't let go!' he shouted, struggling to release himself. 'Help me.'

Logan stepped forward and grabbed Frog's arm, pulling at the weapon as Frog looked pleadingly up at him.

The others looked on helplessly as the light engulfed Frog and Logan, turning them transparent. Then, with a soundless flash, they were gone. A bare patch of earth in the centre of the tent was all that remained.

As soon as the stars appeared around him and the spinning feeling hit his senses, Frog knew that this was exactly what had happened when he and Sir Peacealot had clasped hands around his sword. He was back in the Slipstream. This time however, his head cleared and as he watched shooting stars fly past him and the whirlpools of far-off galaxies turn against a black, velvet backdrop of space, his mind connected events together and in a moment he realised what was happening and what he must do.

He was aware of Logan next to him, his eyes wide with surprise and confusion. There was an acceleration of movement and they were sent spinning downwards into a whirlpool of stars. Frog had just enough time to think to himself, *This is the bit where it all goes dark.* And he was right.

17

Take me Home

Chris opened his eyes. The dark leaves and branches of an apple tree were silhouetted above him against a twilight sky.

'Chris, Chris!' his mother's voice beckoned. 'You've had enough time out there now. Come on, time to get washed up and ready for bed.'

Chris smiled to himself. *'I am definitely laying off anything with E numbers in it. What a dream,'* he thought.

He pulled himself up onto one elbow and the smile disappeared from his face. Spread out in the grass at his feet lay the body of an unconscious Logan.

'Not good, definitely, not good,' said Chris.

Further inspection confirmed the reality of his situation. He himself was dressed in the style and clothes of Castellion, his sword now firmly in its sheath on his belt. His boots bore the stains of black oil, inescapable evidence of what had happened to him. He looked around. In the dimming light he could see the piles of dirt and grass from his excavations, just as he had left them.

'Chris, I'm not calling you again. Get up here now or

there'll be no TV for the rest of the week!' shouted his mother.

He rolled back his sleeve to reveal his watch. 21.21. It was working again. Time really had stood still. Logan stirred and moaned, his eyes flickering in the first movements of waking.

Chris had to think and quickly. 'Mum? I've stepped in some dog mess. I won't be long but it's going to take me a while to clean my trainers.' He didn't like lying, especially to his mum, but he felt that he had no choice.

'You'd better make a good job of it young man and don't take too long. I'll be having a word with our neighbours tomorrow about keeping their dog out of our garden,' she replied.

Now he really did feel guilty; still, he'd face that argument when the time came. What to do now was the burning issue. He turned his attention back to Logan who was sitting bolt upright, a confused expression on his face.

'What happened?' he asked as Chris knelt beside him.

Chris took Logan's arm and encouraged him to stand. 'Listen,' he said. 'You've got to trust me on this. We've gone through the Slipstream and travelled back into my world. I know that this is going to sound weird, but you have to keep quiet and do everything that I say. I'll explain later. Okay?'

'Are we in danger?' asked Logan, surveying the shadowy orchard and reaching for his whip.

'No, no. But I've still got to hide you until I can figure out what to do next,' reassured Chris.

'You have trusted me, young Frog, and now it is my

turn to repay that trust. Tell me what I need to do,' said Logan.

'Firstly, my name here is Chris. Secondly, see those lights?' he said pointing to the house. 'That's where I live with my Mum. Things are going to seem pretty strange to you, but stick with me and you'll be okay. Whatever you see, try not to get alarmed, nothing is going to hurt you. Just don't touch anything, that's all. Now, I've got to get us both up into my room without being seen. Follow me and keep close.'

Chris led the way, up through the orchard, keeping in the shadows as much as he could until they were at the back of the house and crouching beneath the kitchen window. Chris slowly peered into the kitchen. His mother was nowhere to be seen.

'Right, I'm going up to my room to get changed so that at least I look normal. You stay here and don't move. Got it?'

Logan looked blankly back. 'Got what?' he asked.

'No, I mean, do you understand?' said Chris.

'Yes. You said to stay here and don't move,' said Logan.

'And don't touch anything,' Chris repeated.

'And don't touch anything,' echoed Logan

Chris removed his boots and cautiously crept around to the kitchen door. Stepping through into the well-lit kitchen, he reached inside a drawer and fished out a plastic carrier bag into which he stuffed the dirty boots. Tucking the bag under his arm he made for the hallway. He could hear his mother talking on the telephone in the lounge and so he quietly scrambled up the stairs, slipping into his bedroom and closing the door. Switching on the light, he pulled off his Castellion clothes and stuffed them under his bed along with the carrier bag and his sword. Pulling open his wardrobe door, he grabbed a pair of jeans and a sweatshirt and changed into them.

'Chris?' he heard his mother call as she crossed the hall towards the kitchen.

He rushed out of his room and down the stairs.

'I'm here, I'm here,' he shouted, frantically trying to stop her from going into the garden. He leapt the last three stairs and bounded into the kitchen.

She stared at him, angrily. 'What is going on? What on earth do you think you're doing?'

'Just getting changed so I can have my supper,' he explained.

She scowled at him. 'Don't be so ridiculous, get upstairs and take those clothes off. You're not going anywhere until you've had a good scrub in the shower. Look at the state of your face. And those hands, they're disgusting. Where are your other clothes and where are your trainers? You had better not have brought them into the house with dog's mess on them.'

'I've left my trainers outside, they were too smelly,' he said, thinking as quickly as he could.

'And your clothes? Are they covered in dog's mess as well?'

'Yes, yes. I've left them with my trainers.' he panicked.

She turned to go out of the kitchen door. 'I'll get them in the washing machine now, it'll be too late in the morning.'

'No! You can't,' he shouted.

She stopped and turned. 'I beg your pardon?'

He stood there, frantically trying to think of an explanation. 'I think that we might have to throw them away, it was a big pile of dog poo and it got everywhere. I really wouldn't want you to touch them,' he said desperately.

The look that Chris feared came over his mum's face. It was the look that said, '*Now, you really are in trouble.*'

'You haven't had those clothes for long. We bought that sweatshirt for you in America. Why can't you be more careful? Right, get up those stairs and into that shower. Now!' she ordered.

As Chris was escorted to the shower, he was lectured on how expensive boy's clothes were these days and finally told that he was grounded. She then left him with orders to scrub himself clean, informing him, as she went, that she would not be retrieving his clothes from the garden and (much to his relief,) that it would be his sole task to sort out, in the morning.

'Call me when you're clean and dressed in your pyjamas,' she instructed.

As soon as he was sure that she had gone downstairs, he undressed, wrapped a towel around him and leant out of the shower room window.

'Logan?' he whispered

There was no answer.

'Logan!' he raised his voice this time.

'I didn't touch anything,' came Logan's voice from the shadows below.

'Good,' said Chris. 'Now listen. I've got to wash, and then let my Mum think that I've gone to bed before I can work out where to hide you. You'll have to wait there a little while longer.'

'That's all right,' came the reply. 'I'll talk to my new companion.'

Chris nearly slipped out of the window in surprise. 'What, what new companion?'

'A ginger cat, he's very friendly,' said Logan.

Chris exhaled with relief. 'Tabby. His name is Tabby and he's my cat,' he said. 'He'll let you stroke him all night if you're not careful. You stay put and look after him.'

Chris shut the window and caught sight of himself in the mirror. He was filthy! No wonder his mum was so mad. His hair was greasy and matted, his face was so dirty that he hardly recognised himself. He then thought of the mark on his forehead. How was he going to explain that? He splashed some water on his face, rinsing away the grime. The mark was gone, or at least it was no longer visible, and to his relief his eyes had returned to their normal grey colour. Satisfied, he jumped into the shower and turned on the water. Fifteen minutes later, after half a bottle of shower gel and plenty of scrubbing he stood in his pyjamas, staring at his glowing red face in the mirror.

His mum knocked on the door. 'Come on, you must be done by now.'

There was no arguing with her tonight. She brought him up a banana, some chocolate fingers and a small bottle of water with strict orders that he eat his supper, read quietly and then brush his teeth. If his light wasn't out in half an hour, then he would be having no TV for at least a week.

After she had kissed him goodnight, he gave himself five minutes, then visited the bathroom. On returning to his room he put on his dressing gown, then stuffed the food and bottle of water into his pockets. He picked up his rechargeable torch and switched off his bedroom light. Quietly, he sat on his bed, working out where he was going to hide Logan for the night as he had no choice but to wait for the following day to put his plans into action.

He sat in the dark for what seemed an eternity, finally checking the luminous face on his watch. 10.45. He opened his wardrobe and reached down his sleeping bag from the shelf. With it bundled under his arm he made his way to the top of the stairs and paused. He could hear the television, it was a shopping channel; his mum sometimes watched them for amusement (she thought the presenters were so bad they were hilarious). A good sign. It was this time of night that his mum would curl up on the sofa intent on watching one of her favourite programmes, only to fall asleep. Waking up with a start, usually around midnight and half asleep, she would make her way to bed. He hoped that tonight would be no exception.

He reached the hall and peeped through the gap in the door to see her peacefully asleep on the sofa. Then he was off, through the kitchen, out of the door and into the back garden. He turned on his torch and shone it into the shadows.

Logan lifted his arm against the glare. 'What magic is this? It burns like a sun.'

'Sorry,' apologised Chris, and switched it off.

Logan was sitting with his back against the wall, Tabby comfortable on his lap.

'Come on,' said Chris. 'I've thought of where you can sleep.'

Chris led Logan to the old shed. It was a half-brick, half-wooden building that housed the lawn mower and other garden tools. However, it was big enough for Chris to have claimed the back section as a den, where he had covered the floor with cardboard and an old duvet. This is where he would sit, occasionally with his friend Billy Smart, planning world domination and swapping Yu-Gi-Oh cards.

'Here you are,' said Chris, opening the door and switching his torch on to light up the interior.

Logan, who still had Tabby in his arms, stood still.

'What's the matter?' said Chris.

'Will the beam of magic light cast a spell on me?' he asked nervously.

'Look, it's harmless,' said Chris, passing his hand backwards and forwards in front of the torch. 'It's just a tool that we have in my world. I'll let you borrow it tonight and you can see how it works. Now come on, I haven't got long, my Mum could wake up soon.'

Logan looked suspiciously at the torch and followed Chris into the shed as he put the torch onto the workbench and spread the sleeping bag on to the floor.

'There you go and here's some food and water for you.'

Logan stared down at Chris's offering, puzzlement on his face.

'I knew that this wasn't going to be easy,' said Chris. 'Right, sit down here with me and I'll explain.'

Chris introduced Logan to bananas and chocolate fingers, showed him the modern wonders of water in a plastic bottle and how the rechargeable torch worked, then he prepared him as much as he could for what he might see and hear when he woke the next day. Chris also made him promise that no matter what happened, Logan was to keep himself hidden until he came back and collected him in the morning. After bidding Logan a good night, he closed the shed door and made his way back to his bedroom where he set his watch alarm for six-thirty – he had a busy day ahead of him. He lay on his bed, feeling too excited and too nervous to sleep but, before he was aware of it, his eyes had closed and he drifted off into a dreamless slumber.

The next morning, Chris's eyes were open seconds before his alarm could pierce the air. He checked across the hall – good, his mother wasn't awake yet. He crept into the spare double bedroom where a mirrored, wall-to-wall wardrobe greeted him. It was in here that his father's clothes still hung, waiting expectantly for their owner to return. His mum would not get rid of them, she had not yet fully reached the point of total acceptance that she had lost her husband. Chris held one of his dad's shirts to his face and breathed in. Even under the smell of detergent he could pick up the lingering scent of his father. He stopped himself when he felt the tear escape from his eye and trace its way down his cheek.

'Come on Chris, make him proud of you,' he said to himself, and wiped his face with the back of his hand. Quickly, he grabbed a pair of jeans, a sweatshirt and a pair of trainers, hoping and praying that they would fit Logan.

Next, he went back to his room and reached under his bed, shoving aside the dirty clothes that he had pushed there the night before. His fingers found a small plastic box and pulled it out. Inside the box was cash that he had saved from pocket money and odd pound coins that he had been given as homework rewards by his mum. He still had the thirty pounds birthday money that his dad had given him but he had not as yet been able to bring himself to spend. All together it amounted to a tidy sum. Quickly he counted it out on his bed. Fifty-two pounds. He hoped that it would be enough.

After throwing some water on his face and brushing his teeth he got changed and made his way down the stairs, his father's clothes bundled under one arm and his Castellion clothes and sword under the other.

He opened the shed door slowly to see Logan, sitting cross-legged, in his hands a couple of Action Man figures that Chris kept in his den. Logan was examining them curiously, inspecting the detail of the faces with amazement. It was a priceless scene and Chris wished for once that he had a camera.

Logan looked up. 'Please tell me that these are not some poor souls who have been cursed.'

'Don't worry, they're just toys,' said Chris.

'Toys?' Such good craftsmanship is wasted on toys.' Logan replied.

'Never mind them, I want you to change into these clothes, I'll explain why later.' Chris handed them to Logan who inspected the jeans with puzzlement.

'Put them on like breeches,' explained Chris, showing the jeans that he was wearing as an example. 'And hide your Castellion clothes and things under that sleeping bag. I'll wait outside until you've finished.'

Chris stood by the side of the shed, out of view from the house. He couldn't afford any chances of being seen by his mum. There was a lot of huffing and puffing coming from Logan followed by a period of silence which prompted Chris to knock on the door.

'Can I come in?' he asked, slowly opening the door.

'I do not understand the purpose of these breeches,' said Logan.

Chris stepped inside and nearly howled with laughter. 'You've got them on back to front, take them off and turn them around,' he instructed as he stepped outside once more, shaking his head.

A few minutes later and with a little help from Chris, Logan stood dressed in twenty-first century attire. Chris had demonstrated how to do up the zip on the jeans and had laced the trainers up for him. The clothes couldn't have fitted him better. However, the trainers took Logan a while to get used to and Chris had to march him up and down the shed a dozen or so times before he stopped walking like a bow-legged duck.

Finally, Chris looked Logan up and down, noticing that the mark on Logan's forehead had also disappeared. 'Apart from the eye patch and the scar, you don't look too bad,' observed Chris. 'I don't think that anyone will bother you though. Which is just as well I guess. Come on, we've got some shopping to do.'

'Shopping?' repeated Logan.

'Yes, we're going to buy some supplies and I need you

to be there as a responsible adult, but I have a feeling that anyone who sees you might have doubts about that!'

Chris stepped out of the shed and crept over to the kitchen window, checking that his mum was nowhere to be seen. He turned to Logan.

'Now, stay with me. No matter what you see, it won't hurt you. It's all normal for this world. There'll be lots of noisy cars and people. Don't talk to anyone unless I tell you to. Do you understand?'

'I would feel safer if I brought my whip and daggers,' said Logan.

'Trust me, you won't need them,' said Chris. 'Now follow me.'

Chris took them both up the side of the house and out onto the main road where Logan's first experience of a large lorry thundering along resulted in him grabbing Chris and throwing the both of them through a hedge and into the park.

'Right,' said Chris as he pushed himself out from Logan's protective arm. 'I can see that this is going to take a while.'

Chris led him to a bench by the bandstand where they sat for a while and he educated Logan about roads and traffic, especially large lorries. Logan listened intently, then he turned his head in awe as a green-keeper motored by, riding a large lawnmower.

'Look at me,' instructed Chris. 'I don't know how long we have to get back to Castellion and whether we'll be in time or not to save our friends but the quicker we do this the better. You can ask me questions later, but for now it's best that you try not to take too much in of what you see and hear. There are things in my world that don't belong in yours.'

'What exactly are we here to do?' asked Logan.

'We're going to a shop to buy some fireworks.'

'You have to go to a shop to buy your fire and make it work?' Logan asked, wide eyed.

'No. These things shoot up into the sky and make lots of coloured lights and loud noises,' explained Chris.

'Ah! Like dragons. We're going to buy some more dragons,' Logan said, smiling with satisfaction.

'Sort of,' said Chris. 'Look, I need you with me because they won't sell these things to children of my age. They'll only sell them to an adult or, someone who looks over eighteen, so it's really important that I give you the money and you pay for them. I'll pick what we need but you really have to keep quiet and do as I say. Now, here's some money, put it into your pocket and look after it.'

Logan looked at the bundle of notes and coins that he was handed, then stuffed them into his jeans pocket as directed.

Chris looked at his watch. 8.50.

'Right, we'll cut across the park, it'll keep us off the main road for a start. Keep your head down and follow me. If anyone even tries to talk to you, just smile at them, that should do it,' said Chris.

Twelve minutes later, they were standing outside 'Big Bang', a party shop that specialised in fancy dress costume hire and also sold fireworks all year round.

'Okay,' said Chris. 'We're going to walk across to the firework counter and I'm going to call you "Uncle"

Logan, just to make sure that the assistant understands that we're together. Then, I'm going to pick out half a dozen fireworks. Let me do the talking, all you have to do is give the guy the money. Got it?'

'Yes,' said Logan, putting his hand in his pocket. 'I have got it here.'

'I mean, do you understand?' said Chris.

'I understand many things,' replied Logan.

'Never mind. I just hope this works,' prayed Chris as he pushed open the shop door and they both walked in.

Later that day, at his local pub, the shopkeeper regaled his encounter with Logan to his mates. 'The guy was a cross between a Hell's Angel and a hippie, over six foot tall, long greasy black hair, scar across his face with a weird eye patch on, but the most intimidating thing was that he didn't stop smiling at me, and as he left he said. "I am a free man. Thank you for your dragons."

Chris managed to get them both back to the shed without incident, however, on checking the kitchen for his mother's whereabouts, he found a note that simply read:

I've gone shopping. Back before eleven. The TV is out of bounds, so is the computer and you're definitely grounded.

He couldn't stop himself from turning the note over and writing on the back:

Sorry mum, be back soon. Gone to save the world – theirs, not ours.

261

Back in the shed they both changed out of their clothes, Chris hiding them under a dusty workbench as they put on their Castellion attire. While he was in the kitchen, Chris had grabbed them both a couple of drinks, some crisps and a Mars bar each which they had consumed quickly, Logan reacting to the chocolate in much the same way as Sir Peacealot had. Chris used some old newspapers that were stored in the shed to wrap up the large rockets that they had bought and he rolled them up into his sleeping bag, making a secure bundle, tying it up with a ball of twine that he had found. Once they where ready, they made their way back down to the orchard and to the place where they had appeared. Chris checked his watch again. It was now 10.35.

'Okay,' he said nervously, drawing his short sword. 'If we hang on to each other, with the bundle between us, we shouldn't lose it and we'll get back together. Are you ready?'

'If it means riding through the stars again to save Castellion, then I would do it a hundred times over,' said Logan. 'Yes, I'm ready. Take me home.'

Chris plunged the sword into the ground and the now familiar sensation pulsed through his body. He gripped Logan and felt Logan's arms flex around his shoulders as they plunged, headfirst, into the swirling light that engulfed them.

18

The Blackwater

'I think that I'm getting used to this,' said Frog as he opened his eyes and stared up into the dark folds of the pavilion. The wind was still howling outside and buffeting the sides of the tent. He looked around. Sir Peacealot, who had decided to remain and wait in hope for their return, was getting to his feet and Logan was just sitting up, shaking his head in an effort to clear his thoughts.

'I don't think that I could ever get used to doing that,' he said.

Frog looked at his watch. 10.36.

'How long have we been gone?' he asked Sir Peacealot.

'I cannot be exact, but my reckoning is about two hours.'

'Where are the others?' asked Logan.

'They have been moving our people back to the foot of the hills, ready to take flight if we are overrun. This weather has not reached the other side of the hills where all of the horses are stationed, it is from there that we will organise our retreat to Castellion Stronghold,' said Sir Peacealot.

FROG

'We'd better go and find the others,' said Frog. 'And you'll need to bring that.' He indicated to his bundled up sleeping bag lying on the floor.

As he pushed open the flap, the blizzard of hail and freezing conditions greeted him, the vicious wind piercing his clothes and chilling his bones in an instant. They made their way to the groups of Rangers, Maids and bowmen, all wrapped in as many layers of clothing and cloaks as was practical for fighting in, but Frog could see that they were still desperately trying to keep warm blood circulating through their bodies. Eventually they joined one of the groups where Lady Dawnstar was briefing some of the commanders. On seeing Frog she broke off from her conversation and wrapped a friendly arm around him.

'I'm so glad to see that you've made it back to us, you too, Logan,' she shouted over the wind. 'Can you tell us what it was all about?'

'Yes, but first of all, where's Fixer and Ginger?' asked Frog.

'I've sent them back over the hill in readiness of our retreat. It's no use putting them in further unnecessary danger,' explained Lady Dawnstar.

'I know that Fixer has her own tinder box, but how many others have one?' asked Frog.

'All Rangers carry their own flint and steel,' said Logan.

'Good, we need twelve people, six with flints, and six of the best bowmen,' said Frog.

'You still haven't told us what this is about,' said Lady Dawnstar.

'I need you to do everything I say, we will only get

264

one chance at this and if it works, the Hidden People and the Frozen Wastes will be history.'

They gathered closer around him, listening to every word as he revealed his plan.

Logan had arranged for eight Rangers and six Bowmen to meet with himself and Frog in one of the pavilions, along with Lady Dawnstar and Sir Peacealot.

Frog had already taken the stick out of one of the rockets and he carefully handed the colourful cylinder to one of the Bowmen and asked him whether, if it were attached to an arrow, it would be possible to fire it into the air. The bowman weighed it in his hand and held it against his longbow. He passed it around to his fellow bowmen and after a general discussion they agreed that, despite its bulk, they were confident that they would be able to fire it quite a distance. They would, however, need to make their arrows twice the usual length.

Frog repeated his plan to them. The Blackwater would burn easily once a blazing flare made contact with it, the surface fumes would be enough to ignite it and spread the flames quickly. However, the rockets needed to explode before they hit the Blackwater so that the fuses would not be smothered by the oil. He was sure that the fuses would burn strong enough in the air and wouldn't be put out by the wind and sleet as they travelled to their target. He also told them clearly that they stood the chance of being badly burned if they fired the rockets too late.

'What we're doing is really dangerous. Because of what's in them, these things can do serious damage,' he pointed out.

'What is in the coloured cylinders?' asked a Ranger.

'Fiery dragons!' said Logan. 'So make sure that you let them fly.'

The bowmen looked at the pile of rockets and took a step back.

'It's all right, they're on our side. You've just got to release them,' said Frog.

It took the bowmen a short while to collect suitable lengths of wood from their stock and fashion the long arrows. Frog watched, amazed as they showed the craft and skill of master bowmen. The rockets were then tied firmly to the arrows.

The plan was to fire one rocket into the sky so that they could see as much of the battlefield as possible when it exploded. This would be the signal for the other bowmen to fire their rockets out in different directions, as low as possible so that they would go off above the ground and ignite the Blackwater. It would need two people to light the blue touchpapers, one to shield them from the wind, the other to ignite them with a spark. The bowmen had to get their rockets set on to their bows quickly and wait for the yellow flare to burn. This, he emphasised, was when it was most dangerous because the rocket would be within seconds of exploding and releasing the 'dragons' as Logan had put it. The timing was crucial. They must pick their distance quickly and accurately and send their arrow and the rocket swiftly on its way. As soon as they had done so, they needed to run for the safety of the hills, far enough away from the Blackwater which, hope-fully, would ignite and turn the whole valley and plain into a sea of boiling flames.

A bowman asked Frog how he knew that this would all work.

'I don't,' replied Frog. 'But it's all we've got.'

They moved to the edge of the Blackwater and spread out into groups of three, Logan and five of the Rangers, ready with their flints. Lady Dawnstar, Frog and Sir Peacealot stood alongside with the rest of the Rangers, ready to shield the rockets with their cloaks.

Don't try this at home,' Frog mentally reminded himself.

The wind, as if sensing their plans, suddenly turned and swept down from the hills behind them in an attempt to push them out into the Blackwater.

'Now!' shouted Logan. 'The wind is behind us, it will help send the arrows on their way.'

The bowman held the arrow down and Frog wrapped his cloak around the crouching Logan and the rocket. With a sudden flash, the touchpaper ignited, sending yellow sparks out and nearly setting light to all three of them. Quickly the bowman raised the blazing flare, pulled back on the bowstring and sent it soaring into the sleet-filled sky The orange glow disappeared and was extinguished from sight.

Disappointed, Frog turned to Logan. 'Let's hope that one of the others has better luck,' he said. 'Let's get to the next bowman ...'

He was cut off by a series of muffled explosions and blinding flashes which fell earthward and gave glimpses of a landscape that was filled with an advancing swarm of frozen figures. They were seconds from being overrun by the massed legions of the Hidden People.

Logan pulled up the end of his cloak and pushed it into Frog's hand. 'Keep hold of that!' he shouted. 'Run!'

An orange flare shot out to the right of them then, another to their left. They put their heads down and moved forwards and had only gone a few steps when a white curtain of wind hit Frog and knocked him sideways, causing him to stumbled and fall, the rock-hard ground cutting into his knees, his hand losing its grip on Logan's cloak. Frog looked up and caught a last glimpse of Logan's grey shape fading into the swirling gloom. He tried to call out, but his voice was lost in the howling wind. Trying to stand, he slipped again, his legs numb with cold and pain. The wind whipped at him, blowing back his hood and tearing away his cloth mask, pellets of hail struck his exposed face drawing pinpricks of blood which froze on his skin.

Two more rockets streaked out into the storm.

'*I'm either going to freeze or be burnt to death. It's not supposed to end like this,*' he told himself, bringing his arm up for protection. '*I don't want to die, not here, not yet.*' He lay down on his side, curled up into a ball and closed his eyes.

'*I'll wake up in a minute and everything will be all right. It'll be just like that film,* The Wizard of Oz. *I'll wake up at home, in bed.*'

Logan was scrambling up and away from the valley, the force of the storm weakening as he got to the higher ground. He was greeted by rows of worried faces standing at the top of the ridge, Fixer and Ginger among them.

'Where are the others?' asked Fixer.

'They should be right behind me,' replied Logan as he joined them.

Lady Dawnstar and Sir Peacealot, along with the other Rangers and bowmen gradually clambered up the slopes and formed a group together.

'Where's Frog?' asked Ginger. 'What's happened to Frog?'

'He was right behind me,' said Logan.

'You mean that you didn't make sure he was with you, that he was safe?' shouted Lady Dawnstar, angrily.

The colour drained from Logan's face. 'He was there, I swear he was right behind me. He had hold of my cloak, I felt him pulling at it as we climbed.'

'Well, he's not here. He's down in that hell hole, freezing to death,' said Lady Dawnstar. 'And I'm not going to let that happen to him.' She stepped forward, but Logan stopped her.

'I lost him. I'll find him,' he said sternly, turning back.

There was a rumble from the swirling storm that covered the valley and the Blackwater plain below them. In the distance they saw coloured stars, shooting up into the sky. Then more, this time from the left and right of the vale. They saw the white mass turn orange and then a blood-red carpet swept out in all directions, back towards the mountains, out across the expanse, forwards and towards them. The storm gave way to a moving sea of flames that seemed to lick at the very sky itself. A wave of heat hit them, causing their wet clothes to steam and hang heavily on them.

Lady Dawnstar turned to Sir Peacealot.

'Can you sense him?'

'Nothing,' he replied

'Nor I. Just a cold emptiness,' she said, bowing her head and gathering her arms around Fixer and Ginger.

Logan collapsed to his knees, striking his fists into the ground with anguish and remorse. The others looked out onto the devastation, a burning, smoking, steaming hell on earth for as far as they could see. Nothing, human or otherwise, could survive the ferocity of the destruction. The Blackwater had risen and Frog had released its awesome power. There was no victory in their eyes, only a sense of loss which engulfed them all as they realised what had happened.

19

Lord Maelstrom

'As I have put out the sun, I will also snuff out the light of Castellion. Soon the Darkness will be complete, frozen across this world for eternity.'

Lord Maelstrom's voice seemed to come out of the very ground. It boomed through the thick black air and resonated through their bodies. The men and women of the southern army fell to their knees, their courage smothered by doubt and fear.

'Know my power and surrender to me,' continued the voice.

Even the creatures and wolves of his army cowered in fear as the air was filled with an unhealthy orange light which spread out from the southern sky. Black shapes swarmed around a burning object, growing in size as it approached. As it drew ever nearer, its detail became clear and terrible. Black dragons flapped their leathery wings in escort around a chariot of fire pulled by two more of the great beasts, their eyes burning a deep red, great chains lashed around their scaly necks as reins. Standing in the chariot was the formidable figure of Lord Maelstrom.

His tall, wiry frame was clothed in a sickly green

material that glistened. The cloak shifted in the heat of the flames which danced and licked at him but did not burn or scorch him. With one hand he swept back his hood and revealed the skeletal features of his face. The skin was tight and pale, his eyes were white with black pupils. Strands of long silver-grey hair hung down in clumps, the bald patches between revealing rune signs, tattooed into his scalp.

'Your king is dead,' he announced, pointing to the body of King Hector which was now lying on the ground with Gizmo kneeling over it.

'I will claim his body and soul as a testament to my victory.'

Gizmo stood back and the king's body rose slowly into the air until it was floating at head height. Then, a golden glow surrounded it, the brightness turning it transparent until it simply and quietly disappeared.

Lord Maelstrom's face filled with fury.

'You dare to rob me of my prize? You have interfered for the last time, you meddling wizard.'

Two black dragons opened their mouths and flames streaked towards Gizmo, who quickly pulled his silver cane from his robes. With it, he drew a circle in the air and a blue translucent orb formed itself over and around him. The flames bounced off and were extinguished by the orb's protective shell.

'Do you still think that you can save this miserable world and prevent me from crossing the Dimensions?' hissed Lord Maelstrom.

'While I still breathe and while the light of Castellion still shines through myself and the Chosen, we will not bow down to you,' replied the wizard.

'One by one, the Chosen will fall, two are gone already, the light that you speak of is dim. Do you not see your army already bows down in my presence?' mocked Lord Maelstrom.

'They may falter, but their pride will never allow them to surrender. Their king may be dead but their fight is for their future, their freedom, their world.' Gizmo turned and addressed the army. 'Is that not so? Is the Light of Castellion not alive in you all?'

Those that had cowered, those that had bowed their heads in fear, rose up and with them a new strength flooded through their ranks. As they stood proud they banged their swords on their shields and stamped the ground in resounding acknowledgement of this new-found strength and in defiance of their enemy.

'Fools!' thundered Lord Maelstrom. 'Look to the north and behold your final downfall.'

Gizmo turned his face northward and the sea of faces behind him did likewise.

Silhouetted against the orange horizon, growing ever closer, was the unmistakable shape of a dragon, one of Lord Maelstrom's black and corrupted instruments. The speed of its arrival was unnatural and within seconds a human form was recognisable, hanging limply from the creature's claws. As it approached Lord Maelstrom, the flames on the chariot were extinguished and the dragon hovered overhead, finally dropping its ragged cargo into the chariot alongside the Dark Lord.

Gizmo already knew who the figure was and even though he did not show it, he knew that now there was little hope left for the future of Castellion and the Dimensions.

'I could have easily let him die. But it would make this useless,' said Lord Maelstrom, holding out the Rune Stone. 'Without his blood to soak it in, I would not achieve the ability to cross over the Dimensions and conquer them at my leisure.'

With his other hand, he reached down and lifted up the figure, holding it by the scruff of its sodden and filthy cloak.

Lord Maelstrom's mouth split open revealing rows of sharp and broken teeth in a vicious grin of triumph.

'Behold, my victory. You shall witness the joining of his blood and the Rune Stone. All armies shall fall before me. And you, feeble Guardian, shall perish with a final vision of his death in your eyes.'

Gizmo looked up, helpless, at the limp and ragged body in the grip of Lord Maelstrom.

Frog's eyes slowly opened and stared back at the wizard.

274

20

Into Lord Maelstrom's Hands

As Frog huddled on the ground, he hoped that the nightmare would end and he waited for a quick release. He felt the air around him turning warmer, the rush of wind buffeting him and he braced himself for the furnace of the fiery Blackwater to burn him to cinders.

Instead, he felt himself being grabbed roughly by the shoulders and hoisted into the air. He watched the ground fall away beneath him as it turned into a sea of boiling flames. He looked up to see that his rescuer was a great, black dragon and he opened up his mind to communicate with the creature and thank him.

A hateful, hissing voice invaded his mind.

'Do not offer me thanks, you little worm, for I am your doom. My master, Lord Maelstrom, tasked me with your capture. If it had been left to me, you would be roasting in flames. A fate that I take great pleasure to exact on all humans when I am able.'

As if to emphasise the fact, the dragon let two streams of liquid flame escape from its nostrils.

Frog struggled even though they were now high above the black clouds.

'Let me go!' he screamed, both mentally and verbally.

'I am tasked with delivering you alive, but I can inflict much pain on you should you give me cause. So keep still and do not bother me,' came the voice, and a searing pain shot through Frog's shoulders as the dragon tightened his claws.

Frog, aware of the dangers, closed his mind to the dragon and mentally reached out to the others, the Chosen. Despite his best efforts, he could feel nothing, no form of response. Then, to his dismay, the awful thoughts of the dragon cut into his senses.

'You are dead to them, you cannot connect with them. I will ensure that none of your thoughts reach out. All that they will feel is a cold empty space if they should reach out for you. You are a mere human and your skills are no match for one such as I. Now, be still lest I flex my claws again on your flesh.'

Frog closed his mind. He thought of his mother, and of his father, his friends back home, and he filled his mind with images of his other world. Soaking in the pleasures and memories, he calmly spoke to himself, searching for a way to give him the strength to survive.

'A mere human?' he thought. *'I'll show you what a mere human can do.'*

No response came from the dragon, such was the enduring strength of the boy Chris, who survived inside the boy who had become Frog.

He focused his mind further as he swung helpless in the dragon's grip. He thought of what he carried on himself. He still had his sword and the talisman around his neck. He slipped his hand into the pouch at his waist and his fingers found the glass whistle that Lady Dawnstar had given him, many months before. He also found the leaves that Fixer had given him. Carefully he placed one in his mouth and sucked in the sharp flavour, letting it spread through his body, its powers building his strength, restoring his health, healing his wounds.

Very soon they were descending through the pale orange clouds and as they emerged he viewed the great armies, spread out across the land below. He saw other black dragons, hovering menacingly in the sky, and a blue orb containing the wizard, floating defiantly in front of a flaming chariot, which contained Lord Maelstrom.

Frog felt a dark probing presence, searching for his thoughts. Quickly he focused on his innermost and secret memories, drawing a protective barrier around his mind, creating a void. As he was carried ever closer to Lord Maelstrom, he closed his eyes and hung limply from the dragon's grasp, waiting for the right moment. A plan was forming in the deepest recess of his brain.

He was dropped into the chariot and heard Lord Maelstrom announcing his intentions and then a rough hand gripped his cloak and raised him from the floor of the chariot.

Frog's movements were swift and sure. He opened his eyes and let his thoughts flow out to the wizard, and at the same time he pulled out his sword and plunged it into Lord Maelstrom's arm. A scream of rage and agony tore through the air. As Frog was dropped back into the chariot, he grabbed the Rune Stone from Lord Maelstrom's hand and threw it towards the wizard. Not waiting to see if it was caught, he reached for two things. First, the talisman. Its Magik instantly made him invisible. Secondly, he raised the small glass whistle to his lips and blew with all his might. There was no sound, but Frog thought that he saw a transparent ripple flow out through the air.

His senses were brought back into focus as the chariot rocked violently. Lord Maelstrom lashed out and tried desperately to remove the sword which had become luminescent in his arm. His voice rising to piercing shrieks, he was shouting in a strange language, trying to summon the darkest of powers to his aid. Frog looked over the side of the chariot. He was maybe five or six metres from the ground. He hesitated to jump when his mind was made up for him. One of the dragons reared up, hissing and growling. Its hind legs caught the chariot and tipped it sideways.

A short, squat creature standing beneath the chariot had a surprising end to its life as its neck was broken by an invisible weight that landed on it, seemingly from nowhere.

Frog rolled to one side, slightly winded but otherwise unhurt. He found himself in the front lines of Lord Maelstrom's army, a collection of twisted and ugly animals that were either reptilian or monkey-like in appearance. He rose up and charged forward towards the blue haze that surrounded the wizard. Astonished creatures were knocked sideways by an unseen force as he pushed and shoved himself through them until at last he was racing across the short, open space between the armies and found sanctuary amongst the comparative safety of some of

Castellion's knights. Once there, he turned and looked back.

Lord Maelstrom was now standing on the ground. The luminescence from the sword had spread up his arm and into part of his face. The chariot was in pieces, the two dragons that had pulled it snapped and clawed at each other, causing chaos around them. Lord Maelstrom was facing Gizmo who was now a few metres in front of him, the orb pulsing blue, flashing streaks of lightning, his robes rippling with static. Gizmo held the Rune Stone aloft and Frog heard his name being called.

Frog let go of the talisman. Knights stood back in surprise and wonder as he became visible. He ran to the wizard, who reached out and took Frog by the hand. The orb extended its light around him, his clothes and hair crackled in the static. Lord Maelstrom raised his free arm upwards and a bolt of lightning streaked down from the orange-black clouds, connecting with his fist. His eyes grew wide with madness and his face contorted in fury.

'Kill them!' Destroy them all!' he screamed.

His army rose into action with a frenzy, surging forwards. The black dragons swooped down, snorting flames. As one, Castellion's army raised its shields and swords, arrows rained from its archers into the oncoming foe and the final bloody battle for Castellion's future ignited into action.

Lord Maelstrom's body was gradually becoming transparent. It seemed that pieces of him were fading, melting away.

'I will not be defeated. I will take my revenge!' he raged.

279

He brought his arm forward, his fingers out-stretched, pointing at Frog. A lightning bolt snaked forward as Gizmo brought Frog's hand into contact with the Rune Stone.

'Behold, your end is nigh. Your powers came from the Rune and so they shall return,' commanded Gizmo.

The lightning diverted away from Frog and struck the Stone. A streak of raw energy began stretching and sucking Lord Maelstrom along its blue-white vein and into the core of the Rune Stone itself until, finally, a flash drew the last particle of him in and the Rune Stone returned to its dark, solid shape.

Frog's sword hovered in the air before them.

'Take it, young Frog. It is yours, it will always be yours to keep and guard,' said Gizmo.

Frog reached out and gripped the sword by the handle. It was surprisingly cool and the metal blade now looked plain and clear. More and more of Castellion's fighting men and women made their way past them, eager to join the battle. Frog could see in their faces that they were exhausted but their pride and courage was driving them forwards.

'What now?' Frog asked.

'Sheath that sword, this battle is not for you,' said Gizmo.

Frog did as he was told.

'What will you do with that?' Frog asked, pointing at the Rune Stone.

'It will be returned to its rightful place, all in good time,' said Gizmo as he concealed it in the folds of his robes. 'Now, we need to see how we fare.'

The orb carried them high above the armies and

allowed them to survey the situation. Castellion's army would progress well in some areas, but as soon as they made ground and pushed the enemy back, the great black dragons swooped down and scorched the earth, killing many fighters at a time. Then the swarms of dark creatures and wolves would surge forward again and retake the ground.

'They can't keep this up for much longer, their strength is running out. Can't you help them?' pleaded Frog.

'The best of my Magik is spent. Most of my energy is keeping us protected in the orb. Even I cannot make any difference, the fight is spread over such a large area, the dragons are too powerful,' explained Gizmo.

As Frog looked out, he saw a new threat approaching from the now grey dawn of the eastern sky. A dark cloud was surging towards them, its shape billowing and shifting as it moved.

'Oh, no! Not more of them?' he cried. 'Our army won't be able to fight this off .'

'They won't have to,' said Gizmo.

'What do you mean?' said Frog.

'You called them,' said Gizmo.

'Called who?' asked Frog.

'The Bird Men and their flocks.'

The dragons were so busy, burning and terrorising, that they had no idea of what hit them.

In their feathered clothes and hanging in harnesses from the talons of great birds, the Bird Men swung through the air. They blew into their noiseless, glass whistles, giving unheard commands, directing the birds silently but with deadly effect. Great clouds of smaller birds swarmed around each dragon, smothering its wings while hawks attacked their eyes, pecking and clawing them out, until, in the end, the blinded beasts plummeted to the ground to be immediately set upon by great white eagles that tore at the leathery wings. Finally Castellion's knights were able to move in and put a swift end to the now wretched dragons.

This was when the army that was Lord Maelstrom's broke its ranks and ran, scattering away as fast as it could, with Castellion's army chasing at its heels, cutting creatures down as they ran, showing no mercy but taking no pleasure.

The sky began to clear, the black and grey clouds shrinking away as the sun lifted itself over a clear horizon, its warmth energising Castellion's brave fighters.

'The commanders will reorganise their people now and put this battle to an end,' said Gizmo. 'We must return to Castellion Stronghold, there is still much to be done.'

The orb brought them back to the ground and faded around them. Frog noticed that the wizard looked older; his eyes were not as bright, his movements slow and deliberate.

'Are you all right?' asked Frog with concern.

'Tired. I have used up much of my strength and energy and this has been an immeasurable test for me. Even so, it was an even greater test for you. But as it was foretold, your bravery brought the final defeat of Lord Maelstrom.'

'I don't think that I was brave.' said Frog. 'I just wanted to survive.'

Gizmo put his arm around Frog's shoulders as they made their way back to the encampment. Here, Gizmo found a young squire tending to some horses and sent him in search of some clean clothes for Frog. The squire shortly returned with a bundle wrapped in a cloak and handed it to Frog.

'I know who you are,' said the squire. 'You're the one they call Frog. You were brought here by the black dragon and it was you who killed Lord Maelstrom. You saved us all.'

'Don't believe everything you hear,' said Frog, glancing at Gizmo. 'Things are not always what they seem. It took a wizard to save you, I just did my bit.'

'Well, thank you anyway,' said the squire excitedly. 'I've managed to get you some clean clothes although I'm sorry if they're a bit big.'

'Thank you,' said Frog. 'You're a better squire than I could ever be.'

The young squire smiled at Frog, bowed and ran off towards the scene of the battle.

After Frog had washed in some cold water and changed into the clean, but oversized, garments, he joined Gizmo who had saddled up his horse and was mounted, ready to ride. The wizard couldn't help but laugh as he saw Frog approaching, his tunic hanging over his knees and his cloak dragging on the ground.

'I feel a right twit,' said Frog.

'You look every bit the hero to me,' said Gizmo. 'Now, climb up with me, we have a long ride together. As we travel, you can tell me about the events in the north and how our companions have fared.'

He gently pulled back the reins and the horse broke into a gallop, carrying them with ease, chasing the shadows of the rising sun.

21

Don't Call Me Little

The army of the north had started their journey back towards Castellion Stronghold, leaving the burning Blackwater plains behind them. The smoke was visible for miles and the flames could be seen on the horizon for many nights to come. The weather had suddenly changed after the firestorm had exploded into its raging inferno and the wind had dropped to a calm breeze with the hail and sleet melting into a fine mist before stopping altogether. The sky was a pale pre-dawn colour, the dark clouds had begun to dissolve and were replaced by columns of acrid smoke.

The intense heat of the fire turned the soil into a coarse, grey sand and for several months afterwards it would remain warm to the touch. The Frozen Wastes were pushed back to the mountain ranges and if any of the Hidden People survived, they were never seen again.

Sir Peacealot and Lady Dawnstar rode on horses at the head of the returning army with Fixer and Ginger sharing their mounts, clinging on as much for comfort as they did for safety. Logan scouted ahead with some of his Rangers, looking for any dangers or unfriendly forces that might be lying in wait for them.

There was a subdued atmosphere even though the battle had been won. For some, the cost had been heavy, particularly as many of the Maids, Rangers and bowmen had fallen victim to the Hidden People's touch and had been turned into the frozen dead. Their friends and comrades were forced to destroy them in order to survive themselves.

Fixer and Ginger had not spoken a word since the loss of Frog. Lady Dawnstar and Sir Peacealot had focused on briefing the remaining commanders and on organising the march home, the loss of both Frog and Sir Dragonslayer heavy on their minds.

The moment that Frog opened his mind to Gizmo and plunged his sword into Lord Maelstrom's arm, Lady Dawnstar raised her head as if jolted from sleep.

'Did you feel that?' she asked Sir Peacealot.

He looked at her, his expression searching for a meaning.

'I sense ... Can this be true?' he asked.

She smiled back at him. 'It is, I'm sure it's him. He's alive!' She dismounted and looked to the south. 'I don't know how, but he has survived and I sense that his thoughts are strong.' She paused and a frown appeared on her face. 'He's with the wizard and ... '

'Lord Maelstrom,' finished Sir Peacealot.

'What is it? What's going on?' asked Ginger.

'It's Frog. He's alive,' said Lady Dawnstar.

'How do you know? How can you be so sure?' asked Fixer.

'Trust us, we know,' assured Sir Peacealot. 'But he's involved in something much more dangerous than we've seen here.'

Logan thundered towards them on his horse.
'Can this be true? Do I really sense him?' His face
was more alive than it had been since they left the
Blackwater.
'We feel his thoughts too,' confirmed Sir Peacealot.
'But there is still great danger, we must ride to
Castellion Stronghold.'
Lady Dawnstar climbed back onto her horse, nearly
sending Fixer flying in her haste. She turned to face
the commanders.
'Sound the horns, we may still sweeten our victory.
Gather your strongest and most able fighters, give
them the freshest horses, we form a cavalry to ride
with speed, for there is other work to do, our comrades
in the south need us.'

The scene at Castellion Stronghold was one of siege.
Large packs of wolves surrounded the castle and great
war engines and catapults threatened the towers and
buttresses of the outer walls.
The great wolf, Fangmaster, had convinced Lord
Maelstrom to let him take an army to encircle and cut
off Castellion Stronghold in preparation for his arrival
and Lord Maelstrom in his greed for victory had sent
the wolf and hundreds of his hordes through the
passages and canyons of the west, to execute the plan.
Fangmaster's orders were to surround the great
fortress and wait, but Fangmaster had other ideas. He
wanted the victory and the spoils for himself. As far as
he and his brethren were concerned the only good
human was a dead human. Lord Maelstrom's plans to
drain his enemies' souls and add them to his army,

building up an unconquerable force, were, as far as Fangmaster was concerned, a waste of a good killing opportunity. They enjoyed the sport of hunting the humans down, feasting on their blood and tearing down their homes and fortresses. That's what he and his wolf packs lived for. Besides, when Lord Maelstrom turned up to the open gates of Castellion Stronghold with all resistance conquered, he would thank the wolf and reward him.

The task, however, was not going as easily as he had expected. Contrary to what he had thought, a strong garrison had been left to defend and protect the Stronghold. They had been there for many days now and had been bombarding the occupants with the remains of the cattle and sheep that had been left to graze in the surrounding fields and subsequently slaughtered by the wolves. Instead of breaking the spirits of those inside the Stronghold, the result was both surprising and infuriating to Fangmaster. Every time a salvo of carcasses was sent flying over the walls there was a round of jeering and taunting from the battlements.

'Thanks for the fresh supplies.'

'Any chance that you could pick us some vegetables as well?'

'Sorry we can't invite you to dinner.'

This was followed by howls of laughter from the soldiers and guards.

'I want those doors burnt down and the Stronghold taken, by tomorrow's dawn,' Fangmaster snarled at his captains. 'I don't care how you do it, but if you fail, it'll be your throats that I'll be ripping out!'

Previous attacks on the walls had resulted in the wolves' huge war towers being set alight by an onslaught of burning arrows, the great charred remains collapsing into useless heaps. The plan now was to push one of these towers up to and against the great wooden portcullis and entrance doors. If the tower was set alight in the same manner, the doors would surely burn as well. If not, they would use the tower to scale the battlements and invade the Stronghold.

A large wooden assault tower was brought up and positioned, ready to be pushed straight at the stronghold doors. Fangmaster had his captains assemble countless wolves ready to throw their weight at the tower. On his command, they would move in behind it and drive it forward to its goal. Although speed was of the essence, Fangmaster was prepared to sacrifice as many wolves as it took to carry out his plan. Such was his ruthless and barbaric nature.

They waited until darkness fell and then, with a chorus of howls, the packs moved in, shoving and heaving the creaking structure forwards. The castle troops had been watching and waiting and, with the sound of trumpets, ranks of archers let loose clouds of arrows down into the struggling creatures. As one fell another would quickly replace it until wolf trampled on wolf, the fallen bodies crushed by the surge of replacements until the wooden tower crashed against its target.

Still the arrows rained down and still the hoards moved forwards, clambering up the beams and struts, swarming towards the battlements. Then, in desperation, cauldrons of burning logs were tipped down onto the structure, setting light to wolves and wood alike until very soon the frame, portcullis and doors were ablaze.

The surviving wolves were called back to where Fangmaster watched the flames lick at the doors, the timber sparking and flaring.

'Call all of our packs back from around the stronghold, I want every wolf positioned here, ready to pour through the entrance when I give the order,' he growled.

'But we'll lose so many as they try to clamber through the still burning timbers,' pointed out another wolf.

'When the tower collapses in a burning heap, the soldiers will realise, too late, what is happening to their precious doors. They'll put the fires out, cooling the flames enough for us to clamber through. The doors will have been weakened and won't withstand the weight of our numbers. Look, the metal bolts and hinges already glow white-hot with the heat,' said Fangmaster.

He was right. Not long after the tower had folded in flames, the cauldrons appeared again at the battlements, but this time water poured down until the flames receded and clouds of steam concealed the wreckage.

'Now! Now! Now!' howled Fangmaster.

The gathered throng charged forwards, a filthy grey mass of yowling, baying fur. The billowing cloud concealed them as they collided with the scorched and weakened doors, row upon row of bodies, crushing against the wood until with a resounding *crack!* the great gates splintered apart, disintegrating and allowing the tide of savage animals to spill into the first courtyard.

The archers were ready and waiting, their commanders with foresight having organised them into position around the encircling and overlooking battlements. Before the first rows of tumbling, leaping creatures had a chance to assess their new surroundings, hissing swarms of arrows flew out and found their targets. Volley after volley was fired into the flood of wolves which refused to cease or falter. Some of the creatures were gaining ground, climbing over the heaped bodies to scale a flight of steps or to dart through a gap in the thinning barrage of arrows to find refuge in the stable buildings which were thankfully empty of any horses or ponies.

The commanders gave the order to fall back to the second battlements that protected the inner courtyards and gave access to the central halls and the heart of Castellion Stronghold. It was here that the families from the outlying villages, the elderly and the young, were now sheltered. Never before had the outer walls been breached and the commanders prepared their soldiers for hand-to-hand combat. All could see that the odds were against them and that they were vastly outnumbered, but they held their ground ready to fight to the end.

Two explosions resounded from outside the walls, the ground was rocked and the grey mass of wolves faltered, a sense of alarm spreading from their rearguard, the sound of trumpets rolled through the air and echoed around the inner walls, sending the wolves into a panic. Castellion's army leapt into action, attacking the wolves, forcing them to move back as gaps in their ranks opened up.

Outside the castle, Fangmaster was cursing his commanders as they joined the now disorganised and unruly mass of wolves, running in all directions, looking for an escape from the burning balls of flame that landed and exploded among them. In their panic many of them were driven into the path of the oncoming army of thundering horses and their riders, a cavalry of shining Maids of Steel and fearsome Rangers, bearing down at great speed, their swords high above their heads, the blades catching the rays of the now unveiled sun. Dawn had come quickly on this day and with its brightness came vengeance and retribution.

Frog stood on the hill, watching the action develop. Beside him, Gizmo was arcing his arm.

'I think that I can manage just one more,' he said as he released another fireball from his hand. As it flew into the sky, it streaked its way towards the now fleeing army of wolves. He sat down on the grass, wiping his hands in satisfaction.

'That's it, my friend. My powers are all but drained. I must take a nice long rest when this is finally over,' he said wearily.

Frog sat down beside him and placed a hand on the wizard's arm.

'Is this it?' Is the war with Lord Maelstrom really over?' he asked.

'It would appear that both the north and south have been saved, we just need to sort these wolves out, but apart from that, I don't think that there's anyone else left that will be capable of causing such trouble.'

'Where's Storm?' Frog asked with concern.

'I last saw him with the tail end of a Madbagger between his teeth, then a number of creatures closed in around him. I'm afraid that I was rather involved with Lord Maelstrom to see further. It's been a while, and I can only guess that he perished in the battle,' the wizard replied, sadly.

After a few minutes silence between them, Frog turned and looked at the wizard.

'Does this mean that I can go home?'

'Soon, my boy, soon. We just have one or two things to arrange, but, yes, your work here is done. We have much to thank you for.'

'It's not that I've had a choice. Although it has been a great adventure for me. Scary, but exciting,' said Frog.

The wizard turned to him. 'You've always had a choice, young Frog. You could have left us at any time and not come back.'

'I don't understand. How?' he asked.

'Free will. Had you closed your mind to us, had you refused to take up the task and the responsibility, then you would have crossed back through the Slipstream and into your world, even before you were given your sword,' explained Gizmo.

'What would have happened to Castellion?' asked Frog.

'I think it would have been a very different future for us all,' mused the wizard.

They both sat there, wizard and boy, watching the wolves as they were encircled by the defenders of

Castellion. Some leapt in attack and died, some turned on each other in bloody frustration, until eventually they cowered and grovelled in submission and surrendered.

'What will happen to them?' asked Frog.

'I'll put a restraining spell on them and they'll be made to collect and bury their dead. After that they'll be put to work repairing the damage that they've caused,' said Gizmo.

'But surely you'll never be able to set them free?' asked Frog.

'Things can change, young Frog, you never know. Someday we may be able to trust a wolf,' replied Gizmo.

'I wouldn't bet on it,' said a menacing voice behind them.

They both turned to see the tall and repulsive Fang-master, a wickedly sharp spear in his hands, its point only centimetres from the wizard.

'One twitch and I'll run you through old man,' he said menacingly.

'What do you want?' asked the wizard.

'You must have the Rune Stone. Give it to me.' He pressed the spear so that the metal blade was touching the wizard's throat.

Frog slowly slid his hand to the hilt of his sword.

'I wouldn't even try if I was you,' warned the wolf. 'Or I'll have you searching a *dead* wizard's robes for the Stone.'

Frog moved his hand away from the sword and Gizmo reached inside his robes and brought out the Rune Stone.

'Give it to me, now!' Fangmaster reached out and snatched it from the wizard's hand.

'Now, you, little boy. Come and stand in front of me,' he ordered.

Frog climbed to his feet and approached the wolf who, in a swift movement, dropped the spear and grabbed Frog, spinning him around so that his back was pressed against the wolf's stinking and matted chest. The crooked blade of a hunting knife appeared in his hand and came to rest at Frog's throat.

'Where that fool Maelstrom failed, I will succeed. At my hand, the blood of this little boy will be spilt onto the Stone. I will inherit the power!'

'Don't call me little!' shouted Frog and brought the heel of his boot down onto the wolf's bare foot with all his might. He felt the bones crack. The wolf emitted a ferocious howl and as his grasp relaxed, Frog twisted himself free and dived between the beast's legs, but not before the knife had sliced through the air and caught his hand, a cold tingling sensation searing through it.

The wolf spun around as Frog scrabbled backwards along the ground, trying to free his sword which had become caught up in his cloak.

'Enough!' screamed Fangmaster as he plunged the knife forwards.

Frog stared helplessly into the slavering grin of the wolf when, suddenly, it was gone. The long hairy arms dropped to the wolf's sides, the clawed hands released the knife and the Rune Stone, and they fell to the ground. The body stood headless and motionless for a second or so and then slowly crumpled sideways into a heap on the grass.

Frog looked up to see Sir Peacealot, Logan and Lady Dawnstar, astride their horses, her long sword stained with the wolf's blood. Then, from behind the horses, two figures ran out, shrieking and shouting with glee.

Ginger and Fixer fell on Frog, hugging and embracing him until his breath was taken away. He hugged them back with all his might, all three of them with unashamed tears of joy rolling down their cheeks.

Fixer was the first to notice the blood.

'You're hurt, you're bleeding!' she said in alarm.

Frog brought up his hand and held it out. Blood pooled in his palm and he noticed that his little finger was now a bloody stump.

'I hate blood,' he said. Then he fainted.

When the world came swimming back into view, he was propped up on Lady Dawnstar's lap, the sour taste of Logan's elixir on his lips.

'For someone who likes to live dangerously, it's a bit late to be afraid of blood,' she said, smiling.

'My hand?' said Frog, bringing it up to inspect it.

It was wrapped in some of the special leaves, bound up with a thin material that looked like cobwebs.

'Don't worry my boy, those leaves and my Magik will soon have it healed, although you'll have to make do in future minus most of your little finger. I'm afraid we couldn't find it, otherwise I'd have popped it back on for you,' said Gizmo.

While Frog recovered, they all sat and exchanged stories, filling in gaps for each other, sharing the loss of the king and of Sir Dragonslayer. Recounting the dangers and the victory.

And so it was, on that grassy hill, with a clear blue sky above them and a warm sun shining, that they stood reunited, holding hands in a circle. The wizard, Sir Peacealot, Lady Dawnstar, Logan, Fixer, Ginger and Frog.

The golden light returned, but this time it radiated from the Rune Stone that Gizmo had placed in the centre of their circle. Its brilliant tentacles reached out and touched their foreheads, bringing Ginger and Fixer into the Chosen. Anyone looking up from the vale below could have been forgiven for thinking that a second sun had risen over the hilltop.

22

10.38

Over the coming months, Castellion Stronghold was repaired and all of the valiant and brave survivors from Castellion's armies returned to their lives and homes scattered throughout the land. This was not before a mass victory celebration was held with great ceremony and procession, inside and outside the grounds of Castellion. The scene was very much the same as it had been during the gathering of the armies prior to the great battles. The meadows and plains outside the Stronghold were filled with tents, marquees and pavilions, the colours and ensigns of the knights and clansmen dominated by the emblem of Castellion, a pale blue background with a golden-rayed sun in the centre which seemed to radiate a sense of new-found security and strength.

Frog returned to his position with the other squires at the stables and on his return was overjoyed to find his horse, Thunder, in one of the stalls. He was well fed and nourished and Frog could find no evidence that he was any the worse for wear from his journey back to Castellion Stronghold, indeed all of the horses from the expedition had safely returned.

Frog, Ginger and Fixer had happily and proudly regaled the stable hands and young squires with their adventures but not until it was recognised that there were losses among them. Lofty and Snoop had perished in the confrontation with Lord Maelstrom – both had insisted on going to the front lines with their knights and they died carrying out their duties to the end. Ginger and Fixer were particularly sad at the news as they had grown up with the boys, and as a mark of respect, banners bearing the insignia of Lofty and Snoop's knights were hung on the stable doors.

Indeed, a ceremony was held to remember all of the fallen. Gizmo assembled the Chosen, gathering them together on the hill where Fangmaster had met his sudden and just end. In the centre of the hill, a deep, oval pit had been excavated, surrounded by colourful, roped garlands. From this point, the wizard's voice carried out to the assembled throng around him and in the fields below.

'There is no victory without sacrifice. We stand here today through our courage and belief, but those that are not with us gave their lives as forfeit, without question, without condition. On this hill will be erected a monument, not only to our fallen king but also to the lost squires, servants and stable hands, the clansmen and women of this realm. Over the coming days, a token of remembrance for each life will be put into this barrow and sealed beneath the monument. Today, we will place the first of many such items.'

He raised and presented King Hector's crown into the air for all to see and then gently dropped it into the pit. A dragon master approached and presented a delicately carved dragon broach to the assembly.

'The clasp of our lost dragon master, Sir Dragonslayer,' he announced, solemnly dropping it to join the crown.

A small procession of commanders from the ranks of Maids, Rangers and bowmen followed, each one presenting some item of a fallen comrade.

Over the next week or so, numerous friends and kinsmen of the fallen visited the barrow to place a personal article in respect and dedication.

Numerous banquets and celebrations followed and Frog, Ginger and Fixer attended as many as they could. They did so not because they were required, but as they had endured so much together, they wanted to experience the company and stories of those that they had not had the honour of fighting alongside.

It was on one such visit to a camp fire feast that some Rangers, who had been scouring the southern battlefields for lost companions, returned, their horses weary and their wagons dusty from the long journey.

They joined the gathering, eagerly helping themselves to food and drink, sharing news both sad and welcome. One of the Rangers approached the group that Frog was sitting with. He was carrying something, cradling it, wrapped up in his cloak.

'What's that you've got there?' asked a fellow Ranger.

'He's poorly hurt, I found him lying amongst a group of dead wolves, his fur all matted and caked with blood. How he got to be in such a place, I don't know. There's a long, deep gash to his side, how he's survived at all is a miracle.' The Ranger pulled back the cloak to reveal a weak and injured black cat.

'Storm!' shouted Frog.

'You know this animal?' asked the Ranger.

'He's the wizard's cat,' said Frog. 'We need to get him to the wizard. He'll be able to heal him.'

The Ranger carefully wrapped the cloak around Storm and handed him to Frog.

'I think that's a task for yourself,' said the Ranger. 'I'm not too sure if the wizard will take too kindly to me handing him his half-dead pet.'

Frog carried Storm to Gizmo, as quickly as his legs would carry him, shouting out the wizard's name in his mind, sending out images of Storm.

In less than an hour, Storm was stretched out in front of a roaring fire in the wizard's apartments, having been fed a concoction of raw meat and Magik by Gizmo.

'He'll live,' beamed Gizmo. 'Although I suspect he'll have to take on smaller prey in future and he may be a bit slower than he used to be.'

Frog knelt and ran a careful hand along the cat's fur. An unnaturally loud growl of pleasure escaped from Storm. Frog slowly pulled his hand away and stepped back.

'I don't think that I could ever get used to that,' he admitted.

The wizard was now facing Frog. He held a cloth bundle and a small carved wooden box.

Frog looked at the box. 'Are my things in there?'

'Yes.'

'And, are those my proper clothes?'

'Yes.'

'Is it time for me to go home?'

'Yes,' said Gizmo, smiling kindly. 'Follow me.'

The wizard took them down a long spiral staircase and along passageways and corridors until they emerged through a small door in the castle walls and out into the bright moonlight. The path that they took led them up to the now familiar hill, a newly-built, tall, golden obelisk at its summit.

Waiting in silence were Fixer, Ginger, Logan, Lady Dawnstar and Sir Peacealot.

Frog bit his lip and put on a brave face.

'We'll have to stop meeting like this, people will talk,' he said jokingly.

Five puzzled faces stared back at him.

'Frog-world humour,' explained the wizard.

'I'm not in a laughing mood,' said Fixer. 'I'm going to miss you. We're all going to miss you.' She let one small tear escape from the corner of her eye.

'Frog's time here is now fulfilled,' said Gizmo. 'He must return to his own world, his real life.'

'But why can't you stay? If time doesn't move in your world, then it doesn't matter how long you stay with us,' pleaded Ginger.

'Eventually, he will grow old enough that it will show when he returns. Nothing can stop him ageing, in either world, in any Dimension,' explained Gizmo. 'Besides, Frog has family, he has sacrificed more than enough time without them. His heart yearns for them.'

'I want to stay, but I must go home, can you understand that?' asked Frog.

Lady Dawnstar knelt in front of him. 'It is hard for

302

us to lose something precious. You have given us much more than friendship and you will remain with us, in our hearts and minds. You will not be forgotten.'

She leaned forward and kissed him on the cheek. This time, Frog didn't blush. He threw his arms around her and squeezed with all his might. After a few moments she gently pulled away and stood back.

Frog put his hand into his leather pouch. 'I'd better let you have this back,' he said holding out the glass whistle.

She folded his fingers over it. 'It's yours to keep,' she said.

Frog looked at Gizmo, who nodded in agreement.

Next, Logan placed his hands on Frog's shoulders. 'You'd make a good Ranger with a little more training,' he smiled. 'But as I won't have that pleasure, I've had this made for you. I'm sure with some practice, it will be useful, even in your strange world, which, by the way, was the scariest adventure that I've ever had, but it was worth it for the taste of your chocolate!'

He produced a small leather whip from his cape, presented it to Frog, stepped back and bowed.

Fixer and Ginger moved in front of Frog and without tears or sadness all three embraced each other.

'We haven't got anything to give you, I'm afraid,' said Ginger.

'Except our pledge, that should you ever need us, in this or any other world, we will find a way to reach you,' continued Fixer.

'Thank you,' said Frog. 'It goes without saying that I will gladly do the same for you.'

Sir Peacealot knelt, as Lady Dawnstar had, placed

303

one hand on Frog's shoulder and looked into his
eyes.

'You are a remarkable young man. You rose to every
challenge and accepted responsibility. Your courage
and friendship has been beyond value and I am proud
that you have been my squire. I will adopt your colours
and emblem in honour of our bond. You freed me and
brought me home and now it is time for us to free you
and send you home. Farewell, my young friend, and
thank you for bringing the Light that freed us from
evil.'

'Turn to me now, young Frog,' said the wizard. 'I give
you back what is rightly yours.' He handed Frog the
bundle and the small wooden box. 'Just whisper your
name to it and it will open and close at your will, this is
my gift to you. Take all that we have given you as a
testament to your valour. Now, draw your sword.'

With a shaky hand, Frog pulled the short sword
from its sheath. The blade was burning with the now
familiar blue and white light.

'Return the sword to the earth and take your journey
home,' instructed the wizard.

Frog took one last look at the six faces that now
encircled him, then he plunged the shining steel blade
into the ground.

This time, a curtain of light wrapped itself around
him and he was enveloped in a transparent beam. He
could still see the others, watching him as he was lifted
by a rush of air and up the narrow tube of light. As he
rose, the ground fell away into darkness and above him
he could see a small orange disc, growing ever closer,
ever larger, ever brighter. It wasn't long before he

realised that the disc was in fact the sun, its brightness reflecting on the light around him, turning it hues of gold and red. He closed his eyes against the glare, expecting to be thrust onward and upward when, suddenly, he was standing still and on solid ground. He felt his sword, still in his hand, but free of the earth. As he clutched at his bundle, he brought a hand up to shield his eyes as he tentatively opened them.

Dappled sunlight greeted him, a soft warm breeze shifted the leaves on the branches above him. Something moved against his leg and he looked down.

'Tabby!' he cried in excitement.

He dropped the bundle and sheathed his sword, sitting himself cross-legged on the ground and scooping the cat up on to his lap. He sat there hugging and stroking the purring animal as he looked back up through the trees to the house.

'I'm home, Tabby. I'm home,' he said.

He allowed himself a while to clear his head and gather his thoughts. Finally he looked at his watch. 10.38.

'It's amazing. I still can't believe it,' he said out loud. 'Two minutes. I've only been gone two minutes!'

Putting the cat down, he gathered his things and crept up towards the house. He reached the wall beneath the kitchen window just in time to hear his mother approach the back door and enter the kitchen. He held his breath, weighing up his options.

His mother's voice sailed through the open door.

'Gone to save the world, indeed,' she said as she read what he had written on the note earlier. 'If you've gone out, my boy, it's you that will need saving. Chris. Chris!' she shouted as her voice receded into the house.

Chris quickly decided that he could not risk going into the house, let alone try to get into his bedroom. He headed for the shed and slipped inside, closing the door quietly behind him. Unfolding the bundle, he took out his clothes. As he changed back into them and put on his trainers, he realised how strange it felt to be wearing them again. He had got so used to the loose-fitting attire of Castellion that his jeans felt tight and uncomfortable and his trainers felt stranger still.

He used the sacking that they were wrapped in to bundle up his Castellion clothes and folded them around his sword, the dragon-skin waistcoat and the whip.

He held the box to his face and whispered. 'Chris.' Nothing happened. He paused for a moment and then whispered again. 'Frog.'

The top of the box silently hinged back to reveal his Tamagotchi, marbles, half a rubber, conker, wine bottle cork and finally the chewing gum. He pushed the objects into the pockets of his jeans, then, placing the glass whistle and the talisman and neck chain into the box, he whispered to it again, 'Frog,' and it silently closed.

There was an old chest of drawers in the shed and the bottom drawer was used by Chris to store any toys that he and Billy might use in their den. He pulled it open and, pushing a radio-controlled car and a frisbee to one side, placed the bundle and the box as far back as possible and slid the draw shut. *Plenty of time to figure out what to do with it,* he thought. *Now it's time to face the music.*

306

He walked around the house and into the kitchen, standing just inside the door. He took a deep breath and called.

'Mum? Mum, I'm home.'

He heard the door to the living room open and his other's footsteps approaching along the hall. Then he was in the doorway, looking at him intensely.

'Hi Mum,' he said, giving a feeble little wave. Then it hit him, right in front of his face. Four and a half fingers!

'What's happened, Chris?'

'I can explain, Mum. Honest,' he said.

'*No you can't,*' said a voice in his head.

'I thought you said that your clothes were ruined?' she said, looking him up and down, ignoring his hand.

'*She can't see it,*' he thought. '*Otherwise she would have gone ballistic!*'

'The truth, Chris.'

His mind was racing in overtime. What a twit he was. He should have changed into the other clothes that were still in the shed.

'I ... I ... I ...' was all that would come out of his mouth.

'Well?' she asked, impatiently.

The idea popped into his head and before he could help himself it was coming out of his mouth.

'I felt so bad about what had happened and what you said about looking after my clothes that I put everything into a bag and took it down to the launderette, first thing this morning. I wanted to be wearing them as a surprise for you.'

Her expression changed to one of suspicion.

'You put your trainers in the washing machine?' she asked.

'Yes, and then in a tumble dryer. They're still a bit warm though,' he added.

'Where did you get the money?' she quizzed.

'I've got loads of pocket money saved up. I used some of that.'

'So, what was that note about you going to save the world?'

'I meant that I was going on a mission. I didn't want to spoil the surprise.'

She looked him up and down again. After what seemed a long silence, she half smiled at him.

'Okay, well done for trying to put things right. But, you're not completely let off. That garden's still a mess, you'd better finish what you started.'

'Thanks, Mum.' He ran forwards and wrapped his arms around her.

'It's so good to be home,' he said, without thinking.

She leaned forwards and kissed the top of his head. 'You are a strange boy.'

He allowed himself to savour the comfort of holding his mum. He wished that he could share his adventure with her, tell her everything. But he knew that he couldn't, not now. *'Maybe one day,'* he thought. He finally stepped back and, holding out his hands, he said, 'Mum, can you see anything wrong with me?'

She frowned and a worried look came over her face.

'What is it? What's the matter?'

'Nothing. I just wondered if you thought that there was something wrong with me.' He wiggled the fingers on his left hand.

'You mean apart from your unpredictable episodes of disobedience and your untidiness?' she said, her face relaxing. 'And if that's a new rude sign that you've ʼicked up from school, you can stop it now.'

'No, I'm not being rude, just testing something, at's all.'

'*She can't see what's happened to my finger, she eally can't see it,*' he thought.

'Well you go and test it in the garden, I want that mess cleaned up by tea time.' She turned to unpack the bags of shopping that she had brought in.

As he reached the kitchen door, he said. 'I love you, Mum.'

'And I love you too,' she said, looking after him, but he was already gone.

He ran down the path to the trees at the bottom of the orchard, where it had all begun, the piles of grass scattered everywhere, the tools from the shed lying where he had left them. Suddenly he felt tired and his eyelids grew heavy.

'*I'll just have a rest before I start,*' he thought and sat himself down, propping his back up against a tree trunk and letting his eyes close against the morning sun.

That was how his mum found him, an hour or so later when she brought him a drink and some sandwiches. Before she woke him, she took a moment to study her son. He looked so peaceful. '*There is something different about him,*' she thought. '*But what is it?*' There was a small flash. '*His forehead, there's something on his forehead!*' She leaned forward to look closer and a beam of sunlight reflected through the leaves and dappled across his face. The mark was gone in an instant. *'Just a trick of the light,'* she assured herself. She gently shook his shoulder.

'Chris? Chris? Wake up, it's time for lunch.'

Chris slowly opened his eyes and smiled as his mother's face came into focus.

Epilogue

During the autumn of that year, a group of ground staff, working at the Royal Botanic Gardens at Kew in Richmond, England, were clearing a long untouched area of land, just behind the famous Pagoda. A series of oriental-style water gardens were to be constructed as a new feature for the following spring. It was here that one of them discovered a metal, life-size figure of a woman, her features resembling an old witch, her hand outstretched as if casting a spell.

The statue was carefully unearthed and taken to the research centre for examination, and after a series of tests it was concluded that it was crafted by an unidentified artist, its age unknown. Because of the fine detail and craftsmanship, it was decided to erect the statue on a sandstone plinth in a wooded grove, adding some novelty value to the woodland walk. There it spent its time, amusing those that stumbled across it and putting fear into smaller children who wandered too close and gazed upon the grotesque facial features.

Then, the following year, a gardener, while planting a young willow sapling near one of the recent water features, unearthed an object in the shape of a small, metal, twisted wand with delicate markings engraved around it.

Again, despite extensive research, its origin remained a mystery and it was stored in a cabinet in the science centre with other artefacts that had been discovered over the years. There it remained until, one evening, after the gardens had closed to the public, a science student had an idea as to where the wand belonged. She removed it from the cabinet and walked out into the gardens, following the woodland path until she finally reached the witch's statue.

She hesitantly reached up and placed the wand into the witch's outstretched hand. It fitted perfectly. As she stood back admiring the now complete statue, a green glow began to spread along the wand.

The next day, the gardens were closed to the public as police interviewed staff about a murder and a missing statue. The girl, or at least her remains, had been found that morning by one of the ground staff who had been emptying the litter bins on the woodland walk. She had been identified only by her clothes and a small silver cross which she wore around her neck; otherwise, it would have been impossible to know who she was as she had aged beyond recognition.

The plinth had been reduced to a pile of sand, and one word had been angrily scrawled across its surface:

REVENGE